A CERTAIN PARADISE

JAMES RYAN

Perfect Wind Publishing
London

All characters appearing in this work are fictitious. Any resemblance to real persons, living or dead, is purely coincidental.

Cover design by Anthony Palden Burnley

Perfect Wind Publishing
London
perfectwindpublishing@gmail.com

ISBN: 1470091658
ISBN 13: 9781470091651

To those who pointed out
truth and beauty
I thank you.

To those who showed
how to purify the heart
I thank you – so very much.

To those of us
who took advantage of others
and to those of us their prey
May my tears wash away
all the iniquities and pain.

To those who bought joy
May your laughter penetrate to the
very ends of the universe.

To the reader of this book
May you be happy
benefit all beings.

CONTENTS

Please note - thoughts are italicised

THE FIRST WEEK

TUESDAY

NIGHT

Morton recognised the fact that he was in ill humour and that fact gave him a deep feeling of satisfaction. *This time I'll give no quarter* he mused to himself. He became aware that his shirt was soaked in sweat and tried to rearrange his short plump shape in the narrow airline seat.

Disgusting tropical weather. According to his watch they'd be in soon. *Six minutes.*

He realised suddenly that he didn't know where his briefcase was. Bending forward he saw it under his seat. He sat back again only to feel his wet shirt. *Disgusting weather, disgusting situation.* He made a mental note to try and preserve this mood intact throughout his stay - he considered it one of his major directorial skills and wondered if all the world's great leaders hadn't intentionally been of the same disposition. *Two minutes to land.* His passport was on top of all the papers in his briefcase, the key to his briefcase was in his left trouser pocket ... he felt for his safety belt, a step ahead of all the other passengers, and pushed it together with a satisfying click. His face was set in exactly the same expression he'd noted in his teens on a painting of Napoleon leading the French on horseback into Russia. *Into battle.* He urged the plane to land.

~

Garry was playing dominoes. He'd been playing for an hour when he looked up hearing a plane coming in.

"Here it comes" said one of the other taximen.

"Here's trouble" said Garry laying down a double five.

"Give me a rum".

"No man!"

"You playin'. Play!"

"I finishin' the game! Play!"

The pieces were slammed down noisily on the board. The game finished as the plane came to a standstill. They stood up together and went over to the old wooden building that served as reception for Entropica International Airport. The pieces were thrown in a plastic bag and posted with the board in the airport mailbox.

Garry walked over to the immigration area and waited. In a moment the arriving passengers entered and he saw Morton come in looking angry. *'E white face red and 'e sweating a lot.* He smiled to himself as he walked up to the barrier.

"Mr. Morton", he said, "nice to have you back!"

"Is it?" said Morton, looking over the row of dark smiling West Indian faces.

"Of course" said Garry. Garry stood taller than the rest of the taximen and was beginning to put on weight.

"Well it's nice to see you Garry. Is the taxi still working?"

"It's outside, Mr. Morton. I'll go there and wait for you."

"Good man."

Morton turned to the line for the immigration desk. Garry went back to the check in area and the bar.

"Rum and water" he said sitting down on his usual stool. *I wonder if Nan'll be on the road tonight.* He drank it down. *Maybe under the trees.*

He paid and went outside. Morton came up and Garry took his bags. In a moment they were sitting up front in the twelve-seater bus looking out of the large wind screen gliding through the warm tropical night. As they passed through Point Village, Garry caught sight of Nan in a short frock barefoot by Lambert's shop. She lived with her grandmother in a small wooden house behind. She was well built and beautiful - a future carnival queen - fourteen and still at school but already taking man as Garry well knew. He had a feeling she'd be there when he got back - there was no money in the house. He pressed down on the gas. They flew through the night.

At the hotel Morton climbed out and was immediately irked to see there was no one to meet him aside from the receptionist, a young woman.

"Thanks Garry. Nice drive in." Morton took out his handkerchief and dabbed his face. "Glad to see you're keeping up the pace."

"Oh you know how it is." Garry unloaded the bags.

"Come over to the bar for a drink."

"Thank you sir but I've got to get back."

"Your wife's well?"

"Yes fine. And how is Mistress Morton?"

"Excellent health."

"Well good night sir." He closed the door and drove off back up the road.

Approaching Point Village he slowed and turned down the stereo. He saw her among the trees. He stopped. She didn't move.

"Nan" he said quietly. She came up to the bus intense, her eyes lowered.

"Nan" he said again with a smile. She looked up into his eyes. No attitude, expression or thought defaced her exact beauty.

"Get in" he said.

She went round and got in.

He moved off slowly, turned the stereo back up and headed for the darkness of the trees above Sapphire Bay.

WEDNESDAY

MORNING

The hotel was halfway down the island, twelve miles from the airport which lay at its westernmost point. The island was part of the long volcanic chain that divides the Caribbean from the Atlantic. They had exploded from out of the world's deepest sea as earth on fire millions of years before and then condensed into black rock - barren sentinels in an empty sea. Their form was often conical, or like Entropica, a series of linked cones rising to heights of four thousand feet and more. They contained deep fissured valleys. Time had softened them. Rock had caused rain and weathered to soil. An extraordinary abundance of life had come. Plants and trees in the greenest of tropical greens - coconut, mango, passion fruit, banana, mahogany - flowers and songbirds of the brightest colours. And the sea's edge had been ringed by white coral sand thrown up from the reefs of the island's shallow waters.

The resort was set on gently sloping land behind a sandy bay. Fifty units of octagonal shape were set in landscaped grounds with a huge circular swimming pool, restaurant and office buildings. To the right a small harbor had been dredged extending a natural inlet from the sea. To the left land was being graded for a new building and adjacent to this a bridge was being constructed across a lagoon. A high pink-grey wall built of local stone enclosed the white-washed buildings in their green and lovely grounds.

The resort had been open for almost a year but the final phase of construction was still in progress. Money had come from English financiers. Most of the original managers had been English and had returned to England. The two remaining ones stood on high ground overlooking the hotel. Fair haired but bronzed they could have been brothers. Both sported angular moustaches and were dressed in white T-shirts, white shorts and tennis shoes. Peter was in his thirties and Bill in his twenties.

"Did It arrive?" asked Peter the construction manager.

"It resides in unit eighteen" replied his friend Bill the harbour manager.

"Is It horizontal or vertical?"

"Still horizontal I believe."

"Well in that case I'm off for breakfast – Alf!" he shouted to his mechanic, "back in half an hour!"

"Any spare toast Dogsbody?"

"Of course old chap. Come along: we'll feed you directly after the cat."

∾

Morton struggled with his sheet and threw it off. He felt bad. He became aware the bed was damp. It was hot. He grabbed for his watch - *9.25am*. He sat up slowly and reached for his thermometer. *Eighty six degrees, eighty six degrees. It's always damn well eighty six degrees.* He went to the shower. The word 'imperative' kept coming to him. He switched the shower on. *Imperative, imperative.* By the time he'd found the correct balance of hot and cold water it was time to get out. He stepped out and dried off. He remembered it now. He'd worked it out last night over a brandy. *It is imperative that the hotel staff service is improved*. He'd call a general staff meeting scheduled for immediately after lunch. He started thinking out his speech as he got dressed. *It's absolutely imperative* he said to his imaginary audience *that for the sake of the hotel and for the island itself we improve the hotel service*. He was aware that some of the people working at the hotel were a little slow and weren't familiar with his range of vocabulary. *So much the better – they needn't understand everything*! He determined to use his key phrase several times. They expected unusual phrases from the number one man.

He dressed, picked up the phone and dialed 203.

"Hello" came the reply.

"Is that the restaurant?" said Morton.

"Yes sir."

"This is Morton. Tell King I'm ready for my breakfast."

"Yes sir."

"Who's that speaking?"

"Yes sir."

"No, I said who's that speaking?"

"Winston sir."

"How are you Winston?"

"Fine thank you Mr. Morton."

"Good Winston, I'll see you later." He replaced the handset and unlocked his briefcase.

He took out his papers from his briefcase with a quiet sense of mastery. He knew full well that virtually the whole hotel staff would happily run up and down thinking they were doing well but having no real notion - only the vaguest idea about the real situation - the real natural quantitative unforgiving aspect inherent in all human enterprise. He had one sheet of paper for each hotel department. On the left side of each sheet was the mark 'debit' and on the right side was the mark 'credit'. Morton knew that the debits were larger than the credits and this secret knowledge filled him with a familiar yet unaccountable feeling of satisfaction - a rather agreeable masochistic sensation. It was he alone who had battled to set up the hotel and now it would be he alone who would knock it into financially sound shape. The hotel manager and department heads had a lot of explaining and fidgeting to do and he relished the thought of the awkward meetings ahead.

He picked up the phone again and dialed 163 for the hotel manager.

"Hello."

"Where's Mr. Allen?"

"He's not in yet sir."

"Not in yet! When's he coming in?"

"I don't know sir."

"Well tell him to call me the minute he gets in."

"Yes sir."

He remembered the West Indian conventions.

"Who am I talking to?"

"Jacky."

"How are you Jacky?"

"Fine thank you sir."

"Good. I'll be over to see you later. Goodbye."

~

In the absence of their manager, Alf, the mechanic, was relaxing with his friend Jim, the welder. They were sitting smoking in the front seats of what was left of an old Landrover body in the back of the workshop. They'd climbed in and closed the doors. Their faces betrayed that half smile characteristic of successful truancy.

"The White Wonder come then," said Jim.

"Yeah, Jacky say 'e come last night. Garry carry him."

"How long he stayin'?"

"Peter don't know."

They were silent for a while content in their smoking, sitting and listening for approaching footsteps.

"Peter going to get hells, this time - the backhoe not running. All the lawn mowers done mash up..."

"... an anyone who jump in the pool jump back out with red eye!" added Jim and they laughed delightedly together. They relaxed quietly for a while and smoked another cigarette. The phone rang. They both started and jumped up out of the Landrover. Jim picked up his chipping hammer and in an instant the workshop resounded with life and work. Alf picked up the phone.

"Hello."

"Is that the workshop?"

"Yes."

"Let me speak to Mr. Finch."

"He not here right now."

"Where is he?"

"Gone to come back."

"Gone where to come back?"

There was a pause.

"The sewerage lift pump station."

"Tell him to phone me as soon as he returns."

"Yes sir."

"Who's that speaking?"

"Alf sir."

"Is the backhoe working Alf?"

"No sir."

"I'll be up soon to find out why not."

"Yes sir."

"Goodbye."

"Goodbye sir." Alf put down the phone.

"The White Wonder" said Jim with a smile.

∾

Up in the hills overlooking the hotel complex a young man was rolling some dry marijuana leaves in a dry banana leaf. He sat near his grandfather's small wooden house wearing only a piece of cloth around his waist. His body was beautifully muscled and his skin very dark. Under his long brown locks, two eyes shone out with an unnatural brilliance.

"Sweet 'erb, sweet, sweet 'erb" he sang to himself as he stripped some narrow lengths of banana leaf to make ties for his work.

"'Eh sister!" he shouted as his girlfriend's sister walked by up the road.

"Me got something for you."

"Keep you' rubbish dirtiness to you'self boy!" she shouted back. He continued with his work.

"Yo!" His friend Chip sat down beside him shaking a box of matches.

They lit up, smoked and leaned back.

After a while they began to feel very good. Everything seemed just right. The wind rustled the palm trees above them. They could hear school children and cattle in the distance and the sun lit up everything in bright colours. Shadows danced around them. Even the air seemed to possess a special quality.

"You going work today?" said Chip.

"Yeah, when the sun up so" said Zackie pointing overhead. There was what seemed to be a long pause. Then Chip said, "Oh."

"What the food is?" said Zackie.

"I-tal soup" said Chip with a big smile. Both of them were smiling now and continued to do so even until after the soup was finished.

"It cool up here in the hills" said Chip, "Babylon die..."

"Babylon I comin' today" said Zackie.

In the adjacent unit to which Morton was going through his figures while awaiting breakfast two maids were working and talking very quickly.

"Yeah man she cut off she hair to wear wig for she man."

"Then she a bald head in trut'" said Edna.

"An' the time she take to pluck she eyebrow ..."

"Tellin' you..."

"... that she got no time to do no kinda work."

"Ah so."

"An' she buying so much bottle a cream for she face, an lipstick for she mout', an eyebrow pencil, O Lord ..." she broke off with a chuckle.

"An she still look like a ram goat!" exclaimed Elba.

"In troot!"

"An' the man Bates 'e come by she and take she and leave she and go look wife from that Maduro girl ..."

"But she still think she get a ring from he!" exclaimed Edna.

"What's this noise?"

Morton was standing in the doorway.

"Good morning Mr. Morton."

"What's all this noise?" asked Morton looking from the short plump Elba to the tall slim Edna.

"What noise Mr. Morton? We here cleanin' this room."

"It sounded like there was a party in here."

"No Mr. Morton" said Edna standing back so Morton could look passed her, "only Elba and I is here."

"Well you must have been talking at the tops of your voices."

The women looked at him evenly trying to penetrate the reason for his presence.

"Well look" said Morton taking another tack, "one of you go to the kitchen for me and find out what's happened to my breakfast. Tell King I'm waiting. And tell him to send coffee for two - in fact you girls can fetch it for me."

"Yes Mr. Morton." said the girls at once.

"And how's life treating you girls?" said Morton warming to them now that they'd changed from hindrances to accomplices.

"Alright" said Edna.

"Alright. Is that all?" asked Morton jovially. But then perceiving that this remark had no meaning for them and that from here on the conversation would be a struggle he stood aside so the women could pass and waived them through with a smile.

~

Morton was just finishing his eggs when there was a knock on the door and Steadman Allen, the Entropican hotel manager, entered all smiles. Like most island men he'd been raised to work land and look after animals but at school they'd discovered his sharp intellect and sent him to the States on a presidential scholarship. Five years after returning home he was Permanent Secretary responsible for development in the Entropical government. That was when Morton had met him in the original negotiations for the establishment of a multimillion dollar resort on the island, and found to his surprise that he was up against a negotiator he wasn't quite sure he had the edge on.

Steadman was now in his thirties and getting chubby. The odd white hair stood out from his dark brown head.

"Ben - so nice to see you!"

"Nice to see you too Steadman. I didn't realise you came in so early on a Wednesday. It's only 10.25 a.m. Have some cold coffee."

Steadman laughed.

"So sorry I couldn't meet you last night Ben - we had a Rotary meeting that went on into the early hours."

"Oh I see. And how are your ladies?"

Steadman laughed again, a good hearted belly laugh.

"No seriously Ben the meeting finished late ..." He paused, "How's Mrs. Morton?"

"She's fine thank you Steadman. So what's the latest at Tamarind Tree?"

"Peter tells me the construction is on schedule. Occupancy has fallen to fifteen per cent - it's the end of the season I suppose ... what else ... Oh yes! I have this idea Ben - you know what could be really big around here ..."

"Yes I do Steadman – the debits. I have the latest ones here". Morton lifted up a pile of papers and looked mournful.

AFTERNOON

By the time the sun was overhead Zackie, dressed now in a shirt and jeans, started to walk down to town. A typed memo had been distributed to all department heads:

"June 12. All hotel staff to assemble at 2.30 p.m. in the hotel restaurant for speech from Executive Director".

The temperature rose to 90 °F and the trade winds, which had blown day and night since last November, quietly died away. It was the beginning of summer, the end of the tourist season. The seven day a week routine was over and the staff were ready for the change.

In the main office building Morton and his hotel manager talked with some intensity over familiar and well aired topics. At 2.40 p.m. they judged that all the onsite staff were assembled and walked over to the restaurant.

On entering the dining area Morton was immediately aware of a laissez faire attitude quite out of keeping with the spirit of his prepared speech.

Steadman motioned him to a chair and he sat down angrily and looked about with eyes full of recrimination. When Steadman had finished his introduction he started off his speech in a voice full of severe determination, having quite forgotten the warm paternalistic approach he had planned.

"When this hotel opened it justly had a fine reputation for many things," he paused meaningfully, "one of these was its high standard of service..."

The maids sat together, the gardeners and maintenance men sat together, the reception staff sat together. Someone at the back started giving out chewing gum.

"... moreover we cannot continue in this way, simply cannot..." A huge bee buzzed around the meeting and then banged into a window. It kept on banging into it.

"... cleaning services. But that's just it. We can't do it this way, so we decide there'll be another way ..."

The bee now had everyone's complete attention. It was so close to the edge of the window and to freedom.

"... is evident. But it cannot be stood for, won't be stood for..."

Surely God give the damn bee brains enough to make it back outside.

"... what's more it's imperative that we don't give in to these base urges ..."

Morton's face was very red. The bee finally made it outside, someone's chair creaked and a gardener fell off backwards. Everyone laughed. Morton smiled a bit but drove on.

Bill was looking out the window. Grey clouds were looming up in the east. Far out in the Caribbean he could see dark patches appearing on the sea's face. *Wind coming.* He looked back at the meeting and felt it a terrible waste of an afternoon.

"... and so for the sake not only of the hotel ..." Morton's change in tone bought him back to the present. *He's like a tape recording.* He moved uneasily in his seat. *In order to show the importance of this meeting Morton's going to keep us here for two hours minimum. That means five o'clock start. The nearest clouds are over Margarita Island – ten miles – wind in an hour. Sunset at 6.30pm – an hour and a half.* Having settled in his mind he could still have an evening's sail he turned his attention back to the meeting.

"... and it is therefore absolutely imperative that we pull together in our effort to make this the best hotel on the island - no in the Caribbean - not just for ourselves - not just for the hotel, but for the nation as a whole."

Morton sat back somewhat moved by his own words. He pulled out a tin and an old pipe and started, with evident practice, to transfer a small portion of the contents of the tin into the pipe.

"Now are there any questions?" he said looking up.

There was an uneasy silence.

"All quite straightforward to you is it Stew?"

Everyone laughed. Stew was considered the hotel dunce. But he had a kind nature and smiled back and said

"Thanking you."

"What about holidays?" said Edna.

"Well what about holidays Edna?" countered Morton.

"Well Mr. Morton we haven't had any this year."

"Come and see me in my office please Edna..." Morton lit his pipe and let out a puff of smoke. There was another silence. Outside a scrambling noise could be heard on the main staircase. Someone was coming up. Someone heralded by singing:

"I-man, soca music."

Zackie appeared on the top step.

"Why so many people here none eating?" he said half out loud. He gazed about himself while remaining by the staircase. Then he heard his name called:

"Zackie."

He stepped forward. It was a white man called his name. He recognized him. He'd seen him somewhere before.

"Good day" he said.

"Late for the meeting Zackie?" said Morton.

"I come clean the kitchen."

There were giggles from the back.

"Good for you Zackie. At least someone knows why he's here. Carry on."

Zackie disappeared through the swing doors into the kitchen. But every now and then some odd disjointed phrase from a sweet reggae song would rise up over the partition wall and fill out the empty question hour.

~

EVENING

Before the last of the salaried staff descended the staircase with Morton for a discussion at the poolside bar there was a small tri-coloured sail flapping in the late afternoon wind at the end of the beach. Caught by the sun it appeared to give off its own light. Stripped to his swimming trunks the helmsman pushed his boat into the water and set the rudder in place. The sail was tugging at the boat. 5pm. He pushed off, jumped aboard, put the dagger board in the slot and pulled the sail in. The boat sped away from the beach and into the sea and clear wind. It heeled and he sat out to windward bringing her round to face the waves. Warm spray covered him again and again. He felt free and new. The problems of the land were as an intangible nothingness.

Another identical boat was rounding a buoy to the north, a mile away. *Red Hat.*

He tacked and sped north to close it. *The dagger-board's stalling too soon - I'll have to try another one. The luff's too tight; the mainsheet clamp's too low.* Ten minutes later the boats were sailing within hailing distance.

"Eh, honkey!"

"Nigger boy!" His friend, a young businessman.

They came alongside and stalled out together, riding the swell - smiling happily.

"How long you been here?"

"A' hour."

"Let's take a pass round the buoys."

"Starting from where?"

"Here!"

"Right. Reef, Quarantine, Wreck to starboard. Finish at Reef."

"I'll wait for you before I go."

"In your dreams boy!"

"HA!"

They pulled in their sails tight together - both boats gathered speed as they made for the first mark. For half an hour they knew only the wind, the waves, the feel of their boat, the position of the other – the simple perfection of it all. Red Hat finished ten boat lengths ahead.

"Phew - nice race!"

"Jammy sod. Your sail's bigger than mine."

"No sir! You got your mainsheet tie in the wrong place."

"What!?"

"It should be to port for the boom." Bill looked across at Red Hat's Boat.

"You always have yours like that?"

"Maybe". Red Hat flashed a boyish grin.

"Who you steal that boat from anyway?"

Red Hat laughed.

"You think you can win the championship in a hotel boat?"

"Yeah because you ain't so damn fast."

"Beat your ass today"

"Yes - well I didn't have the sheet positioned in the right place on the boat this time - but I will next time."

They laughed together. “I gotta split, it’s getting dark.”

“See you.”

The boat gurgled and rolled down the evening waves. The stars were coming out as he reached the channel. He could hear crickets and tree frogs. The channel was a lighter patch in the darkening sea. He slid inside the reef over the shallow waters of the bay and up the beach. Someone was standing at the top. Peter. They pulled up the boat without speaking. When it was away Peter said

“Nice sail?”

“Beautiful.”

“You win?”

“No.”

“Morton’s looking for you”

“Where is he?”

“At the poolside bar”

“Well I’m heading east then”

Bill was shaking with cold.

“Come by us for a coffee and warm up”

“Thanks but better keep outa range. I got plans for tonight”

“Oh yeah?”

“Yeah”

The spars and sail put away, Bill dressed quickly. They walked to the car park and said goodnight.

~

Morton was beginning to feel hungry and the conversation in the bar was becoming tedious to him. He made his apologies and left. Returning to his room he showered and stood drying himself in front of the huge full-length mirror.

His well rounded belly was reflected back at him. His face and forearms had been reddened by the day’s sun but the rest of his body was still quite white.

He didn't much like this reflection. *Well I'm looking stout. I need some exercise. Too much damn work.... those light bulbs are badly placed..... most of my friends are fatter.... stout heart!.... when the workload diminishes I'll exercise more.... golf perhaps.... the important thing of course is the mind.... keeping the intellect sharp and doing useful work..... creating wealth and dividing it up. There's the key issue.*

He dressed for dinner and appeared before himself again wearing a blue and white striped shirt with gold cufflinks, grey trousers neatly pressed by the hotel staff and shiny black leather shoes. His silver grey hair was brushed neatly back from his temples giving him a distinguished air. His pipe jutted out squarely from his jaw.

Yes our bodies age and die but the fruit of our work lives on... the immortal Morton.... quite distinguished.... the clothing rather makes one overlook the fullness of form.

But on entering the restaurant he rather got the feeling that the silent watchful eye, that is the birthright of the island people, did not in any way overlook this fullness, this portliness - this visible evidence of his having, for many years, taken too large a share. A certain weariness came over him. The maitre d' flitted about him like an attentive peacock. Sipping a medium dry sherry he went over the day's work in his mind. It seemed to him that getting results out here was heavy going. *It's the heat. And there's no tradition of industriousness. In England the worker is praised. Here the dancer is praised. Life as a dance! An everlasting carnival! What an absurd notion! At least Krishna had one or two good ideas.*

He looked round at the restaurant staff. *How to save them from themselves? That's the key issue.*

His hors d'oeuvre came and he wasted no time in making a start on it. *If the islands had been home to the Industrial Revolution would there not be a proper respect for the work ethic? I wonder..... and yet they have their churches here. They must teach the importance of hard work - striving is central to religious life.*

He paused to pour some water. *Is it part of their religious upbringing? Maybe not! It's tambourines and hand clapping here. Our church taught us the virtues of helping others and helping yourself. Damn cold there in winter. I never saw the vicar smile once - tough old bird.*

"The duck sir"

Morton looked at his magnificent plate of duck a l'orange.

"Thank you Wilfred"

The important thing is to get them in a position of responsibility quickly. Then they'll soon shape up. A major West Indian resort run just by islanders. What a marvelous inspiration for the others!..... Yes that's the way...

He finished his main course and had dessert.

"Was that satisfactory sir?"

"Yes Wilfred - a very satisfying meal of a very high standard. Well prepared and served"

Yet, unhappily, there were some part of himself that was not quite satisfied. He lingered over a liqueur twirling the syrupy liquid in the dainty glass, relaxed and at ease for all the world to see. But that little part of himself that was not thoroughly satisfied lingered there with him too. He returned to his room and, pulling out his briefcase and securing pen and paper, he started to write.

THURSDAY

MORNING

The clouds that had brought wind in the evening brought rain in the night. In the early hours of the morning a cool wind came and then rain fell on the island making a gentle even sound. It fell on the hotel, on the houses and yards of the islanders, on the kept fields and on the scrub land and forests of the island's high slopes. First spotted, then dampened, then wet, the island's face started to run with water. The cattle in the lower fields stood up and turned away in dumb endurance. Every surface ran with a film of water – homes, villas, shops, bars, offices, churches and roads, their gutters coming to life and gurgling again. Crystals of salt adorning the decks and deck-houses of ships, yachts and fishing boats in the harbour were dissolved, washed away, run overboard back into the sea. The sound of running water came to obliterate that of falling rain. Water ran over the saturated land to the ghauts and sped in urgent torrents to the sea turning the coastal waters milky brown.

At first light a pale rainbow arced out from the hotel into the sea. The gardens and buildings had taken on a wonderful, radiant yet delicate beauty as though the land itself had been cleansed of all past wrongdoing.

Rain dancing on the sea's face. Rain, morning rain. Rain, morning rain.

Morning in a small wooden house in the country - Jacky was awakened by her mother. She lay there for some moments absorbing the deep luxury of lying in her own bed in her mother's house surrounded by loved ones and the things she cared about. A beautiful soft languid feeling still held her and she lay there listening to the sounds of her mother preparing for the morning, trying to remember her broken dream - the bed and the sleep and herself still almost one thing. Her mother's voice came to her again.

She sat up, blinked, stretched and pushed the wooden shutters open. It was cool outside. It had rained.

She put on her house coat ready to help her mother prepare breakfast. They lived quietly together - mother and two daughters. Her mother worked in a supermarket in town. She worked at reception for the hotel. Her younger sister was still at school. She went to an area partitioned off from the main room which served as a kitchen and went up to her mother and kissed her and held her. Her mother stood there motionless for a moment feeling her daughter's warmth and softness.

"Come on girl you' too soft. You slow this morning. Hurry get breakfast or the bus go leave us." She said this in a matter of fact voice but there was a sparkle in her sweet eyes. And that sparkle she had passed to her daughters for safekeeping as it were, for them to pass to their children in their turn.

In Jacky's eyes virtually no one could be suspected of anything but the highest motives and the greatest sincerity. Anything that appeared otherwise was either not properly understood or just a temporary aberration. In fact it was in large part for her manner rather than for her academic prowess that she was chosen by the hotel. Guests with complaints would go to reception and, so thought the hotel manager, their complaints would dissolve before the presence of this girl – and the fact she probably wouldn't be able to understand the exact nature of the complaint would be all for the better.

They said their prayers over breakfast and ate. Afterwards Jacky cleared away, washed up and set the room straight. As she worked she sang and as she sang she thought of the coming day and of what she would wear for it. She went to her room with a basin of water to wash, stopping first to plait her sister's hair. Icilma was glad of this - she liked to look smart for school.

They were on the road in good time. Standing under their huge tamarind tree with several other town workers, they could hear the bus in the distance. It turned the corner, its wheels and sides covered in dirt from picking up country people on the wet and unsurfaced roads.

The sliding door opened in front of them. They climbed in and sat down - Jacky in front of her mother. The door closed, the bus moved forward into the working day. *What will it bring?*

The countryside above and beyond the towns, villages and kept fields was largely scrub, acres and acres of it, thick and impenetrable. The town people called the country people 'bush people' and their minibus the 'bush bus'. The only person who didn't use this name was the owner-driver himself, a young man from Watley village. Having put all his cash, hopes and pride into the vehicle, he painted down the sides:

'Top Road Runner - King Taxi man.'

The front and back were suitably adorned with golden crowns. Nevertheless the people continued with their impiety - it was the 'bush bus'.

The bus pulled up outside the hotel gates. Jacky opened the door and climbed out. A man closed the door behind her and the bus continued with her mother in it - but she didn't look back. A nervous energy ran through her. *Please help me today Jesus.* She stood by the roadside for a minute waiting for her breath to become more regular, then she crossed over and entered into the gates and into the hotel. She passed through the varnished hardwood doors into the air conditioned world of the offices. Her heart was pounding. In the back office a chubby woman in middle years was bending double cleaning the floor.

She didn't change position to look at the newcomer.

"Jacky that you?"

"Yes Mistress Skeritt. Good morning to you."

"Well girl and aren't you dressed up today!"

Jacky smiled and flushed. They talked together happily for some time. Mistress Skeritt finished her cleaning as the young girl arranged her desk and personal belongings. When the inter-office door opened to reveal the accountant Jacky became aware that her turbulent feelings had all but subsided. She hardly had time to say her practiced "Good morning Mr Osborne" when the phone rang and she at once left the back office for the reception desk.

"Good morning, reception, can I help you?"

"I want a ham and egg sandwich and coffee in my room."

"I'm sorry sir, there is no room service."

"No room service!"

"No sir."

"Then how do I eat?"

"The hotel restaurant is open sir."

"Oh yeah. Well how come I was just there and it was closed?"

"Was it?"

"Yes it was. I can't wait all day to eat. I'm here on business. Get me a sandwich sent to my room." And with that the hungry guest slammed down his phone. The accountant was standing over her.

"Any trouble Jacky?"

"A man in villa 26 said he wants a ham and egg sandwich and coffee in his room and the restaurant is closed."

"Phone the restaurant and see if they are open. If they are phone the man back and tell him. If not phone the food and beverage manager."

"Yes Mr Osborne" replied Jackie grateful for the help and somewhat over-awed by this speedy piece of logic. *I wonder if I ever be so efficient.* She dialled the restaurant.

"Hello King Kong!" came a shout in her ears.

"Good morning Mr. King. Can you tell me please are you open for breakfast now?"

"We here but we hiding."

"Oh.... well are you serving breakfast? A man in villa 26 tell me he was just there but you was closed."

"Tell him come back."

"He say he want a ham and egg sandwich and coffee."

"No ham."

There was a pause while Jacky took this in.

"Thank you Mr King." She closed the connection and dialled villa 26.

"What is it?"

"Good morning, reception here sir - they are serving breakfast in the restaurant now."

"Oh, so I have to go there and get it..."

"Yes sir there is no room service..." Jacky paused. "and there's no ham either."

~

By the time Morton arose and stood bleary-eyed on the red Italian tiles of his patio the sun was well risen. The night rain was evaporating from every square inch of the island and it was already quite humid. *Ugh... I don't seem to be getting used to this at all. It's like a huge steam bath you can't get out of.* He returned to his room, switched the paddle fan to maximum velocity and, pouring himself some iced water, drank it down with a grunt. *Five past nine.* He had to meet with the Minister of Labour at noon. Before that he planned to take a tour of the hotel – he'd drawn up a schedule for his day's work last night. Feeling quite out of temper he would have preferred to be going around the various hotel departments giving everyone a well-deserved rocket - but as it was he had to face a meeting that would require all his tact, restraint and careful judgment. Steadman had been at pains to emphasise to him the delicacy of the negotiations.

Yes the first thing is the establishment of a cordial businesslike atmosphere. That damn Labour Law! That damn politician Daley and his damned idealism.

Five months ago the projections for the hotel looked quite good. They could expect to see a profit within three years and real income after five. But the publication of the new Labour Law changed all that. It required overtime rates to be paid on all work done outside normal office hours. Their wage bill would increase overnight by 50% on half of their work done - an immediate cost increase of 30% with a productivity increase of zero. The law seemed to be targeted at those businesses run by expatriates. It certainly seemed to be ignored by locals. It made Morton fume. *It's just the legacy of slavery. I wonder how many times a day Daley uses that word? Doesn't he know it was banished from the island a hundred and fifty years ago?*

Morton knew the history but did not understand the pain. There was a knock on the door. Breakfast was served on time and was evidently carefully prepared. Morton thanked the waiter, laid out the contents of his tray hotel style, poured himself some coffee and started on the grapefruit. He felt his role to be almost a messianic one - the bringing of sound financial advice to the island, cutting through this stagnant pond of dark idealism. He was glad he allowed racial feeling no room in his heart. *The average person is like a sheep - you lead him here or you lead him there. Some are black and some are white but they all follow.*

It flashed to him that sheep will only follow sheep but he chose not to pursue his analogy any further. Instead, realising there was nothing left to eat, he placed his knife and fork together, wiped his mouth with the embossed paper serviette, stood up and started making his preparations to leave.

∾

"Bill."

"Yeah."

"It's Peter."

"What's up?"

"Some bastard's gone off with my theodolite."

"Well I'm neither the bastard nor the thief. I've got my own telescope thank you."

"Well keep an eye out - it's been taken today - I want it back."

"Okay."

Bill replaced his receiver and continued to sort out his own discrepancies - there was an unaccounted 150 gallons of premium missing - he was responsible for the fuel pumps in the harbour - and his books had to be ratified by the accountant on Friday. Gossip spread quickly on the island.

The phone went again.

"Harbour office."

"Good morning Mr Baker. There's a message just come in for you from overseas - shall I read it?"

"No thanks Jacky. I got to come over. How are you?"

"Fine thank you. And Mr Morton is looking for you for some figures."

"Okay."

"And there was an outside call for you from customs."

"What happened to that?"

"I tried to put it through but your line was busy. Oh.... hold the line please."

"That's okay I'm coming over." He put down the phone but didn't otherwise move. *There's something about that girl... she has a sweet smile, but she's not a real good looker - a little dumpy really... and our conversations are straight-forward enough, there's no flirtation.... but there's something there....*

He sat for some time looking out of the office door only half aware of himself. *Perspective!...Yes that's what it is. Whenever she speaks to me things fall into place. Sensing her goodness, her value, other things take their natural order. And right now urgently required figures come to the end of that natural order!*

Danny the deckhand came in. A keen dinghy sailor, he'd worked at the harbour for a year, his first regular job since leaving school four years before. He'd quickly become an asset to the company.

"Boat six has water up to the cabin sole."

"What! Where's it come from?"

"I don't know."

"You checked the stern tube?"

"Yeah."

"Through-hull fittings?"

"No."

"Is it fresh or salt?"

"How should I know?"

"Taste it. Maybe someone left a hatch open last night - it rained a lot."

"The hatches were closed."

"When's the boat due out?"

"Noon."

Bill checked his booking chart.

"God dammit!"

"Garry just dropped some people at reception."

"An old couple?"

"Yes."

"Hell! Well go back check it out. I'll be over in a minute."

Bill sped over to reception, slipped passed a Swedish couple into the back office and picked up his mail and messages. As he passed back through reception Jacky stopped him.

"Mr Baker. This is Mr and Mrs Heidelberger. They..."

"Oh Mr and Mrs Heidelberger – we've been looking forward to your arrival. How was your trip?" said Bill shaking hands.

"Very long and very boring. We wish to wash off. We will leave our suitcases on the boat first. Please show us."

Mr Heidelberger bent forward to pick up his suitcases.

"Ah yes of course but first please come and join me for a coffee in the restaurant - I would like to look at your contract papers."

"Oh. There is a problem?"

"No but I'm afraid there may be some paperwork error. Therefore I wish to correct them" said Bill unconsciously following the Swede's way of speaking. He showed them to the restaurant and ordered coffee for three, drank his down and informed them he would take the contract to his office for ratification. He then sped over to boat six and jumped aboard. Danny's legs were visible on a quarter berth. The rest of him was in the engine compartment.

"Find it?"

"Yeah."

"What was it?"

"The hosing on the water intake was punctured. I find a next one."

"Nice work. It's going okay?"

"Seem so."

"I got the people in the restaurant having coffee. Try and get the place dried and cleaned up. They're itching to get on board."

Bill jumped ashore and was going down the dock when he stopped and turned back.

"And run the engine. Make sure it's okay."

In the office he found the contract file. He located the Heidelberger contract and was leaving the office with it as the phone went.

"Bill."

"Yes Ben how are you, didn't have a chance to..."

"Have you got the figures for me?"

"Er, yes, they're here on my desk. I'm just finishing them off."

"Well bring them to me before noon today please."

"Okay."

"Is everything going well?"

"Fine, thank you."

The Heidelberger suitcases came into view, across the doorway.

"Excuse me Ben I have to go. I'll be over there at twelve."

"Finished your coffee?" he said looking up at the Heidelbergers.

"Yes, but we are here for sailing. Please show us our boat."

"Of course. The contract appears to be in order. Please follow me."

He took a suitcase and led them round the harbour to boat six. Danny had just completed running the engine and checking the gauges. Bill passed him the suitcases.

"This is Danny. He's just been doing the final engine check."

Mr Heidelberger looked down into the cabin.

"The floor is not dry. Why is it?"

Just before noon the hotel's most prestigious motor vehicle crackled over the gravel, stopped at the main entrance and then proceeded on its way downtown. Morton was at the wheel. Aware of the eyes of several of his workers he was careful not to make any mistakes. *They have an acute sense of the absurd and it would never occur to any of them to conceal their mirth.*

Peter watched him go from the construction area.

"Make sure you don't crash the ruddy thing" he said out loud, "we don't have any spares."

He turned to his masons.

"Okay lunchtime. See if you can find out anything about my theodolite. If we don't know anything by afternoon I'm calling the police in."

They looked down on the ground in front of them. Peter turned on the hose and cleaned his hands and arms. The water sparkled in the sun. In a moment he was by his apartment door taking off his sandals.

NOON

The winds that passed over the hotel ran up the slopes of the volcanic hills till they reached the crest and then, reduced somewhat, tumbled and swirled downward, coursing away to the west and the gentle turquoise bays.

The worked land near the crest was green and fertile. Work was done by hand - the fields were steep - too steep for machinery. Not that the farmers had money enough for tractors. Zackie's grandfather stood in one of these fields. His sons were long since gone about 'big business' - office jobs in America. He would be the last unless Zackie stopped his stupidness. He knew Zackie loved the land.

In his left hand was a hoe and around him were old blue-grey work clothes that waved in the breeze. His trousers were tied up with string, the zip was broken and there was a gap. But on his head his favourite beret, set at a rakish angle, covered the short trimmed grey wool of his hair. The stubble on his chin was the same colour and stood out against his dark skin. Yearly his body stiffened a little more and bent a little more as if the earth itself was slowly drawing him back. His eyes were marvellously clear and humble - yet there was no certainty in them. He was standing up to his waist in bush looking at an avocado pear tree. *Yes she bearing again, she fruitful still.* His thoughts came slowly. The breeze came to him up the hillside, cooling his sweat. *In a short while Mistress Allen* - for that is how he referred to his wife both to others and to himself - *will go carry them Tamarind Tree thanks be to God.* Speaking in this way to himself he turned back down the hill. A pair of birds flew close by and landed on a tree ahead. He felt their passing and his eyes followed their path and rested on them for a moment. They looked back at him. *They waiting on me.*

The earth was dark, moist and ready. He continued with his row making ready for planting on the dark side, away from the sun. There was work enough for the day. *In a couple of day they will needs watering a little.* He cast an eye towards Stella, his donkey, tied at the very edge of the field. He remembered his pales under the house and raising his hoe bought it down into the land opening it, ready for seed.

~

Out on the end of the harbour breakwater two girls were sitting on the stonework eating sandwiches out of paper bags and drinking cold sodas from cans. Pelicans sailed around them waiting for the fish to come within reach. “I love ’e you know. I know it from today.”

The sea broke a few feet away. They were watching the waves come and go, feeling a wild vitality rise in them, at once both dreadful and delightful.

Jacky was breathing quite deeply. She looked at the harbour. *Yes. Yes I will…. definitely… yes.*

"But does he love you? He a different colour remember."

"He feel something yes."

"He have a white girlfriend he come here with."

"I know."

"And what about Weston?"

"Weston he bad. He doesn't love me. He have other woman and go by them! He just come by me when he ready and go away again. I stupid to see him. I finished with him and she doesn't love him. I know."

They could see bright coloured fish moving around the reef below them. For some time they watched them changing places at the reef face.

Rubina said "I hope you can get him."

Jacky said "I don't know how."

An empty can rolled away, ran up against a stone wall and was stopped.

Both Morton and the Labour Minister felt they knew more about the other's motives than the other knew about their own and each felt himself to be negotiating on the side of 'righteousness' and were resolved not to waiver from their position.

It was midday and 92° as Morton climbed the last few concrete steps to the Minister of Labour's second floor government office. He took care to conceal the effort it was costing him. In England two days before it had been 56°. His cottage didn't have stairs. He gave his name to the young woman in the outer office and as soon as she left to announce him he sat down. He could hear Daley's deep voice in the adjoining office. It was a voice often charged with emotion, a voice rarely heard at a moderate level. Morton was shown in.

Daley was a huge man, tall and imposing like an upright grizzly. His black three-piece suit lent him a forbidding air. The many buttons of his waistcoat seemed barely able to constrain him. He lunged forward from the back wall with both arms outstretched.

"Ah, Mr Morton, so nice to have you back on our island!"

"It's a pleasure to be back." They shook hands and Daley motioned Morton to a chair, which was at a level substantially below his own. Morton sat down.

"And how's the great Entropical government? Progressing towards Utopia I hope" chided Morton rather pleased to be engaging in a battle with someone of some intelligence.

"Well as you know we try to get a little closer by the end of every day" Daley smiled "and I must congratulate you again on your hotel - it is evidently a great success."

Morton paused for a moment to reflect.

"I wish it were but we've a long way to go yet I'm afraid, a long, long way" and as he said this he realised more acutely the carefulness with which he must now choose his words. From his pocket he pulled pipe, tobacco tin and matches. These implements Morton found, apart from being pleasant to the taste and giving him, he rather hoped, the aura of a Master Mariner - he was a keen sailor himself - were useful conversational tools as they could be tampered with, knocked out, puffed on, looked at, relighted and sucked on with apparent absorption during critical moments in an argument when a little time was needed for thought.

"Ah, I'm pleased to see you've bought the peace pipe" said Daley.

"Yes we all want peace don't we?" said Morton "a piece of this, a piece of that."

Daley laughed a deep belly laugh and Morton couldn't help smiling very broadly for some time at his own joke. Eventually he was obliged to distract himself with his pipe for fear Daley might see his sweet side and mark the weakness.

"Well in truth" Daley decided to lead off the real discussion feeling it better established his position, "the only way to get real peace is to have a stable government, and the only way to have a stable government is for the laws of the land to be obeyed..." He looked Morton in the eyes. His eyes were bulging - anger was there.

"...your hotel is a transgressor in this respect."

"I think you're being a little unfair to us" said Morton. The atmosphere in the room had suddenly become businesslike. "I know you're in agreement with us that the hotel has been a benefit to the island..."

"Of course."

".... and after all a government can't be in a position to govern if there's virtually nothing there to govern.... the government has expanded as the commercial sector has expanded. The two are so closely interlinked I find it hard to consider them as separate entities. Really we're both struggling towards the same goal and I feel we'll always be able to reach amicable agreement because of this."

Daley sat back without speaking. Morton lit his pipe and feeling rather pleased, prepared to continue.

"The Labour Law was set up by the will of the people." Daley's voice was raised. "As such it is unchangeable unless the people themselves should choose to change it!"

"Well then I think they should start choosing" Morton cut in "it's no use having legislation which appears spiritually pleasing if it bankrupts the country and ruins the nation."

"Bankruptcy!" Daley shouted.

"Bankruptcy!" his anger had spread from his eyes to his face. This was an argument that he hadn't properly foreseen.

"You are trying to tell me that your hotel is going to go bankrupt!?"

Morton chose not to speak for a moment giving Daley time for his rage to pass and to allow his words to have more gravity. It was a sentence he had prepared beforehand.

"I sincerely believe that our company cannot and will not ever be financially sound if the new Labour Law is interpreted in its very strictest sense."

"The Labour Law was set up" Daley continued ignoring Morton's point, "to protect the working man against corporate abuse. As Minister of Labour it is my duty to see that it is properly enforced."

"With all due respect" Morton cut in, "the Labour Law was set up very fairly to cope with the traditional enterprise working conventional weekday hours. But the hotel's case is exceptional, conventional hours are only worked by a few of the staff. The majority are working irregular or unusual hours."

"All the more reason for better compensation."

"Yes but we can only pay so much. We're already paying well above the national average. We can only sell a holiday for so much without pricing ourselves out of the market. And this dictates in turn the price we can pay for the services we require."

There was a silence and Morton mistakenly imagined Daley must be reassessing his position.

"Tell me Mr Morton, where did the money come from to build this hotel?"

Morton puffed on his pipe anticipating a trap.

"You know where it came from - profits from a diverse and hardworking English investment company."

"And will this government control where the profits of this company will go?" Morton realised too late he'd phrased his reply badly.

"Well as you know that is taken care of by your corporate legislation and corporate taxation policies." He hesitated, and not wanting to pursue the possibilities for change in these areas, continued hurriedly, "the blunt fact of the matter is that if we stick absolutely to the letter of the law it will cost our company an additional 30% in wages and this is a cost we just can't meet. As it is we're paying above average wages. The staff still work for us. They haven't all left. We're not abusing them. We're not a bunch of ogres. But we really cannot put up our labour bill any further and still hope our hotel will be considered by North Americans. It won't. We're in direct competition with the Virgin Islands, with St Martin, with Puerto Rico with the Dominican Republic - you name it we're up against it. I've spoken with the tour operators in New York. They've been very open with us. We stick to our prices for the coming year or they're not interested."

The figure of 30% agreed with Daley's own estimate. After a pause Morton continued,

"The absolute maximum we could offer our staff for irregular hours and overtime would be 15% extra. Even that's a risk I, as a businessman, hesitate to take. But I want to underline my sympathies with your principles, your objectives." Morton noted the flicker of pleasure Daley couldn't quite conceal.

"But it's the absolute furthest we can stretch."

Daley didn't speak for a moment. He looked out of the window so Morton couldn't see his eyes.

"And what about cutting costs in other areas? I believe you still have several highly paid managers."

Morton recognized this as an oblique reference to his two remaining white managers.

"Well of course cost efficiency is important in all areas not just labour..." His English managers were paid more than four times the average worker's salary. He himself was getting ten times as much "... and we do expect to be soon reducing our expatriate management staff..." He held out this further carrot and looked Daley straight in the face.

"How soon might that be?"

"It could be arranged within six months."

Both sat back and considered their position. Daley decided he had a workable compromise. Getting rid of two expatriates was a bonus he hadn't foreseen.

The secretary knocked on the door and coffee was served, rather late. The conversation became easier and rested on other topics. When it was finished Daley stood up and Morton, taking time collecting his pipe and briefcase, did the same.

"I think the matter has now moved forward and we should meet again quite soon. Meanwhile I shall confer with my colleagues. I'm glad we are able to better see each other's point of view."

"Very well" said Morton, "I shall expect to hear from you." He'd expected to have to offer at least 25% and he'd got away with fifteen. And he had an excuse for replacing his last two irksome English managers. He was pleased and taking care not to show it.

~

AFTERNOON

Clever and good-looking Hilton had just turned twenty. After a late night at the hotel he'd woken at noon and now lay in bed listening to his stereo. He liked to spend time in bed. The shutters were still closed but a little daylight penetrated into the room. Beads of sweat formed on his forehead. He wasn't feeling too good .... *I's no use they think they can fool me with their fanciness – 'Trainee Accountant'. It sound so big and pay so small! They have me for 'oman. They have me keeping book. They have me for answering phone. Me nah want that. Three months and I still keeping book! 'oman work! I going to butt up against Osborne today. Is time they move me on to other things. I tell him, kinda easy like, it time to check out the bucks they paying me.... maybe it a mistake or something... or I have 'o explain I gotta think of moving on, right .... is true they can't keep me down.* He looked across at the mirror and was satisfied by the reflection of himself that his thoughts were true. Similar thoughts had been coming to him for weeks. The office girls were an additional thorn in his side. They treated him like a kid brother. But he reckoned he would soon be above them and one of his jobs would be to control them...... *An opening gotta come where I can move in and do my own thing, make some good bread, have a big office and so on, get some respect, build a concrete house, fast wheels and chicks boy.... oh yes chicks like peas.* He smiled to himself. Mosquitoes buzzed around him and tried to land on his damp skin. It was evidently getting late. *Yeah man I got the talent - who else my age got the brains? All the teachers check it out. Work at the hotel is a' insult. A smally, smally job on a girl wage and always seeking to correct, correct, correct. They just want to play smart. Soon we see who the smart man be – huh! A girl wage. They can stick their honkey hotel....*

"Hilton! Hilton! Get up boy." His elder sister's voice coming from outside the door, loud and incontrovertible.

"It after three. You able do nothing but dream?"

"An' who you think bringing the bucks in this house 'oman?"

He sat up.

"Me needs a clean shirt."

Unbolting the door he went outside to an enclosure made of four sheets of galvanised roofing and turned on the pipe. Standing on the rocks under the shower his hostility washed away with his sweat. He felt cool, refreshed, ready to go. Back inside he faced his mirror and set his hair in place working straightforward and single-mindedly like a fashion artist putting the final touches to his latest work. He dressed in a contoured shirt, high wasted slacks and striped leather shoes. *Entropica Dread man!* He felt pleased.

After eating his food he washed out his mouth and padlocked his door - more from family than thieves - then stepped down into the road and bright sunlight. From the shade of a neep tree he watched the local schoolchildren slowly making their way towards him and back to their homes. They looked ill kept from the heat and their play in the schoolyard. A small group of girls was coming up his side of the road. One of his present favourites was amongst them. *These chicks can make themselves something else for the disco but right now Entropica Dread man got the advantage.* He looked down at himself. As his favourite drew near he stood forward a little, standing quite erect and still, breathing slowly. She carelessly let her eyes run over him. He stood there with a distant look in his eyes and then as she passed said,

"Hey li'le sister."

She turned, not caring to hide the pleasure of being stopped.

"You an' I goin' to get together soon."

She looked at him for a second and then carried on up the road to catch up with her friends. As they fell in together again there were giggles. One of them looked round smiling but was evidently embarrassed as well.

Dread man just going to make that little thing this week.

Garry's taxi was coming over the top of the hill - now doing service as a local bus. It stopped exactly by him. He opened the door and climbed in with a single step and took the front seat. Reggae music filled the taxi.

"Music machine!"

"'s'appenin'?" said Garry.

"Everything bootiful."

Garry glanced at him. Hilton seemed very pleased with himself. He'd seen the schoolgirls going by.

"Find any nice chicks lately?"

"Yeah - one or two."

"Anything sweet?"

"That Sweeney thing."

"Oh Nan."

"Yeah man she just heading to give me a little sexing this week."

"Uh huh."

The taxi reached the hotel gates as the day workers were coming out. It was almost four. Hilton jumped out and slammed the side panel with the flat of his hand as a farewell. Bright eyed and bushy tailed, the natural centre of energy and attention, he greeted everyone as he passed through into the back office. Jacky was fiddling with her bag. She'd cleaned up her desk ages before.

"Okay chil' you can go" said Hilton walking passed and into reception with the air of a chief executive. Jacky left without saying goodbye. Somehow this overpowering male presence made it stick in her throat.

The phone went.

"Hello reception can I help you?"

"Kindly tell Mr Finch I want to see him in my office at once and tell Mr Baker to be here waiting at 5 p.m."

"Very well sir."

Hilton dialled Peter's home number.

~

Garry's taxi pushed its way slowly west through the end of day traffic carrying the hotel workers that lived at Point back to their homes.

This was the time of day when cars could be seen parked up in the main street any old how, young men running here and there shouting with beers in their hands - feeling ready to fete - the work and heat of the day over. An occasional car, idle for some time, might suddenly scream off burning rubber. Women were on the street minding their own business but looking a ride and perhaps the chance of a man - then climbing in some car gesturing and laughing delightedly. Everyone was glad to have their work finished with for the day - even those without work felt glad the working day was over!

Car stereos and portables were playing – rockers! People shopping, meeting easily and talking all kinds of 'stupidness', glad to be together. The young men yanking:

"Eh brother man s'appening?"

"Coolin' it, coolin' it."

"Right on. Gonna be checkin' you out later."

"Dig it. Hey gotta be moving along a little."

"Yeah - later then."

"Right."

And then at a distance –

"Keep the beat under your feet."

An old man, resting on his front gate, looked out from his yard and smiled - glad to be done with all that.

Edna and Elba were squashed together between two others on the back seat of Garry's taxi. They were sweating a lot, just wanting to get home and wash off.

"The girl, she better have her work done today."

"Who, the girl Val?"

"Yeah, she a devil bitch when I gone out. If I catch she again..."

The taxi stopped. Everyone looked forward. They were held up behind two cars going opposite ways - the drivers talking. Garry pressed his horn. Up front somebody shouted out a side window, "Move up, move up."

King walked up behind the taxi where it had stopped and pushed forward the sliding window on Elba's side.

"Eh, Elba I ready for you now," he said in a low voice. Everyone in the taxi turned round to see who was ready for Elba. King standing there by the window - a big smile on his face.

"Don't harass me boy!" she returned with a nice mixture of annoyance and delight.

He reached his hand in the window and down into her shopping bag. She grabbed for her bag but too late. He was looking at what he'd got. Some matches. The two cars ahead started to move. The taxi started forward. King stood there in the road.

"Give me back me matches."

"I bring it by you later."

"I vex you! Don't come by me tonight!"

"An' I got something else for you."

Elba turned forward and said "Huh!" as though she'd suffered a great indignity.

"I don't want 'e up by me round me house no place at all" she said out loud so the whole taxi could hear.

Edna said in her ear "You give 'e a nice fight first."

Elba couldn't help smiling a big smile but then she made herself look serious again. Even so a little smile kept playing on her face, just coming and going, beaming out every now and then, all along the road and the rest of the way home.

NIGHT

Bill was leaving his office to take the Sunfish out when Hilton phoned with Morton's message. He went over to the boat and made some adjustments based on what he'd learned the previous day. It looked better. He unrigged it and carefully stored the sails and boards away. There was now only one possible evening left for practice before the championship.

By 5:45 p.m. he'd been waiting at reception for three quarters of an hour talking with Hilton and resenting the loss of time. Every now and then angry voices could be heard overhead. A door opened upstairs - voices now easy to understand. Peter clambered down the stairs. He was seething with anger, his eyes jumping and his words coming in short bursts like machine-gun fire:

"Asshole! He wants you now. He's up to something!"

"Up to what?"

"You'll see! Come by me later."

"Okay."

Bill climbed the stairs and knocked on the door.

"Come in, come in Bill. Sit down."

Morton pointed to a seat without looking up.

"And how's the marine department?"

"Well, you know," said Bill, "paddling along..."

Morton relit his pipe.

"Yes I'd say it is judging by the figures. In fact I'd say you've forgotten which way you're meant to be paddling."

"What figures are you referring to?"

This was Morton's cue. He sorted through the papers on his desk.

"These are the figures" said Morton in much the same way that Moses must have said "These are the commandments."

"You'll notice," he said passing them to Bill, "that the debits are substantially larger than the credits."

"So they are" said Bill, "but it doesn't say what the accounting period is."

"June to December of last year."

"Well it's scarcely of value then."

Morton noted this impudence but restrained himself.

"And exactly why is that?"

"Because as you know it's the off-season except for part of December. If you want meaningful figures you'll have to extend the accounting period."

"Oh so you think it's all well and good just to spend, spend, spend providing it's the off-season."

"I didn't say that"

"The blunt fact of the matter is" said Morton, "you're not fulfilling your role as manager." He paused. "You've gone way beyond your budgeted expenditure for the period."

"As you know I never agreed that budget. It was set up by your accountant in England. He didn't seem to really understand what was going on."

"Peebles may have made one or two errors but his overall drift was right and you've gone outside it. The reason we brought you out here in the first place was to put your sort of expertise in control to work here, so that you would really control the department and train up new men. But I really can't see much evidence of that control."

"As you well know it was the off-season - that's when we provide a maintenance facility. I'm not going to haul a boat, find its shaft is out of alignment, its bearings need replacing and the anodes gone and say 'Oh well we only got enough money to antifoul it'."

"Now you're getting silly."

Bill looked warily at Morton. "Everything we spent is in the accounts files. Every receipt is there. I'll answer for them one by one if you wish."

"Nobody's trying to go behind your back and check everything" said Morton looking for a new opening "but there's a slackness here. I see it in your department. I see it in the food and beverage department. I see it in the maintenance department. I see it in sales. It's rife throughout the hotel. Rife!"

"And how is that slackness reflected in the figures?"

"What income do we have for the period? We have 34 bareboat charters, 310 harbour fees and 45 day-boat hires. Out of a potential of what?"

"Yes, well as I said it's the off-season..."

"And exactly what have you done to get the people here to use the boats?"

"With respect Ben, I thought that was your job."

"Oh don't give me that rot! I've heard it so many times before. My job is to promote the hotel overseas yes - but how many people are staying in the hotel without even knowing they can go sailing? How many? - tell me that! And how many are sitting in the other hotels which have no facilities doing nothing because they don't know what we have? Go on, tell me Bill, how many?"

It was Bill's turn to pause and now. Morton was getting heated and he didn't want to press him now. And while desiring to appear zealous he didn't want to take on what he guessed Morton had in mind - to spend his evenings going from table to table in the other hotel restaurants selling sailing.

"Well it's hard to say. As you know our hotel manager sees to our guests and the other hotels..."

"Yes, go on Bill, the other hotels..."

"Well I believe we could best reach them by printing a handout."

"Good lad and carrying it round to them and selling watersports. And why hasn't this been done before?"

"Because.......because we have no authority for exceeding our budget" said Bill with a smile.

"Well you have now. Get it done. Let me see a draft of it. When can I have it?" Morton was already tidying up.

"Would tomorrow be too soon?"

They both smiled now.

"Noon" said Morton.

~

Bill walked up to Peter's apartment in the darkness. *Looks like I'm still okay for the jolly old racing.* He was feeling quite pleased. *Conversations with Morton are always amusing in a peculiar sort of way. It's like a chess game - you can see your opponent's men but you're not quite sure why they're there. But then, come to that, you're not always too sure about your own sometimes. Still - you have to keep an eye open - you can lose quite unexpectedly.*

He knocked at the door. Peter's wife Marjorie opened it.

"I guess you're ready for a drink too" she smiled.

"Sure thing."

He stepped inside and closed the door.

"Let me have a beer please."

Peter was sitting in his armchair, his anger largely quenched now, but his eyes still shining wildly out of a ruddy face.

"Well, what did you think?"

Bill took his beer and drank it half down.

"Gee whiz that's good. I don't know. Same old garbage as far as I can see."

"He didn't for instance imply anything he hadn't implied before?"

"Can't think of anything original that was said by either party."

"Well it seemed to me" said Peter, "the bastard wants me off the island."

"Oh yeah?"

"Yeah."

"What makes you think so?"

"He kept on coming back to how I wasn't doing things right and how I should now be looking to other things and all the while giving me a special meaningful look in the eye..."

"Oh yeah?"

Bill thought for a minute, a little slowly. Things didn't seem so clear after a beer.

"You know now you come to mention it he did say something similar to me."

"What did he say?" said Peter vainly trying to conceal his delight at finding his friend in the same boat.

"Can't remember exactly. Something about I was brought out here to control and I wasn't doing it - oh yeah - and to train up the locals to take over from me."

"Sounds familiar."

"Yeah well it's just the usual rubbish. We've been hearing the same since the day we arrived."

"And he didn't say anything about the Labour Department wanting us off the island?"

"What!" Bill looked up surprised. He suddenly felt cornered. The conversation was no longer merely an amusement. A move had been made he hadn't even seen.

"No he didn't.....but I guess he figured you'd let me know."

Peter watched his words taking effect.

"I wonder why the Labour people want us off now."

"Well you know Daley – he'd rather see us keel hauled, but repatriation is a second best."

"Oh boy," said Bill, "I ain't ready for this yet."

෴

Point village just before dawn. King is suddenly awakened. There's an electric light bulb almost in his face. Where is he? He looks round and makes out Elba sitting on the bed facing him. He remembers, sinks back and turns over.

Elba hits him on the shoulder.

"Get up boy! Get up! Get outta me house now before you ruined me reputation!"

He sits up, blinks his eyes and smiles. He finds his clothes, still damp, stands up unsteadily and puts them on.

She goes to the door, unhooks the two latches and stands aside for him to pass. He hugs her up from behind, steps out into the night and finds the road. There is already a faint lightness in the east. It had been a good night. He walks, runs, skips and dances down the road - light and carefree. There seemed to be less gravity than usual.

~

Morton felt he was making progress. He was beginning to see his mark on things more clearly - things were pointing in the right direction. He'd spent a pleasant evening over dinner at Steadman's home. Steadman's wife served them and somehow her sweet feminine presence flowed in the gaps that separated their spiky male egos and they'd felt particularly close. Steadman had even congratulated him on his negotiations with the Minister of Labour, and praise from Steadman was rare indeed. After dinner they sat outside on the patio overlooking the sea. Morton sipped their excellent brandy, drank coffee and puffed leisurely on his pipe. For a time they reminisced about the early stages of the development, their initial hopes and fears. Some silence had even been allowed to reign giving their concerns a certain perspective. Steadman drove him back and said goodnight.

He'd imagined he'd simply undress and exchange his present daze for a pleasant doze. But it wasn't to be. A mosquito came upon him just before sleep did. He tried to ignore it at first but it was persistent. He turned over but it found him again. He put his head under the sheets but it became too hot. He exposed himself again and the mosquito landed on his head. He took a few swipes without success. Maybe there were several of them. He had to be fresh for the morrow. How to hit a mosquito in the dark? He could put on the light but that would only make him wider awake and attract more insects. He decided to ignore it. But it persisted. *It must know the exact location of my ear drum. A mosquito flaps its wings at 250 flaps per second. That accounts for the buzz.* The buzzing was so loud it had to be almost in his ear. He took another swipe. Silence. He thought he felt something in his fingers, but a second later the buzzing started again. Then it stopped again. He lay on his back. This time he really was going to go off to sleep. But just as he was almost there the buzzing came back. He tried to will it to fly away but it landed on his forehead. Thoroughly annoyed he reached for the bedside lamp. His pyjamas were sticky.

What time is it? The clock was close by. *Five past two*. Finding a magazine by his bedside, a woman's journal, he started to read.

FRIDAY

MORNING

Imperceptibly the light of the morning sun dispelled the night. Its loom came up from out of the eastern sea and the island slowly appeared from out of the night and stood there - dark and immobile - a silent unchanging presence amidst the vast stretches of stirring, moving but endlessly empty sea.

Half an hour later the orb of the sun appeared throwing a yellow lance before it like a magic wand. The island took on colour and life and its quiet face stirred in the morning breeze.

Ah! Sunshine - morning! Yes morning, sweet morning. Thankyou. Thankyou again. Yes, thankyou so very much. You must have known - we had become as castaways - lying unconscious in a strange dark land. But now we have come to ourselves once more - we, the actors, have awakened - can see again - and, remembering where we left off, continue with our play.

Edna was woken as usual by her children. She'd been listening to them tossing and turning for some time, wanting to get up. Her husband had threatened them to be still and as they all slept in the same room this was no idle threat. But they were asleep first and awake first and longed to get up.

There was a daughter, Alicia, and two sons, James and Junior. Edna was proud of them and glad they were all by her husband even if he did have other women and children outside.

Alicia was eight and the eldest. She was useful round the house now and could mind Junior. She was clever too - her school books were neat, she got good marks, praise and pleasure in her schooling. Her school satchel hung over the bed she shared with her brothers. But Edna loved her for being a loving daughter and told Elba to make some quick as insurance and better too than the paper ones they'd started selling downtown.

She looked at the crack between the shutters and the window frame to see how light the day had got.

"Alicia."

"Yes Mammy."

"Put on the water to boil."

Alicia pushed James out of the way and got up and went to the kitchen, lit the gas stove, poured water into a saucepan and set it in place.

"Junior!" Alicia was standing over her brother "get up."

James jumped up and went straight to the living room to see if anyone had moved his car. It was still there. He looked at it affectionately and then set it on the floor and started to run it up and down.

"James! Stop that noise!" His father's harsh voice came to him through the intervening partition and made him jump. He hid the car under the side table and went meekly outside and made ready for school.

"What time is it Alicia?"

"The clock say twenty minutes past six Mammy. The water ready Mammy."

Edna stretched and got up. She took the water off and poured it into a tub, added cold water, and washed herself. Then she dried off, put on her housecoat and started to cook breakfast.

Tyrone got up when he could smell corn beef frying. He sat by the table, his beautifully formed body kept in shape by hard physical work on building sites. He rarely had much to say. Edna passed him a Milo drink and his breakfast. Then she cooked breakfast for herself and her children.

Alicia and James were soon dressed for school in clean pressed uniforms. Even if they had lived in a mansion they couldn't have been turned out any better.

"I taking Junior by Alice for the day so have he ready to go out now."

"Yes Mammy."

"And James, what's the matter today? You looks sick boy."

James was sulking. He'd taken his car and put it in a box to take to school. At school he and Fish would play with their cars together. He didn't look up, didn't answer.

"Don't be looking like that when I get back or you get licks for true!"

She put the dishes to wash and started fixing up her hair for the new day.

∾

The harbour office was occupied earlier than usual. Bill was at work on his watersports leaflet. He wanted everything completed as early as possible so that he could get away to practice in his boat before the next day's races.

After a while Danny arrived and went about his business on the dock.

At about nine Bill became vaguely aware of voices by the office door.

"Say this here the harbour office?"

"Yes," said Bill standing up, "can I help you?"

Two plump middle-aged American couples stepped into the office. It took a little time. The leader was wearing a captain's hat.

"Can we day charter one of your boats?"

"Certainly you can - what do you have in mind?"

"Can we have a skippered day-sailer for the day for the four of us?"

"Yes - we have 'Blue Eyes' - she's that 36 foot blue sloop there." Bill pointed into the harbour.

"That's the one we wanted. When could she be ready by?"

"We could be ready in half an hour and you'd have the boat till 5 p.m."

"Uh huh. Can we go to Bird Island?"

"You can go where ever you please provided the skipper agrees and it's safe and feasible."

They agreed terms and the four left to have coffee in the restaurant. Bill walked up the dock to Danny.

"Danny check out 'Blue Eyes'. We got a day charter leaving in half an hour. I'm organising the food and drinks. They've paid."

"Okay."

"And guess who's the lucky skipper..."

"Oh no."

"Yes. I'm sorry, I'm working in the office today. You can handle it easy enough. The winds are light. They're talking about Bird Island. They're okay, friendly. Give them plenty to drink at lunch and get them back a bit early. I want to be gone by five."

Danny steered the boat out to sea with some misgivings. For one thing he was uneasy as he wasn't yet a first rate skipper - there was the risk involved and the tensions of anchoring or coming alongside or keeping the guests safe while steering the boat through a squall. And then there was the uneasiness of sailing with old white people who you didn't know and who treated you funny - they could be patronising or hostile, over friendly, condescending or indifferent.

But by the time he'd left harbour, raised sail and borne off on the agreed course he found himself glad to be sailing along over deep blue waters with a fresh beam wind. The boat was free of the land and he was free of the sway of his own, sometimes murky, thoughts. The charterers seemed happy. Spray broke occasionally over the bow and the boat surged ahead leaving a white wake. It was a beautiful day, the islands were standing out clearly - there was almost no haze - unusual for that time of year when dust from the Sahara blew across the Atlantic for weeks on end causing the clean lines of distant islands to become indistinct. Ahead of them at about a thousand feet two frigate birds circled effortlessly in an azure sky. He thought about streaming a line and catching the fish the birds were watching.

"Danny."

"Yes sir."

"How much is real estate down here?"

"It varies a lot."

"Yeah - well how much for an acre?"

"I heard some property man say it can be anything from 20,000 to 200,000 US per acre."

"Uh huh! And property - how much is a good-sized house?"

"Well... 200,000. But a man is building a house on Bird Island for 10 million."

"An American?"

"No. I don't know where he comes from - Europe somewhere."

"And where do you live Danny?"

"Back just outside of town."

"And where does the hotel manager come from?" said his wife looking interested.

"Entropica."

"What an interesting man!"

"How much longer before we get there?" asked the other lady.

"Not long - an hour or so."

She turned to her husband and passing him a plastic bottle said "Put some of this on my back George. Put it on thick - I don't want to burn. Can we put an awning up as soon as we get there?"

"I'll put it up first thing after we're anchored."

"The first thing I'm going to do when I get back to the States..." said George's wife "...you know what it is George?..."

George didn't seem to know.

"... is to visit my chiropodist. My poor feet! They're killing me! The walking I've done this past week in this heat! My feet are twice their normal size! And dead skin everywhere and sore red spots."

"What sort of boat is this Danny?"

"A Columbia 36."

"A friend of mine has a Columbia 50 on the Chesapeake. What speed will she do?"

"Maybe 7 knots."

"Uh huh!" he paused. "Are there any cold beers?"

"Yes in the ice box by the galley sink."

"Ted you ready for a beer?"

"Sure thing let's have one now."

George went below to get them.

"George pass up my handbag please. It's where I left it on the bed."

Danny was thinking –

Lord - how these people talk. I wonder why they like to charter a boat.

∾

"Reception – have you contacted Henry Braithwaite yet?"

"Yes Mr Morton - he's coming now."

"Good heavens at last!" Morton put the phone down. He was feeling tired and distracted. His thoughts lacked their usual clarity. *Why is Henry always late? I used to think he was trying to make a point - now I believe he's incapable of being on time.*

Henry was the hotel's foreman carpenter. His father, a Guyanese, had been a shipwright and had come to the island with his family when Henry was a small boy. They'd come on a small wooden sailing ship built in the Grenadines that traded fresh produce between the islands. His father had done well initially but later taken to drink. Henry found his schooldays irksome. He was neither handsome nor popular. The other boys had told him many times none of them had to bang water to reach Entropica. There was some bullying, but he was clever and worked with his father building and repairing fishing boats in the holidays. Twenty years later he had one of the best paid jobs available. He was famous throughout the island for his success and for his brightly coloured shirts - always purchased one or two sizes too big. His hair was receding slightly but he sported an enormous pair of sideburns that reached down almost to his mouth. Recently, he had found himself overweight and with 'pressure', so he was now trying, whenever possible, to avoid unnecessary strain.

There was a knock on the door and Morton looked up to see Henry's dark face.

"Come in Henry sit down."

He came in wiping the sweat from his face and hands with a handkerchief.

"I heard you were looking for me."

"Yes Henry, for the past hour. I want to know what's happening on the construction side *if anything*."

"Everything's progressing satisfactorily Mr. Morton. The form-work for the bridge is ahead of schedule..."

Morton noted his harassed expression and found it hard to make eye contact.

"And what about maintenance Henry? I hear there's all sorts of complaints."

Henry sat silent wondering who'd been complaining to Mr Morton about him. He only glanced at Morton for a second every now and then.

"Come on Henry," Morton cajoled, "you must have something to say."

"Well what sort of complaints?"

Morton hesitated.

"There are a lot of things that have been reported as defective and not properly progressed - fly screens in disrepair, doors not closing, cupboards not opening, shelves bending...."

"It's the weather Mr Morton. The sea breeze swell up the timber all the time. It can't be helped. I only two men on maintenance to fix all these things. The rest is on the bridge."

"And you really can't cope with two men full-time?"

"It's as you see it is Mr Morton."

Morton hesitated to ascertain that he understood this phrase.

"Well in that case if you're ahead on the bridge as you say you are you'd better pull two men off the bridge and put them on maintenance for the time being."

"Very well Mr Morton."

"So can I expect to see maintenance up to scratch within a week?"

"I'll do what I can Mr Morton."

"Very well Henry. I shall be looking to see how you get on. Please find Mr Finch and send him here to me."

Henry left the office with a weak smile.

NOON

"Girl come here help me fin' dis thing."

"Jacky you gotta fin' it yourself - you know I can't leave this desk now. I got a call coming in.... 'Hello Tamarind Tree can I help you?'"

Jacky continued to look through the chart desk drawers for the requested plan. She'd already read so many plan titles since she'd been told to find one she was beginning to wonder if she could remember its title at all. It was a plan for the leisure complex, yes, but what else did he say? Ground floor that was it, yes, and here it was in front of her: 'Leisure Complex/ Ground Floor/Structure.'

Near to tears, she pulled it out with relief. *At last*. It seemed like she'd spent all morning looking for it. She must have been through that drawer ten times already. She'd just finished pushing all the other plans back in so the drawer would shut when the accountant came in.

"Jacky is that the plan? Mr Morton is wondering what happened."

"Yes Mr Osborne this is the one" she smiled at him.

The accountant looked at it, folded it, and took it upstairs.

"You fin' it then girl?"

There was a big smile on Jacky's face.

"Yes, just in time. I look through them drawer...."

The reception phone went.

"Hello reception," Rubina with her telephone voice "yes... yes Mr Osborne."

"You hear that girl? They say they want the plumbing plan."

Mortified, Jacky went back to the chart desk. There was at least one copy of every plan, for every aspect of the hotel since the original architect's proposals, four years ago. Drained of all her confidence, breathing heavily, and with her back to the office door, she started through again.

After a short while she could hear Rubina's voice again.

"Yes Mr Morton is in.....is he expecting you?" Then "Please take a seat sir while I call him for you. Mr Morton, reception here. I have Mr Rogers here waiting for you..... yes sir..... Mr Rogers, Mr Morton says you can go up now."

Jacky heard the sound of the man climbing the office stairs.

"Eh, girl - that Mr Rogers the plumber. They must want the plan for he. Hurry up fin' it now."

~

At noon high up on the hill overlooking the resort Zackie's grandfather walked up the boundary path and lay down his cutlass and a large sackful of coconuts by his house. He took a drink of water from a bottle and settled himself on a rock under the shade of a breadfruit tree. He didn't go in the house feeling his old wife must be away on business somewhere.

Slowly his eyelids lowered on the hot day. He began to doze and the images of his youth came back to him. He surrendered willingly to them and moved amongst them again...

.... he saw his wife, then only a girl, and felt again the perfect wind that blew through their lives then...and then, as though from above, he saw the high fields of the island he strode over in his prime – steep and rocky. Now he seemed to fly over them, over his ground, over his fertile fields...and he remembered, could feel even, the strength he had had, his manliness, and his feeling for his wife...and then he saw a radiance - overhead and around them - their house, the land, the children, the animals - all were coloured in a golden hue - they were in a blessing. They were in the perfection of things and had become it. His wife was a little way away from him. He saw her looking over at him, and the white's of her eyes radiated out a joy - so easy, so boundless - it was all about them.

As his sleep ebbed and flowed he drifted from past to present and back again.

He remembered their labour and their produce coming out from the land - and he saw his wife and her labour and their children coming from her.

And then it must have been Sunday for their small children were standing outside the house dressed in their best and surrounding their mother with joy. And somehow his old face wore exactly the same joyous look hers had displayed all those many years before.

A plane passed overhead and stirred him, rousing him to the rest of the day. Looking up he saw the sun lower in the sky. He stood up slowly and reached awkwardly for his meal tin – all his joints now stiffened from lack of use.

Finding himself refreshed by his rest, the water and bread and his remembrances, he took up his cutlass again and picked his way carefully back down the hill.

AFTERNOON

At 4pm Bill could just make out 'Blue Eyes' sail amongst the twenty or thirty yachts visible from the beach. They were about three miles offshore. He walked along the beach barefoot on the hard sand near the sea to rig his sailing dinghy. At 4:30 p.m. 'Blue Eyes' entered the harbour under engine with her sails put away. Danny handled the boat well inside the dock area. The four charterers, reddened now by the day's sun, looked out from the cockpit with apprehensive smiles. Bill took the lines and made them fast. The charterers stepped ashore with evident satisfaction. Danny was given a generous tip, and they left for the taxi stand in good humour, strolling down the dock, gently bumping into each other as they went.

Bill and Danny stood watching them, smiling.

"Good day?"

"Yes."

"And a good tip. Okay - cover up the main sail and hose her down. You're in charge for the weekend - you know where I'll be. Don't leave the dock that's all. We'll talk on Monday."

"Right."

Bill slipped off to his Sunfish. His work on the advert for the hotel's sea sports had been passed to reception for Morton by lunch. Lunch hour had been spent making a wind bend diagram of the harbour in which they'd race - the trade winds blew from northeast to southeast and predictable veers could be worked out in advance. At 5 p.m. he was 50 yards offshore, out of hailing range, and feeling pleased. It seemed certain he'd be free for the championship. The boat felt more alive. The adjustments he'd made felt good. Looking to windward he saw five Sunfish sailing together and he tacked onto starboard to close them.

NIGHT

It was after dark and Henry was parked up on a dirt track off the main Point road. He owned a black executive Toyota. He'd had the windows tinted black. There were no lights on in his car or outside. He sat with his window open listening and thinking and watching the cars go by on the main road forty yards below him.

After about an hour Bates' car passed in front of him. He felt a tightening in his belly. *The Bates bastard.* When it was out of sight up the road to town, he closed his window, started up the engine and moved down the dirt track. Meeting the main road the car turned left and slid onto the road with a quiet crackling of gravel - stealthy, secretive and purposeful, like a reptile.

Approaching town he slowed down to walking pace. *Bates never go no place special.* He saw the car outside a bar. He carried on down through the town and pulled up outside his usual haunt - the 'Sunset Bar and Restaurant'. Inside he ordered a rum and coke. It was early. There was no one else there. He put a couple of records on the old jukebox to distract himself. Then he ordered another rum and coke and a chicken leg and chips even though he'd recently come from eating his evening meal at home. He sat in a corner drinking, eating and thinking. By nine o'clock the place was beginning to fill up. He went outside and got back in his car and headed back up the main road into town. Bates' car was still pulled up outside the same bar. Parking further down the road he sat still a moment regulating his breathing. Bates was a big guy. He didn't want to make any mistakes. He wiped the sweat off his face, climbed out and walked casually into the bar.

Bates was sitting on one of the bar stools surrounded by some of his friends.

"Eh, Braithwaite!"

"Yeah Bates, Maduro – how's things?"

"Well I dunno yet. Friday night. Should be good."

"Uh h uh."

He ordered a rum and coke and started to sip it. After a while a band started up across the road. By about ten o'clock there were a number of people milling around outside. Bates and his friends got up and crossed the street, paid at the door and went inside. Henry ordered another rum and coke. Later in the men's bathroom he washed his face and set his gold necklace in place, straightened his shirt, and pushed the gold rings on his fingers up against his hand. He had eight thick ones. As he walked back to his car he noted Bates' was still there. After a minute he started up and headed slowly west. He took a right at the government quarry and, switching off his lights, drove behind the crushing equipment. He turned off the engine, mopped his face and looked about him. All seemed quiet. He took the path that lead behind the village to Bates' backyard - hidden as it was by a curve in the valley. The small wooden house was all closed up, but there was a light coming from the cracks in the doors and shutters.

Henry knocked at the door. He called her by her maiden name. Her voice came out girlish and unsure.

"Who there?" But she already knew.

"It me, Henry. I come for you now."

~

It was late. There were small rattlings and bangings. Windows were being closed in a way the waiters judged to be obvious yet ostensibly discrete. The fruit table was dismantled and sent into the kitchen. The bar was cleaned off and the glasses dried. The cash register was attended to.

Morton sat over coffee and liqueurs with his hotel manager and subcontracted plumber. All the other diners had left. Morton puffed on his pipe and eyed the plumber.

"That was an excellent meal and quite unexpected. Thank you."

"Not at all Sunny" said Morton, "both Steadman and I are very satisfied with the work you've done for the hotel..."

"Thank you."

Morton glanced at Steadman, "... but speaking again about the matter we touched on earlier today in my office...

we really must open the new leisure complex this winter and as things stand it's your plumbing that might hold things up..." he paused "...could you possibly see your way to moving more quickly on this project?" Roger's face was impassive.

"We may be able to add some additional reimbursement to you...."

"I'm sorry Mr Morton. It's as I told you earlier. I can't change around now. I have some men on other works."

"Then take on more, why not?"

"I don't so much like to do that. It takes time to check out new men. I know the work of my men right now but I can't rush a job with new men. It's as you know Mr Morton."

Morton knocked his pipe against the sole of his shoe with some force.

"Sunny, you know we can employ our own plumbers."

"That's up to you Mr Morton."

Morton sat back. *It's like talking to a brick wall.*

"Steadman, what do you have to say about this?"

"I think in this case we should let the man get on as he wants. His work in the past has been good. We'll just put pressure on him to stay out in front."

He smiled at Rogers and Rogers returned his smile.

"Don't worry I'll be doing my best. Now if you gentlemen will excuse me my wife is expecting me home."

"Yes, yes of course."

They stood up and said goodnight. Rogers left and the maitre d' came over and was about to speak when Morton sat back down. When the maitre d' had retired he said,

"How the hell do you get a contented creep like that to move." It wasn't a question. Steadman smiled, pleased at Morton's remark and at his frustration. The man was really beginning to get the feel of things out here. It wasn't quite as simple as the terse instructions from England implied.

"Don't worry Ben," he counselled, "we can at least rely on him keeping his word. There aren't too many contractors like that as you know."

"Yes I suppose you're right," said Morton reluctantly "..I suppose you're right".

But he wasn't sure he was.

SATURDAY

MORNING

Early Saturday morning - the weekend heralded by a few cocks crowing as if impatient for action. But no bird takes to the air. Stillness. Even the night sounds have died away.

In the main cabin of a seventy foot wooden schooner Stan Sutton opened his eyes and was at once completely awake. His wife lay asleep beside him in their motionless boat. The chronometer on the oak panelled bulkhead showed 1005 GMT - five past six local time. He got up, slid back the hatch, and climbed on deck – still wearing the swimming shorts he'd worn the previous day. The anemometer moved and stopped.

"What's it like?" - his wife now awake.

"Not much yet. It'll fill in."

She put on T shirt and shorts and went to the gimballed stove to make tea. He went to his warehouse and dragged out three gigantic inflated orange buoys. After a struggle he had them in the chase boat. By the time he had the anchors aboard the tea was ready.

"Need any help?"

"Thanks. It's okay. I can lay them myself. Just get those scamps dressed and organised. They'll be on the boat for a long time today. It'll either drive them crazy or they'll drive us crazy. I'm hoping it's them not us." He drank his tea and looked at the sky again. Yesterday's marine forecast predicted winds east north east 10 to 15 knots - ideal for Sunfish sailing. Tea finished he left their marine home for the chase boat and starting up the main engine watched the gauges settle into place. Having checked the exhaust for cooling water, he untied the boat, pushed off and climbed aboard.

Up on the hill overlooking the harbour Red Hat sat on his veranda watching Stan go out. The big marine diesel could be clearly heard even though it was a mile distant. He watched Stan place the three markers and thought about where he'd place his tacks. His wife called him in for breakfast.

"Still no wind?"

"No" he replied "but it's coming now."

~

The race gun echoed around the hills surrounding the harbour. A puff of smoke rose away from the committee boat. Ten minutes to the first start. Stan reloaded for the five-minute gun, his wife readied the flags. Their children, sitting on the deck-edge with their life-jackets on, watched the big ones racing passed in their boats. It seemed they were in constant danger of hitting each other, there were so many of them, zigzagging in and out passed each other.

The first orange mark lay directly to windward and the start line was set at right angles to it - a small orange buoy at one end and Stan's chase boat at the other. The boats had to pass through this line and go around the three marks twice. Stan had made them in a triangle a mile and a half apart. Nine miles. He checked his gun, flags and stopwatch.

The sailors were in high spirits, the best ones in a focused sort of a way. It was the yearly Entropican Sunfish Championships. There was a good deal of shouting amongst the noise of flapping sails.

"Eh Red Hat!"

"Yo!"

"Steve! You' mast coming down!" Steve was the seventeen year old schoolboy son of a local businessman.

"Garbage! Keep out of my way today. I'm going to be going fast fast!"

They tried a few practice tacks keeping an eye on the wind patterns to windward as the wind slowly increased. The winds inshore were still light and coming in isolated gusts. It seemed best to stay offshore - later on might be better to tack in and play the shifts.

Another gun. They check their watches - five minutes to the start. A blue flag replaced the white one on Stan's boat - they were under racing rules. Bill looked at his sail. It was too full now that the wind had increased but the first chance to adjust it would be between races. The last two of the fleet of eighteen sailed up to the committee boat. Each had in two lightweight youngsters with anxious expressions on the faces. The helmsmen checked their watches and headed for the line.

The start gun and the first boats crossed over. Bill was through the line on port keeping an eye to leeward. After thirty seconds he was ahead and to windward of the rest of the fleet and tacked on to starboard to cover them, moving quickly and carefully. He got the boat going fast on the new tack and glanced quickly astern to see the whole fleet behind him. Steve made a poor start but tacked quickly onto port seeking stronger winds. Bill held on for a moment covering the fleet and watching Steve's progress. Seeing it was good he tacked to follow. Red Hat and Trini tacked with him.

The best four sailors worked their way to windward through the waves and increasing wind keeping their boats sailing fast and occasionally glancing at each other, the rest of the fleet and the wind patterns up ahead. Red Hat was moving up through them and each looked at their boats and Red Hat's to see why he was going faster, but after a few minutes he remained level.

They sailed with their feet in the boat but their backsides over the deck edge to keep the boats upright against the wind. This made for hard work on the stomach muscles and the wind was increasing. Steve was the lightest and as the wind increased it became harder and harder for him to sail his boat upright. He watched ever more intently for a wind bend and after a minute was sure he was being headed away from the first mark. This meant he could tack onto the now more favourable starboard tack and relax for a moment in doing so. He tacked and was confident as he settled down onto the new tack that this one was best. He renewed his efforts and by the first mark was ahead with Red Hat, Bill and Trini in close pursuit.

They raced off down the new leg away from the wind at high speed. They were close together and weaving to left and right trying to take each other's wind, take advantage of gusts, waves and surf.

Trini shouted "Steve slow down you bitch!"

Steve was delighted with his position and determined to hold onto it but Red Hat was fast off the wind and surfed ahead to gybe close behind him at the second mark. Bill and Trini gybed and they all ran back to the start line to complete the first lap. Racing passed small marker buoys from sunken fish pots they saw that there was little current. But the wind was changing and as they sailed down to the leeward mark Bill noted the wind filling in near the shore and determined to tack in if Red Hat stayed out.

At the leeward mark Steve led Red Hat by a boat's length. They both tacked immediately round it to pursue the same course they'd sailed on the first lap. Bill hardened up and headed inshore. Trini followed but then broke off and sailed to seaward. By the windward mark Bill was ahead of Red Hat and Steve by thirty yards. Going inshore had paid off. He felt good. The boat took off with the gusts, his self-bailer gurgled as it sucked the boat dry and he was catching the waves right and surfing in the gusts. Never had it felt so good and it always felt so good! Diving into the wave in front and cutting across the trough and up into the next wave, a gust and then spray and a white wake streaming out to the others behind, their boats dancing on the waves, dancing in the sun, the sea and the spray.

At the gybe it was evident Red Hat was catching him and by the finish line Red Hat took the gun with Bill second, Steve third and Trini surfing up close behind shouting "You got it Red Hat you got it."

"Close race!" shouted Red Hat.

"Nice oooo oooo oooo!"

Trini went by whooping and yelling.

They relaxed in the bottom of their boats, watching the rest of the fleet surf down to them, they're coloured sails shining, lit up by the sun. One more race before lunch and two after. They headed towards Stan's boat, watching each other, their boats and the sea - minds clear and fresh.

Stan leaned over toward them, evidently sharing in their pleasure, their happiness.

"If there's one thing I can't stand" he shouted over "it's seeing young men slacking."

On Saturdays the shops in town stay open till lunch. It's the busiest time of the week - the workers go shopping and people from all about come to town to lime. The main street, a hundred yards long, is bordered by the island's principal shops, together with a few private houses. Quiet wooden houses set in small fenced gardens appear much as they were fifty years ago – now surrounded by old fruit trees and scented iridescent flowers. Further along, ancient shops with wooden verandas and patterned fretwork are interspersed with huge brightly coloured concrete cubes, recently built and fronted by gaudy new signs.

All unfenced yards are the province of sheep, goats and fowl - they are all of them quite used to small town life. Here and there an old car can be seen, mutely rusting away in the undergrowth, kept near the people it used to carry. Walking along you can smell the baker's fine breads and cakes - glimpse town peoples' laundry skied by the morning wind - recognize familiar faces - island people going about their accustomed weekend chores, their children lagging a little way behind.

Jacky and her sister were in town carefully dressed and happy in their appearance. It seemed to Jacky that almost everyone had taken special care with their clothes. The young men looked especially fine but she also looked at the other girls and older women - their dresses and the way they styled their hair. She kept hers ironed straight. It seemed to her almost like going to church except some people could be noisy, even pushy, showy and in a rush. Rubina was standing at the corner as arranged. She stood talking to a man. Jacky stopped twenty yards short and talked with her sister, every now and then turning to watch her friend. She was looking her sister over to check everything was in order when Rubina came over excited.

"Jack – ky" she drew out the greeting.

"Girl" said Jacky "who you liming now?"

"Not he. Me standing there an 'e come up and say 'is love I love you'. I tell 'e 'e fresh. 'e say 'e carry me beach today!"

"You tell 'e no?"

"Of course girl who you think me is? Huh!"

She turned to her friend's sister.

"Hi Icilma." The girl nodded shyly back not feeling the equal of an older girl who could deal with men so easily.

"Well girl, what you coming town for today?"

"Pink thread, elastic, two pounds flour and salt fish."

"Come with me girl, le' we go by Hot Rod get ice cream."

"And how we going to reach there girl? I things to buy."

"Is walking we walk."

"Then le' we go fast fast."

They set off happy in each other's company. Between the shops they could make out the flapping sails of dinghies gathering for a race in the middle of the harbour. Jacky felt a fluttering inside her.

"Come on" said Rubina and then she sang, "I'm young, but I'm moving on..."

~

They were driving to the beach for the afternoon. A mile out of Cornfield, Henry's wife broke the silence.

"You really disgusting the way you slam the door on me in front the neighbours them."

Henry exuded anger but remained silent. He was finding it more and more necessary to use physical means to get peace in his own house. How could he have foreseen this when he built it all those years before – by far the largest house in the village. Everything was straightforward then. He'd been anxious to leave behind the common jam-up little house of his youth and own a proper monument to wealth and ease. His new single storey house boasted a high roof, giving rise to a vast L shaped living room. The walls were painted grey and the floor covered with red Italian tiles. The imported furniture was still safeguarded in the thick clear plastic covering set in place at the factory prior to dispatch. It was like living in a rather empty furniture warehouse.

Unhappily married for twelve years they were estranged – at sea in the same ship, borne down by their huge cargo of grudges. Unable to see the way out, they'd become prisoners of their own nightmare, powerless to do anything but continue.

And the further they went, the larger their cargo became and the more perilous their position. Anger came to them in waves.

"You a disgusting ignorant man."

The car climbed Runaway Hill to reach over the top road and descend to the bay where they would spend the afternoon. It was Henry's habit to sit in the bar 'chatting rubbish' with the Kapok Bay Bar crowd. His wife would sit along the beach under a tree with her women friends.

He sensed her getting ready to say something.

"Shut up!"

∾

Zackie and Chip were sitting on a smooth volcanic rock by the house. A black car was coming slowly down the unsurfaced road towards them. They watched it coming, the wheels being pushed up into the car by the rocks in the road and coming out again, the dust turning in clouds behind.

"Henry car" said Zackie.

As it approached they looked to see who was inside. A woman. As it came closer they saw it was Henry's wife, could hear hostile voices and see anger in expressions and gestures. Chip waved as the car went by. Henry looked through him. The car carried on down the road.

As if to break the spell of the sourness the car seemed to leave behind with its tracks and dust Chip began to sing:

"If you get down, and you quarrel, everyday
you sayin' prayer, to the devil, I say...."

"Brother Bob Marley, Rastafari, I-n-I one" said Zackie, "ever livin', ever faithful..."

The sourness vanished with the song.

"Me hungry. Le' we go look mango"

"Yeah brother man"

They set off at an easy pace - the sun was high. Zackie took up the song again and his friend joined in. This was their music, Rastafari word, Jah law.

"If you get down, and you quarrel, everyday You' sayin' prayer, to the devil, I say. Why not try help one another on the way Make it much easier You just can't live, that negative way if you know when I mean Make way for that positive day, for it's...."

Chip climbed a huge evergreen tree with a giant trunk and dark leaves and threw down a dozen ripe mangoes. Zackie caught all twelve and shouted "West Indies!"

The mango were not quite ripe and tasted so strong first bite it hurt their mouths.

"We eat till our stomach them tell us to stop."

Afterwards they lay back in the shade of the tree and smoked some ganja. Chip said:

"Me going to get a red tent and then me going to start movin' 'round the hills them livin' with the natural life and the wind....it going to be Rastafari home and me goin' plant it over I-tal an' eat up the I-tal in the tent...an' inside going to be I-rey and cool and everything red-red and me asking a sister come in wi' me an' lie down inside it an' we be together an' then I-n-I break it down and move on an' wave to them baldhead them an' them goin' to say 'How this man goin' on so?' an' I-n-I goin' on so and go so and go..... and me fin' a next place and me watch the star them comin' out an' me listenin' to the wind and me seein' the cloud them passin' over - an' all the lickle life there wi' me too - makin' noise an' listening to themself ....

An' in the mornin' I-n-I wake up and everythin' red-red an' I-rey..."

You needed a car to reach Kapok Bay Bar. As a result many of the wealthier islanders favoured it as their weekend meeting point. Beautifully situated amongst trees and shrubs, it faced west out over the Caribbean Sea from the middle of a mile wide pink flecked, white sand bay.

By late afternoon the bar was full of noise and people jostling about. The bar's radio was turned right up and someone had brought a giant stereo and left it playing rockers on one of the side tables. Most of the patrons were male and had been there for some time. No one was without a rum or a beer. A dozen fellows crowded round the bar betting on a horse race about to be relayed over the radio. At a corner table there was a loud game of dominoes in progress - you had to make noise or you couldn't hear yourself play. Everyone by now had acquired a smile, albeit a slightly foolish or exaggerated one, and were feeling in the Saturday afternoon groove. The sun was falling in the sky and the rays blasted into the bar - but it just seemed to excite everyone more: they drank more and sweated more and shouted more and demanded more attention of each other. They drank together and no one really noticed who paid or for whom. They only noticed when someone ordered drinks and found they couldn't pay. This was a huge joke and everyone laughed and generously chipped in.

Henry and Peter sat at a table in animated conversation. Normally their relationship wasn't very good and they wouldn't have chosen to socialise together - but today they were united in their contempt for Morton. Peter was a little surprised by the depth of Henry's wrath but being united with a local was unusual and pleasant. Henry mopped his face with his handkerchief and shouted for two more rum and cokes. Peter, remembering his wife sitting alone on the beach, drank his down quickly, and got up to go.

Henry said "By the way, what size spanner you need for the brake nuts to bleed Morton's car?"

"Three quarter inch." Peter gave him a quizzical look.

"Okay, see you later then."

They parted with brightly shining eyes and a feeling of kinship which seemed strange to them both.

Peter made a reasonable exit from the bar but landed badly and felt unsteady when he reached the soft sand of the beach. He couldn't walk quite straight.

"Marjorie - going for a swim!"

She looked up from her place some distance down the beach and immediately thought *He's sloshed.* But when the water reached his waist he dived forward into a powerful freestyle. The water swirled about him cool and fresh and all his thoughts immediately vanished. Inner turmoil turned into physical power and he was simply a man swimming out into the bay.

A hundred yards out he stopped and turned back to face the beach which lay exquisite and tranquil before him. The grasses on the hill above the bay changed colour as the winds passed over them. He turned over on his back and watched the colossal clouds floating by over the bay. The sea supported him gently like an old friend. He knew his quarrel with Morton was false, vain, absurd and insignificant. He swam out further round a schooner anchored out in the bay and then back in to the shore to sink down on the sand by his wife. His body seemed to have become very heavy. The sun dried and warmed him. It seemed the whole bay was his friend and his heart went out to the bay and somehow was the bay. A spirit of great good feeling welled up in him and he took care not to move at all but wished he could be there always like that - feeling that everything was in its proper place and somehow taken care of.

Marjorie sat on a towel a little distance off. Having caught the sun she sat facing it, now covered in a thin cotton print dress put on over her modest pink bikini. Her elbows rested on her knees and she looked seaward. The rays of the sun were still on her burning her face and neck more deeply but she didn't move.

Tomorrow I shall have to stock up on food. I should have done it yesterday. I'll have to go to the supermarket to get the New Zealand lamb. She disliked the girls there. They were unfriendly. She didn't know her weekly grocery bill was more than their weekly wage. She practiced in her mind before them. Dignity was precious. *And how much is that? Kindly place everything in a box for me. I have my car outside.* And then she was in her car and wanting to get away and it wouldn't start. Three youths sat on a wall watching her as you might watch some unpleasant looking animal in a cage. *Push push! I need a push. Push!*

"It's beautiful here" said Peter.

"Yes it's lovely isn't it?" said Marjorie looking at her husband with a smile. *It's beautiful yes – but how much longer have we got to stick it out for?*

EVENING

The sun turned red and went down below the sea. The day was almost finished. The island, unbidden, glided slowly toward the night. A cool wind moved over the land and it began to loose its colour. The day's last sounds, clearly born on the dusky stillness, faded out into the unknown leaving the valleys empty.

In the villages men were returning home to eat and rest. Women, standing by their houses, talking and shouting at their offspring, finishing off their work, looked up to see it was already dark, and the lights from the other houses shining out into the night.

~

The gangsters stood in a line smugly confident. It was easy to dislike them. They'd just beaten up some nice Chinese boys. Bruce Lee stepped forward and faced them. Then, in an instant, he span on one foot and kicked the leader in the face.

"The dragon whips his tail!" he said. The cinema resounded with shouts of approval. But he'd only kung-fued one of them. Now he started on the others. Edna and Tyrone watched enthralled. Their weekly outing and the movie was good. They'd been gone from the house for an hour.

In the house, behind locked doors, a light came on.

"Switch it off."

The house to themselves.

"No get up."

They all got out of bed. James climbed excitedly under a small table in the main room. His head stuck out one end and his behind the other.

"I can turn into a cat you know."

Thwack! His sister had seized the opportunity and hit him hard on his behind.

"Mosquito on your bum" she said. James was afraid to cry.

"Keep quiet or Alice will hear." Alice lived next door.

Junior switched on the TV. James was in the kitchen rubbing his behind. Then he moved a chair to the stove and climbed on it and had the saucepan lid in one hand and a chicken leg in the other.

Alicia came in.

"Boy you get lash!"

James smiled back between bites.

"No, me gonna eat this chicken. If they ask who eat it me say a rat."

The television picture came on and their smiles of pleasure with it. The toys stayed neglected.

"Switch out the light." James did it with sticky fingers.

The TV flickered its messages to them in the dark room and they watched with reverence. Figures were moving on the screen.

Alicia got up and changed to a Spanish station. Then she changed it back. James adjusted the aerial. Then they went back to the Spanish station again. They sat and watched and listened without understanding – listening also to the sounds of the house and for their father's car. They were ready to be caught, ready to run and jump and cry and protest and get lash.

But it was good, oh yes it was very good, it was exceedingly good – TV, truancy and chicken.

SUNDAY

MORNING

Sunday and a quiet morning. Like many others the top road is walked by people going to church in small groups – young and old together, carefully turned out and looking their best – clothes pressed, shoes polished, sacred books held close in well cleaned hands. How extraordinary that from these tired old wooden buildings come forth these fresh faced and well dressed aspirants! The lengthy striking of the bell draws them out from their many and varied homes set back and sometimes hidden from the road.

Zackie's grandfather is one who walks to church. His wife has gone ahead in a cousin's car - she carries some weight these days and her heart is not so good so her family insists she takes a ride when she can. He walks with his friend Tuitt, his stiff black shoes clack against the occasional concrete patch in the dirt road. He has on his Sunday best - a baggy pair of old Oxfords and a grey jacket to match. A brown once sporty hat is set on his head at a slight angle. Cupped in his bony hands are his Bible, service and hymn books. There is a lovely dignity and humility about him which cannot fail but move the heart. All about the land smells sweet. Fallen mangoes are in the road and occasionally he treads on one in error. The bell rings and rings. He and Tuitt walk unhurriedly towards it. There is little need for words.

By the church people greet each other and move inside. They bend down and pray and then sit back with a sense of ease. This is truly marvellous that people can come together in true fellowship - the church their own tranquil space. The wind comes in waves through the big church doors and shutters. Coconut trees lining the hills near and far can be seen, their fronds bowing to the wind and rippling in the sun. The organ starts up and they stand and sing their first hymn. They sit again and a young woman reads a familiar passage, then they kneel and pray. After that the minister comes down from the altar and tells them he doesn't like the way the Boys Brigade is getting so small - if the boys have work to do they must do it at some other time or else he'll stop the meetings. Then the organ starts up again, sweet music, they all stand and sing.

The sermon includes an old Testament passage on the rights of herdsman. Everyone sits up and listens keenly and occasional sounds of approval are heard. *No one can thief my goat!* The final hymn and as they move outside the minister is there by the south door.

"Let the words of your mouth and the meditations of your heart be acceptable in His sight."

He shakes their hands as they leave - something is passed on - given to them - and his words stay with them.

~

"Where the bloody hell is everyone for goodness sake? What do they think this is a holiday camp or something? A hotel, any hotel, anywhere in the world, opens seven days a week. So what do they think this is? Closed for weekends? It's like trying to organise a load of juvenile delinquents and I swore I'd never do that again after my children grew up. Where are our managers Steadman? Your managers Steadman? Where the hell are they?

"Don't tell me they all got religion or something. Not that motley lot. Next time any of them enter a church it'll be inside a box. And where were they yesterday? I was here all day. How often do they think I can come out from England to see them?

Good God... They must think we're running a charity or something. If the British, the Canadians and the Americans are stupid enough to give money to the public sector that's their look out - but this is the private sector - we have to be accountable Steadman or we go broke Steadman and you know what that means Steadman for the hotel, for these people and for the island. Maybe Fred is right – they're just a load of charity children."

"Peter and Bill are here Ben?"

"No they're not as you well know and I deeply regret bringing them out here and leaving them here for so very long. I deeply regret it. It was very wrong of me and I'm going to see to it I get them back. I don't know what's happened to them - they were good men when I brought them out here but now look at them - they couldn't organise a piss up in a brewery. The sun's muddled their heads. It's really sad."

Steadman smiled. He enjoyed executive theatre.

"No really Steadman, it is, it's sad, it's pitiful. We build a glorious hotel, we try and advance the island and improve the people's lot - and what do we get...."

Steadman remained silent, still smiling slightly, aware of the tax and investment advantages.

"....disloyalty. That's what we get. Disloyalty. You try. You do your best for people and you turn around and they're..." he paused to puff on his pipe ".... they're not here. They're out enjoying themselves as they call it. But what they don't realize, what they can't seem to realise is that the only real enjoyment - the deep lasting enjoyment - comes through hard persistent work and the satisfaction of knowing that they have a definite job. And if they don't realise that very soon it's going to be too late - too damn late for all of them." Morton looked away and they sat in silence for a moment each thinking their own thoughts.

An image of his college days in the States came into Steadman's mind. *Ben's like a silver pinball. He comes springing up the road in the morning - if you leave him alone without opposition he'll quickly lose momentum, drop to the bottom and disappear and the game is finished. But if you oppose him he'll rebound madly around all day, banging into things, scoring points and looking like he'll never stop and the devil himself is chasing him.*

Steadman was waiting for him to lose momentum. He'd spent last night arguing with his wife and now felt emotionally exhausted.

"Ben, let me take you down Sugar Mill and buy you a lunch."

"And whatever happened to Bill's advertisement, I was meant to have it on Friday – Friday!"

"Ben, let me buy you a lunch."

No answer.

"Ben, let's go down Sugar Mill, I'll buy you lunch. We're both hungry. We can continue our discussions better with a full stomach."

"Very well Steadman, I am hungry yes."

"And there's some dinghy racing in the harbour, a national championship - we can watch it from the terrace."

"Dinghy racing! In the harbour! So that's where he is! The lazy bastard."

AFTERNOON

The pans bubbled away on the propane burners - stewed mutton, tania, fig, ducana and rice. Yesterday a villager had killed a goat and they'd bought mutton from him and flour from the supermarket. The rest they'd grown themselves on the land around the house. Jackie and her sister fussed over the Sunday dinner having set aside their church clothes for later. Their mother had stayed behind for members' prayer meeting.

"I believe that boy Charlie love you."

"Yeah? Well me no love 'e"

"Me see 'e today watchin' watchin' you in church."

"Not true."

"Yes true."

"Hmm."

"You don't love any boy at all?"

"Maybe I like one." Icilma looked away.

"Go finish your homework."

"No, I do it later."

"Go do it now a girl! Later we go church."

Icilma frowned but went to her bedroom. She'd wanted to be cooking the food when her mother came home.

She pulled out her 'English Grammar' book from under her bed. The last entry read:

'Essay. A supermarket.'

She put the book on her knee and started to write:

"My mother work in a supermarket. It have a glass front. It a big shop with hundreds of food inside. It cool inside and you can have a trolley. There are a lot of people shopping and big car outside. There is not enough space to walk through with the trolley with the people them there. Most things we never eat yet. They are for the white people. They always have sales food for less money but is not what we buy. One day I go work with my mother. The young man them put the food on the shelf. The woman sit at the desk and take the money. The boy carry out the box them."

The sound of a car picking its way up the dirt road. Lunch time!

It was like carnival in the clubhouse. The racing finished, the prize giving yet to come, sailors and friends stood in groups talking, drinking, shouting, gesticulating - enthusiastic speech and happy friendship.

It had been Steve's day and the championship settled in the final race. In a fresh breeze he'd given everything and beaten the stronger and heavier Red Hat. Bill had come in third with Trini forth. Many of the juniors had capsized and now talked with great zeal and pleasure demonstrating positions that only a short time ago had seemed quite alarming. Occasionally they glanced with reverence at Steve.

The Commodore, a portly ex-pilot of the Pacific War, had spent the day watching the racing from the after deck of his yacht which was moored close by the racing circuit. As his sun awning was away for repair he'd taken a large supply of iced drinks aboard for the day to help keep cool. He now stepped forward, and in what was perhaps the most distinguished manoeuvre of the day, squeezed himself between the wall and the prize table without knocking anything off. Already partly drunk and with a face so red it could have been a traffic light, he called defiantly for silence. This evidently gave him some pleasure as he repeated himself several times after the room had become quite quiet. Surprisingly, he was then able to give an articulate and appropriate speech on the club and the improving racing standards. He then invited Steve to come forward.

Steve's parents watched with obvious pleasure, but it was a nice moment for everyone.

"But victory is only sweet if the competition is good" said the Commodore handing over the trophy. The best junior then received his prize and went shyly back to his friends. The ceremonies over no one wanted to go home - the atmosphere was too sweet. The boats bobbed up and down outside the clubhouse – inside the members talked happily together.

Bill and Steve fell to talking about the forthcoming dayboat championships. They agreed to race together again this year. They'd won it last year. Steve was called away to show his trophy and Bill was left thinking about last year's championships and in particular the last race. Competition had been very tight throughout. They had to win the last race to be sure of victory. They got ahead from the start and stayed ahead careful to make no mistakes. Then on the last run home, their tangerine spinnaker billowing out in front and their competitors all way astern behind their sparkling white wake, they sat on opposite gunwales and spoke easily for the first time in the race. Steve said

"Bill, do they have boats in heaven?"

"I don't know. I believe they do. Yes."

"Good," said Steve "it's as I thought." They were approaching the finishing line, smiling happily.

"Do you think if we practiced really hard..."

Bill said "Yes I think we could beat Him. I believe we could. Yes."

Nobody with a slight knowledge of her would have imagined she had such a powerful voice. But then no one with a slight knowledge of her would have seen her with her mouth wide open. It was enormous. The children must have been fully a quarter of a mile away when they heard her shout and though they came scrambling quickly back over the dirt roads clutching their sticks and hoops it was some minutes before they reached their yard and clambered up the concrete steps onto the wooden floor of their house and into the room where their mother was waiting. Still jubilant and overwrought from their games with the other children, they now received a few harsh words from their mother which saw their faces drop.

They took off their clothes and stood one by one in the galvanised tub with a piece of soap in their hands trying to look as though they were doing a good job. Edna sat watching them. After she'd dried off and put on underwear, Alicia stood between her mother's long thighs and had her hair plaited and bobbles placed in - fluorescent pink and white. James hair was kept short. Alicia took down the clean blue uniforms from behind the bedroom door and they put them on. Girls Brigade and Boys Brigade. Now they looked clean and smart, little brown limbs sticking out from their blue uniforms, black socks and black shoes. Edna looked them over and was pleased but didn't show it.

"Get the books them and go come back as you is." They left the house by the front door, not as the frenetic street urchins that had recently come in the back, but as the Williams children, members of the Boys Brigade and Girls Brigade of Point Village Methodist Church. They felt special walking down the street in their blue uniforms side-by-side, their holy books in their hands, their clean eyes lighting up the world. Thus they went to church to pray for the God that was inside them.

~

NIGHT

Soon after the sun went down beneath the west horizon the moon arose from out of the eastern sea. Full and round, it ascended the eastern sky decorating the warm tropical night. Silently it sent down its luminous power and silently it drew its waters up.

Ina went to bed early as did most people on a Sunday night. She was Zackie's girlfriend, a well built eighteen year-old. She lived with her aunt in a small four room wooden house on the top road. Her room was now a dark island moving through the bright lunar night. But the moon sent a beam into the room through the cracked and shrunken shutters, and as the moon moved so the beam moved slowly over her body till it came to her shoulders and she was awakened. She flexed her body and pushed open the wooden shutters and was at once looking into the sky and the round whiteness of the moon. Its light washed over her and awakened the room. Breathing deeply she focused her eyes on it feeling her youthful power steadily increase. For some time she stayed quite still absorbing the watchful energy of the night, the black discs of her breasts pointing back at the white disc of the sky. Then in a single movement she pulled a frock over her head, jumped out of the window and left the house. Bare feet over dry earth. In a moment she was outside Zackie's house. She knocked on the shutter by his bed. Wearing only a simple cloth around his waist he opened the door. She stood there before him, her watery eyes looking at him, looking into him.

"That's good." He spoke slowly. She came in. He closed the door and as he set the latch she pulled the frock up over her head and dropped it to the side. It landed on a chair. He pulled at his loin cloth. It fell to the floor. They looked at each other for a moment without smiling and then came together in a strong embrace .

The heat and the insects had kept Morton largely without sleep for four nights now. He lay on his back in his brown nylon pyjamas with the room fan set to maximum. He was embellishing one of his favourite themes .... *therefore it's essential in any society that all are bound together by the need to help each other for the common good under one charismatic leader.... here in the West Indies that team spirit is still only a shadow*

of what it could be in time.... He pursued his subject further and further into the night. After a while he realised he was thinking about the next day's meetings. He saw Bill walk nonchalantly into his office. *And where the hell were you over the weekend?* No words came from Bill's mouth. *I'll tell you where you were. You were out running a little dinghy around some buoys with a group of other little children. Yes children! When are you going to grow up, become adult and bind together as a team for the common good working towards a socially valuable goal...surely the greatest happiness for the greatest good is worth some hardship now...* Feeling drowsy but believing some fresh air would help him sleep he got up and pulled aside the curtains and patio fly screens expecting to step out into dark night. Much to his surprise it was quite light and he immediately looked up to see if someone had left the light on. It was the moon, full and directly overhead. Its brilliance in the islands always amazed him afresh. He remembered his astronomical knowledge. *It must be midnight.* He checked his watch. *Twelve minutes off. Not bad! It's a beautiful night. There's a lot of beauty here alright. The sea has beauty, the trees here have beauty, yes, even the hotel buildings have beauty. It is all worthwhile. We must press forward.*

He went back to his bed and soon fell into an even sleep.

~

MONDAY

MORNING

Marjorie awoke with the alarm clock at 6:30 a.m. Her husband turned over and faced the other way. Monday morning. She felt low. She got slowly out of bed and put on her kimono and went to the kitchen and stood there a moment, a little dazed, pushing her hair into place. She picked up the coffee percolator and smelt it. It smelt of cockroaches. She rinsed it out and set it going. The boiling water would kill any germs. Then she cleaned two of the cups left from the pile of dishes from Sunday dinner. *Ugh.... how many more days in this heat and humidity do we have to endure? England.... cool morning walks along the pavement to school arriving fresh, rosy cheeked and ready. Here you awake feeling tired and even if you want to work they don't let you. And the standard of the schools! It's all pitiful - the low standards, the listlessness, the dampness, the cockroaches, the struggle...... and for what? What have we gained?* She leaned over and turned the gas down. *My friends have houses in England, they have their husbands in secure jobs. But if Peter is told to leave now what do we go back to?*

She poured the coffee into the cups and took them to their bed and sat on the edge.

"Peter"

"Morning darling" he groaned.

"Coffee's here"

He sat up with half closed eyes and took the cup.

Like many expatriate wives she'd come to the Caribbean expecting halcyon days absorbing the tropical sun, but somehow with time she'd become closed to its brilliance, out of phase with her surroundings, disconnected - unhappy. There was nothing to do and nothing to be done about it. She had a maid, they were cheap. But she wasn't allowed to work and there were no children to mind. She had been a teacher in England so she visited the local schools anyway. They were off-putting - paint peeling off the walls both inside and out, broken desks, torn books, beer cans propping the louver windows open and an arrogance or resentment in her escort that made her want to leave quickly. And the other expatriate wives were very cliquey. You had to have been on the island for years to be fully accepted. Her altruism was fast disappearing into a huge pot of petty thoughts, gossip and self-indulgence. On some days even the simplest tasks loomed as great hurdles laid before her and other people appeared as cold hearted spectators ready to scoff should she trip and fall. Today was another day she had to get through. She had to organise the maid and do the shopping. There was a gaping emptiness inside her and she took in some coffee and cigarette smoke and looked around her. Her apartment was her prison. She'd decorated it herself.

Hearing the cat scraping at the door she left the bed. The cat came in slowly through the opened door. She petted it with one hand, smoking with the other.

~

The phone was ringing as he unlocked the harbour office door. He stepped quickly inside.

"Harbour office."

"Good morning Mr Baker. I have an urgent message for you."

"Hello Jacky - how are you today?"

"Fine thank you. I had a radio telephone call...."

"Oh no!"

"...from TT6"

"The Heidelbergers. What's the problem?"

"They say they are on Jailbird Reef."

"Oh no!... What damage?"

"I don't know, they didn't say." She sounded concerned.

"Did you take the call?"

"Yes."

"When did it come in?"

"Fifteen minutes ago."

"Five to eight. That's all?"

"Yes"

"Okay thanks. Oh and Jacky..."

"Yes."

"Oh - nothing." He replaced the phone, switched on the VHF radio and tuned to Channel 16, the call up and distress frequency.

"Tamarind Tree to TT6. Tamarind Tree to TT6."

He wasn't getting through or they weren't listening. He tried again. *Damn. Come in and answer. I wonder what they were drinking. Oh yes we put a half gallon of brandy on board! It had to be that. And Danny not here yet.*

He phoned the shipyard.

"Hello Jake.... yes Bill. We have a boat on Jailbird... Yes that's right. If you see me towing something in your direction in about four hours please clear the hoist.... yes.... Thanks."

He started loading the chase boat – first-aid kit, 1" line, bridle, mask, snorkel, scuba tank, crowbar, pump. *God I wonder if they holed it. Brand new boat. That damn drink.* He started the engine, untied the lines and pushed the bow out and jumped aboard by the wheel.

Well I'm sorry I can't stay to do the office work Mr Morton. He turned the wheel, put her into gear and throttled up. *Urgent business elsewhere I'm afraid. Darn it! But here we go. The Lone Ranger rides again.*

As he passed the harbour entrance he opened the throttle to full revs. A big smile spread over his face . *Hee hee hee hee. What a nice day for a boat ride!*

~

It was Hilton's Day off. He was walking up from town towards the hotel to meet his cousin Elba for lunch. His best friend Leroy was at his side. They could have been brothers - supple and slim, overdressed and pleased in their appearance, they were alert for everything going on around them - too bad to miss something, miss a chance somewhere.

"Yeah man I got her real good" said Hilton smiling with pleasure. "I tell her, easy like, 'You come down by me Saturday night late'. I lyin' on my bed listenin' to the music machine an' I hear two smally, smally knocks. I open the door and it Nan there looking sweet boy in a cat suit with a deep vee neck. She dig the place straight away as I have on the dread disco lighting and she love the mirrors. I play this track for her and boy..." he broke off. Their eyes met smiling. "She sweet and nice uh-huh! We together four hours. I tell she come by me tonight. I give her a little thing."

"Boy" said Leroy enviously, "you's a lucky sonovabitch."

They walked on the road now as the pavement stopped outside the town.

"Eh – s'appenin' to Bob these days?"

"He got he head tie."

"You mean the Fritt's girl?"

"Yeah she have him boy. Every night 'e on her doorstep like a dog. Every night! Some night 'e wait outside by the bushes an' can't go up – 'e 'fraid she or somethin'. Most night 'e up there an' she just ignorin' 'e or puttin' 'e down and 'e just taking it boy."

"Eh, that better never happen to me or I fist she down when I get out!"

"But Bob 'e not get out. She rule 'e. 'e eyes always like 'e somewhere else – 'e tied for true. An 'e give she all 'e money on a Friday."

"All?"

"Yeah."

"You jokin' me!"

"No, I tellin' you. All. Everything. She take all. Garry tell me by Monday 'e broke and beggin' a ride to town. An' you know how Bob always sayin' how 'e goin' to buy a bike an' 'e never buy – you don't notice that? An' 'e get hundred an' twenty bucks a week an' 'e doesn't even have a next pant."

"So she cook up 'e head for true eh?" He couldn't help laughing. "Uh uh uh – poor Bob". Tears of pleasure welled up in his eyes.

"'e better watch out or 'e daydream so much the hotel get a next lifeguard."

As they approached the hotel they could see a middle-aged white man up a wooden telegraph pole. On Morton's insistence, the electrical subcontractor was urgently installing power lines and a step-down transformer to the area designated for the leisure complex. He had his grips on and was leaning back away from his work as he secured an insulator bracket to the pole - a job he'd first done thirty years ago.

Leroy asked "Who 'e?"

"Fred. 'e a' Englishman. 'e a race man."

"'e look like a boy pickin' nut up a tree."

As they went by Leroy shouted up "Eh honkey! I hungry. You lookin' nuts? Throw me one down."

Fred, already heated by his work and the pressure he was getting from Morton, looked down at the two black youths amused at his expense.

"You want a nut?" He feigned searching in his tool box, "here have this two inch hexagonal steel one. It should fit you. Open your big mouth wide."

AFTERNOON

Mid-afternoon and scarcely a cloud on the horizon - the air quite still. The sun's rays pass unhindered onto the island - they have a searing, burning edge. In the nearby fields animals lay motionless in the shade - pigs in the dirt, cows chewing their cud. Goats and sheep, tied by children in the early morning light to small bushes in open land, now kneel down before this huge glaring disc, panting and looking about themselves nervously - they are vulnerable. They will stay tied there till evening when their young keepers return.

There are no seabirds on the wing and only an occasional fish jumps - the sea is tepid. The hotel guests recline in shady areas moving only to collect iced drinks from fridges and bars. For the construction workers it's an unpleasantness that has to be withstood till four. They work at an even pace - not as fast as in the morning, but they keep going. Most wear baggy shirts and pants – a few strip to the waist exposing dark muscles varnished with sweat. But it's hard to maintain determination day after day in this heat. Even the tar on the road goes soft.

"So gentleman exactly why did you choose to try and sink the backhoe?" Morton's voice, although somewhat stern, betrays a trace of pleasure. They are standing in a small group next to where the new bridge is being erected. In front of them the tyre marks show where the backhoe had dug into the soft sandy mud. It now stands clear of the edge and is being hosed down, its engine running. The bulldozer stands twenty yards away and Alf is removing the wire tow he's used to pull it clear. Peter speaks up:

"The backhoe saves us time carrying timber. We just hit a soft patch that's all."

"Well I'm glad it's saving you time, very glad. You must be ahead of schedule then!" said Morton.

Henry stared silently at the hole the backhoe had made. Peter felt his anger rising. He'd been up to his waist in mud. Morton's words had little power as his clothes were clean.

"We're on time," said Peter and then shouted "Alf get that sledge from the store now." Walking off he said, "Excuse me a minute," to Morton though he had no intention of returning,

"Are you on time Henry?"

"Trying to Mr Morton - but you take off two of my best men and that must keep me back."

"Well just make sure the formwork is ready by Wednesday. Then Peter should have the steelwork complete by Friday and we'll be ready to pour cement. Then we'll have a bridge...."

Not expecting a reply Morton turned and started walking toward the offices. As he did so he caught sight of Bill making for reception within hailing distance.

"Bill," he shouted over. He recognised that he was in a good mood for combat. Bill came over.

"I understand you had a boat on a reef overnight and you didn't reach it till late this morning. What happened?"

"That's right. We received their distress call this morning. They went on last night at dusk."

"So how come you weren't out there yesterday?"

"I think they were trying to get themselves off. They only called today."

"And the damage?"

"Deep scratching of the hull."

"Propeller and shaft?"

"Okay. No funny noises. They were lucky. I told them they've lost their deposit but can continue if they make harbour by early afternoon. They didn't see the reef as it was dusk."

"And you consider them capable after they've smashed into a reef?"

"Yes, I think so. They're to keep away from the reefs and use the bigger harbours."

Morton gave him a cool penetrating look. He felt he could trust Bill's judgment in this case.

"And where is your presentation that was due to me by Friday noon?"

"You haven't received it? That's funny, I gave it in to reception."

"To whom?"

"To Jacky"

"Well kindly retrieve it and bring it to my office in ten minutes."

Ten minutes later Bill was at the office door holding a file. Morton looked up from his coffee and waved him in. He was almost seated when Morton said

"Tell me why you were neglecting your duties over the weekend."

"I don't believe I was." Morton noted how uneasy Bill looked.

"Oh, so you consider leaving the harbour in the hands of an inexperienced youth fulfilling your duties to the full?"

Bill looked Morton in the face but sat silent.

"And if those idiots had radioed us on Sunday morning you'd have swept into glorious action I suppose."

"I have to have time off the same as anyone else and he has to learn to replace me. That means he gets time on his own."

"But doesn't it strike you of some importance that if I'm on island for a limited time and you're requested to produce a document you should make yourself available to discuss it."

"Well I was available Friday afternoon."

"And you should have been available all weekend as you well know."

Morton was feeling heated.

"How is your training of Danny going?"

"He's doing quite well. I believe he should be able to stand on his own two feet within the year."

"Very well. That means in a year's time you will have completed your duties here."

Morton noticed with pleasure the flicker of surprise that passed over Bill's face.

"Well to that extent yes."

"And what other extent is there?"

Bill didn't reply but looked away. Morton continued "Really in many ways the expatriate staff have failed to perform adequately. This isn't a criticism you understand. It's just the way things have turned out. It was a poor decision and really as instigator of the management system I feel some responsibility for this, for you all. I think it was wrong of me to get you out here and I intend to help you return to England at the years end."

"I see."

Morton watched him carefully trying to gauge the effect of his words but Bill remained deliberately opaque.

"And now," said Morton, "kindly let me see your work."

After the meeting Bill returned to his office and phoned the site office.

"Peter... yes, Bill here, you were right - we have less than a year."

"He's determined to have the locals run the thing before they're ready."

"I know that. You know that. Steadman knows that..."

"But Morton prefers not to know that."

"Right."

~

Burnt and dishevelled, swathed in bleached-out shirt and shorts, Fred would enter the Water's Edge Bar at the end of every working day with the look of a bomb disposal expert returning from a close encounter. Fifty three years old and with a face reddened and wrinkled by the tropical sun he was of Yorkshire coal mining stock. A competent tradesman and hard worker, he lived alone in a small apartment behind the town. He had come out a married man, but now his former wife lived in St. Thomas with a Thomian.

The bar was a popular meeting point for expatriates. Soon after he'd seated himself with a characteristic sigh at his accustomed table the waitress bought over a cold beer. He took it from her without speaking, as if it was of little consequence to him, a mere formality, but as soon as it reached his throat his body took over and sucked it down in an instant, so extreme was his need of it. Gazing at the empty bottle he felt sweat beginning to emerge from all the pores of his body as if the liquid had been immediately rushed to all the dried out parts and now the body overflowed a little as a sign of gratitude for having been properly wetted. He felt at once more human and a little surprised at the extent of his dehydration. His partner, Jack, joined him with two more beers and after these he was refreshed and ready for some conversation.

"What a day, what a day," he started.

"Yes the sun could burn you up today."

Fred ordered two more beers and continued.

"You know what 'appened today? I was up a pole fixing transformer in place by Tamarind Tree. Their builders were trying to get some formwork for a bridge in place." His friend looked up ready for a satisfying story.

"You know where... it 'as to cross over about twenty yard of their so-called ornamental lagoon. They almost sank backhoe! That was a right laugh! You should have heard them scream and shout. Then in the afternoon they were at it again with their pieces of board and 4"x4" and 'ammers and nails. And at four o'clock what is there to see.... a load of niggers standing in the water with a few pieces of wood floating around them. Load of stupid niggers eh..." he said in a lowered voice "they couldn't build a doll's house." And he broke off into a loud laugh with his eyes sparkling merrily and took a long draft of the beer and then sat back with a big grin on his face. Then he lit a cigarette and felt a deep satisfaction in the predictability of the world when looked down upon from the elevated heights of his very own 'Fred Biggs philosophy'.

"Morton still chasing you down?"

"Yes – he likes to give people a shocking time – what a pest he is! But I'm the only person on site who can give someone a real big shock - if I want to!"

"You wouldn't electrify Morton would you?" Jack grinned at his friend.

Fred thought for a moment.

"I'll decide that after I get paid" he said looking Jack in the eye.

They both laughed. Fred shook his beer bottle and, realizing it was empty, shouted for two more.

EVENING

Not far away in the 'Sunset Bar and Restaurant' Henry was relaxing over his third rum and coke. After an unusually vexing day a feeling of companionship unaccountably overcame him. He found himself looking at the other men around the bar with a new warmth. *Yes we all in the same boat - problems and vexations.* He could see unhappiness in their faces and felt no desire to be the 'big man' there.

"Bad Apple" he shouted to the proprietor, "me buyin' drinks for everyone."

"Henry you is the best!"

"Heineken."

"Me having a next Red Stripe."

"Me have 'o have a next rum."

He took another rum and coke for himself, paid and was repeatedly toasted. After a while he went and sat outside in the newly stirring evening breeze. He sat on the bonnet of his car and his thoughts turned to how he'd been the first person to own a Japanese car in Cornfield village - a compact silver grey Toyota. The whole village had turned out to see it, standing there on the space he'd cleared in front of his house. Everyone wanted a ride and he'd been glad to see in Doris' eyes a greater yearning than he'd ever noticed before. He had had her many times since then. She was nothing to him now. They passed on the road like strangers.

The coolness of evening came to him. He waved to someone leaving the bar. Bad Apple's child was running in and out of a side door. He called to her and she came to him. He put his hand on her head and she looked up with a coy and beautifully direct smile. *All woman's cunning there in that smile*. The child dropped down to squat at his legs. He made to pick her up but she jumped up delightedly and ran off. He felt a strange bittersweetness. Looking down the road he noticed it was empty.

He realized he wanted something else but didn't know what it was. Darkness fell and he felt his mood changing. A disquieting feeling came over him as though he were being surveyed by evil forces. He sensed the good feeling was going and imagining he was its master tried to hold onto it. But it had gone and he was obliged to set off for home without it. He climbed in his car, started up and drove off quickly.

~

Bill had spent the evening quarrelling with his girlfriend, Liz. He'd sailed out from England for his job at Tamarind Tree. Liz had crewed for him and now worked as resident schoolteacher for the children of a Canadian family. He still lived on board. En route to his boat he passed by the Water's Edge Bar.

He saw Fred sitting alone at the bar, saw at once his weariness and dejection and felt better immediately himself. Evidently Fred had been there for some time. He determined to cheer him up.

"What's the matter you old bastard?"

Fred turned to him and then to his cigarettes. Opening the box he snarled "Matter... matter..... what do you mean, matter?"

Bill remained silent. Fred yielded a little and said

"Someone's thiefing me drinks that's all."

Bill laughed and Fred smiled in spite of himself. It was evident the bartender was listening. Bill looked up and said

"Two rum and cokes."

"Rum and ginger, rum and ginger," growled Fred affecting displeasure "you young boys don't know nothin' 'bout drink." Having said this he again felt satisfied with his age and knowledge and settled down contentedly with his young friend to await the drink due to him.

~

The modern concrete block houses the wealthier on the island lived in worked like gigantic storage heaters taking in the heat of the sun during the day, storing it in their blocks, and giving it out at night. Worn out after a trying day and overcome by the heat Marjorie had gone to bed early. Outside on the patio, cooled by a light breeze, Peter sat back in a plastic recliner looking up at the stars. His apartment faced just to the north of east which was where the breeze was coming from. His eyes went unguided to the pole star and he thought he might spend the night there watching the other stars turn around it and thinking out his own best position. *I'll have to start making plans now if I'm to return to England in a year... what to take, what to get rid of, when to hand in my notice, what job to apply for...* the ins and outs seemed endless. The night slipped past.

Some time later he found himself looking at the moon. *You're our nearest neighbour and a quarter of a million miles away. And England is four thousand miles away - eight hours in a plane. But the stars - how remote and cold they seem - and here we are on the crest of the earth, alive for seventy years, turning slowly in the darkness - moving in vast isolation.*

This little examination did not cause the stars to flash, nor the moon to tremble. They shone out in clear indifference, sentinels in a sky at once separated from and included in his perplexity and disquiet. He realized that he'd reached this point several times in the past and was dimly aware that, at least tonight, he possessed neither the wherewithal nor the determination to penetrate beyond it. He thought perhaps that no one did. He stayed there for a few more minutes and then suddenly stretched, gave up his personal recliner and private observatory and went inside to join his wife, closing and locking the glass sliding doors as he went, and pulling the curtains in place behind him. He opened the bedroom door very carefully and tiptoed over to his side of their queen-size bed and then undressed - first taking off his watch and placing it under his pillow. Pulling on his pyjamas he gently eased himself under the sheet against her. Her warmth and scent enfolded him and he soon melted into her and into sleep.

TUESDAY

MORNING

Tuesday morning and Garry's taxi flying eastward full of town workers. On the back seat Edna and Elba sit side-by-side pressed together by the number of people in the bus. Due to their closeness and the stereo they can converse without being overheard by their fellow passengers.

"I hear 'e by you again last night" said Edna.

"Who tell you that?" said Elba looking at once both pleased and surprised. "Someone in the street."

"Yes it' true" Elba looked in front of her and a deep smile of pleasure came over her features.

"You love 'e?"

"'e nice to me boy. 'e sweet like sugar. 'e love me too."

"An' what happened to you girl when you' man get back from St Thomas? 'e won't left the airport an' they tell 'e you there with a next man. You get licks girl!"

"Me don't care. 'e can give me licks if 'e want. You think 'e sit there at night in 'e room in St Thomas lovin' up me photograph? 'e probably have it turn upside down with some next woman address write on the back. 'e bad – wicked!" Saying this she turned to the window and glared defiantly out.

They arrived at Tamarind Tree and headed for the cleaners' store. The head cleaner was already there and the three of them changed into their hotel uniforms and started gathering their cleaning equipment together. Elba, who had been glowering all this time, had all hers but a broom which was stuck on a slatted upper shelf. She pulled and pulled but it wouldn't come down. She could easily have reached it by standing on one of the chairs.

"Come down!" she shouted.

Eventually it came and she staggered back with it against the head cleaner.

"You see," she said "'e really get me vex up sometimes."

~

Close by Bill, with a surly expression on his face, was having trouble getting into his office. Full of self-righteousness, he was still going over the argument he'd had last night with his girlfriend. The door was jammed. He kicked it and it crashed open against the rubber doorstop and rebounded. At this a slight smile came to his lips.

"Stupid goddamn door."

He picked up the phone and dialled the site office.

"Eh Henry! How are you? I'm fed up with this bloody door. When you going to get the carpenters round? When? Today? Oh yeah - I'll believe it when I see it."

He rang off and started pushing the tall wooden shutters open. They hinged vertically providing ventilation and light. He suddenly realised he'd pushed one into an old gardener working on a flower bed outside.

"Good morning" said the gardener apparently not at all put out.

"Sorry, didn't see you there," said Bill "all these shutters and doors are sticking" he added heatedly.

The three cleaning women came passed pushing their trolleys. Two said "Good morning." The third gave him an angry look.

"Women," said Bill, "I don't know - just when you think you have a close understanding and everything's fine you turn around and... and.... they've, they've changed or something."

"And why does that trouble you? What woman you ever meet yet is the same two days running?"

Chuckling happily to himself the gardener returned to his digging.

~

Point Intermediate School was better known as the 'Fowl House' due to its box-like classrooms with their wire mesh windows. The playgrounds were fenced in with the mesh and covered with concrete which had been poured over the same mesh. The school looked quite uninspiring - it is said that even animals in a zoo will react adversely against tedious surroundings - but the government had little money and the Minister of Education was doing his best. There were fifteen teachers for the five hundred pupils and the academic record wasn't marked. The old-time people said the church schools had been better, more disciplined. But most of the children learnt at least to read and write, count, and get along reasonably in everyday life. A handful would pass every year for the high school in town. One or two of these would go on to university - Barbados, Jamaica, Trinidad, the States, Canada or England. But for most of the children it was just where you went after the holidays were finished, more exciting than home with all the other children - and with no other obligation than to sit at a desk. Around the house there were always jobs, and then there was land to work, cattle to mind, clothes to wash, errands to run and the hundred and one things a child was expected to do to keep their household with sufficient for another day - the continual pushing and pulling of family life.

Only a single tree had survived the clearing of the land and laying of the slab for the school playground. That was a fine old mahogany tree which stood, encircled by concrete, close by the boundary fence. Icilma sat under it sharing the single wooden bench with her best friend. It was mid-morning break and the playground was in routine uproar, but they were oblivious of this in deep discussion:

"... their heart going thud, thud, thud."

"Well what they do next then?"

"The man hug up the woman and take off she clothes."

"What all?"

"Yes all."

"Well sir!"

"An' then 'e push her down..."

"Yes?"

"... and lie on her."

Icilma flushed.

"Well that doesn't seem right to me at all. Some man so big they'd crush the life outta you. I'd fight me way out."

"No girl when you down you down. You doesn't get out."

"Oh."

A black car with tinted windows cruised slowly passed, just a few feet away, on the other side of the fence. Feeling observed they looked up but couldn't see who the driver was. The bell rang and they got up together and went to class. Icilma sensed there was something wrong in it, but she didn't know what. Even so she hoped one day she and a boy would be happy.

∾

Fifty years before they'd cut down cedar trees to build the house. Its frame was of white cedar decorated with rounded mouldings and its boarding was of one inch red cedar. Despite its location near the island's summit it had survived every storm and hurricane since that time. Now it stood grey-brown and half neglected not far from the newly cut government dirt road. All the doors and shutters were open. Zackie was sitting in the kitchen which long ago had been painted a powder blue. His legs dangled over the side of the kitchen table and he watched the flickering patterns of light reflected on the wall from sunlight in a basin of water. Ina's aunt, the owner of the house, was down the village selling eggs and buying bread. The galvanised roof creaked - the heat of the morning sun made it expand and work against its fastenings. Sounds came from outside - wind rustling the palm fronds, the fowl in the yard, Ina's cutlass striking the coconuts. And the smell of the summer grass almost as sweet as ganja.

Neat lattice-work capped the partitions that divided the house into four rooms. The family photographs were pinned to the two partitions in the kitchen. There were dozens of them - some faded and curled in distant greys, others new, sharp and colourful. There stands old man Allen by Stonebridge church as though before his maker - the hills stretch out behind him - a banana plantation can be seen. He has long since been buried in the same churchyard. There is Nina, his daughter, in New York with her in-laws. A dark crimson tenement building stands close behind them. But they no longer climb those steps. Alma - Zackie loves to look at - she is so beautiful - but she's married and gone long-time. Below that photo, a picture of Ina coming back from school with her sisters years ago taken by a white man and posted from overseas.

They've all changed - the shutter opened for a moment, closed, and their image was fixed on shiny paper. We look back and remember, a little - but we also forget - so much. As if anyone stays the same for two moments together! But for a time the photos make us remember – how it was. The past comes back to us like a far-away dream. We try to hold on, take a closer look, but we do not see, we cannot see. We cannot reach them as they were any more, we cannot go back. Our memories die away – as our friends and friendships did. Saddened perhaps, we shrug our shoulders, and carry on.

Somehow it was easy for Zackie to be in the present moment all the time - to see we are always here, always were. It didn't occur to him we could be any where else. Like his brothers and sisters he had a kind connectedness with all about him. He'd had had it even as a child, as they did - but deeper somehow. He knew that those who were close to him before were, in some way, still with him now - his former friends and family present with him still - indivisibly one.

The cutlass continued without a pause. She chopped the white meat from the nuts into tiny pieces for the fowl. Black sugar ants left the wiped clean table top for Zackie's thighs. A dove cooed in the distance. The roof creaked, a door banged closed. When she was finished they would share the ginger beer he had bought – ice cubes still floated in it.

~

Jacky's voice came over the phone to Morton.

"I have Mrs. Morton on the line for you now."

Morton could scarcely conceal his irritation and anyway didn't entirely want to.

"About time!" he snapped, "put her on."

There was a click and Morton heard his wife.

"Hello Anne is that you?" he shouted. Her voice came meekly back to him. "And how are you my darling, well?"

There was a pause while Morton listened.

"Yes, yes I know my love, yes ... I know yes ... thank you ... yes, yes very much ... yes ... I know yes thank you ... yes, listen, this is long distance, is the new perimeter wall complete yet? ... what? ... it is complete ... it's not complete ... is it complete or not?" Morton's voice was becoming louder. The overseas lines were sometimes poor.

"It's not complete! .. not complete! Well what's the hold up? ... Is Blackette there? ... well you can tell him I was very disappointed ... yes very ... I know it's always raining ... yes ... no ... tomorrow am I, by God you're right ... thank you ... no don't bother to phone, I'll phone you as soon as I have a confirmed flight."

There was a knock at the door. Peter was standing there holding plans and papers. Morton waved him in.

"Yes my love thank you ... I will yes ... please take good care of yourself till I get back ... yes ... goodbye."

He replaced the receiver.

Peter sat down opposite him across the desk on which he laid his paperwork. He noticed a copy of 'The Prophet' by Kahil Galbraith set at a slight angle on the otherwise empty side desk.

"Good morning Peter."

"Good morning Ben."

"Coffee? No I suppose it's too late. Well, what do you make of cost and time?" Peter picked up a sheet marked 'Leisure Complex - Preliminary summary of Building Estimates' and read out –

"First phase, completion of basic structure, twelve weeks, two hundred and ten thousand dollars. Second phase, completion of complex, fourteen weeks, three hundred and five thousand dollars."

"So you're saying six months to complete."

"That's right."

"Well it's too long as you know. We have to be operational for the season. December fifteen is your target date. I thought I'd mentioned this before."

"It can't be done Ben. With the best will in the world it can't be done. We haven't even finished the bridge yet."

"So where are the hold ups?"

"In order to complete in that time we'd need more men and more machinery. Plus we'd have to order everything from overseas today and assume a perfect delivery sequence. As you know things like that don't happen too often round here."

"What additional machinery?" Morton's voice was flat.

"More cement mixing capacity - another large mixer. Plus another dumper. Plus more hand tools. And we'd have to assume no breakdowns. Then we'd have to hire and train more labour."

"We have to be ready for the season and that means December fifteen. The owners want it. The tourists want it. I want it. Please be kind enough to revise your estimates."

"The price will go up."

"Some things will go up yes. Others will come down. Building insurance and workers liability will come down. Management costs will be reduced on a pro rata basis."

Their eyes met.

"Very well, I'll revise it, but I won't guarantee it."

"Thank you so much." The telephone rang. Peter picked up his paperwork and left.

"Morton here."

~

"Me nah like in here, it stink" said Jim.

"True" said Alf "we finish up and get out quick."

They were working in the pump room under the swimming pool deck. Alf lit two cigarettes and passed one to Jim. Jim opened a stop cock and closed another isolating one of the filters. The pool could continue running while maintenance was carried out. They dismantled the filter together and finding some debris at the base pushed it out onto the floor, added two scoops of chlorine and a third for luck and started to reassemble it. Alf sat back and smoked. Jim did the work. He started off thinking it through as he did it *plate, washer, ring, nut* but ended up rehearsing an expected encounter *'So don't come round me yard again I'm telling you now!'.*

"Well that good" said Alf looking at the rebuilt filter. Jim switched the filter back into the circuit and everything looked okay. Then he isolated the next filter and called Alf over with the spares box.

"Last one" said Alf, "then we get a cold drink. These damn pumps run too hot."

AFTERNOON

Flash floods had damaged Cornfield Police Station in the past but recently a larger waterway had been constructed in the usually dry ghaut under the main town road. It had been made by bending galvanised sheets into a circle, laying them side by side, boarding in the ends and pouring concrete around them. Then the road was laid over the top. The concrete extended up above the road on either side to form two low white washed walls. Henry's cousin Naman was lying on his back on one wall and his friend Bully had taken up a complimentary position twelve feet away on the other. It was the hottest time of the day. Having finished their groundwork they lay in the shade of breadfruit trees. They'd doze for a while and then talk for a while – not looking at each other but at the sky. A car might pass and provide a little interest - they'd look up in a distant sort of way. Young and healthy, they were both dressed in old jeans, T-shirts and running shoes.

Constable Corbett of Cornfield Police Station stood in the centre of the bridge watching them. He had a wooden bat in his hands. He looked like he wanted to use it.

"Eh, get up man! Get up! Get up!"

Naman and Bully looked up quizzically.

"Come on man get up. You can't rest here all day. Get up! Time we play some street cricket!"

He pulled a ball from his ample pant's pocket.

They sat up and looked at their friend.

"No it too early yet. The sun too hot. Naman, you eat yet for the day?"

"No."

"Me neither. Le' we go by your sister see what she cookin'." Bully leaned over and switched on his radio. It came on distorted and flat.

Constable Corbett walked off.

"We play later then" said Bully.

"Right" said Naman.

Bully had the batteries out on the wall to heat up. If you left them in the sun for a while they worked better.

A girl with a town job came by beautifully dressed. They'd been in the same class in school five years before. The car that had dropped her did a U turn and headed back. She didn't look at them and they only looked at her after she'd passed by.

Bully said "Let we go bay tomorrow."

"What for?"

"Fish."

"You think fishermen going to give us anything? You stupid or something? Is sellin' they sell and me nah haul no red man boat up the beach."

"Nah we go fish."

"Me nah come with you sah." Then he paused "Wi' what?"

"A line."

"Wha' line?"

"Me got a line. Me fin' one."

"It have a hook?" Naman looked at his friend. "Easy to make hook wi' a smally small nail."

"Me could beg one from Fishface."

"Nah. He nah give nobody nothin'."

"Yes 'e would so gi' me!" Naman sat indignantly upright.

"An wha' kinda bait? We needs bait."

"Bait no problem. We get bait."

They sat for a moment looking in front of them. This sounded promising - they both felt a little heartened. Life around Cornfield was pretty routine.

Bully collected the batteries and pushed them in his jeans pocket. "Le' we go."

They set off together up the road to get food from Naman's sister.

The minute Morton had finished signing all his mail he picked up the phone and told reception to find out where his car was so that he could go for a drive before his 5pm accountancy meeting. He was to meet with his hotel manager and accountant to hammer out some projected occupancy rates and income for the upcoming year. But first he wanted some fresh air and a chance to further his own pet project for the island. This project, which was as yet only a conceptual plan, involved demolishing sections of older housing in the main town and villages and replacing them with inexpensive modern block housing. Each house would be set in its own land in a row near a government road - that way they could all be at a set distance from the road and more easily be connected to government services without wasting land. Many of the older houses were away from the road and didn't seem to be part of a regulated scheme. He planned to speak soon with the new Minister of Development, but first he'd put his ideas to Steadman to get his response. And before that he wanted to do a dry run by himself.

When he looked up from the maps and papers he was putting together he was surprised to see Ogel standing there.

"Ogel - what are you doing here?"

"They send me here to drive the car for you Mr. Morton."

"But I didn't ask for a driver the incompetent idiots! I asked for a car." Morton looked at him severely. Then he softened and said

"Well seeing as you're here you may as well drive me. I have to survey the ghaut villages and the top road and be back here by four thirty precisely." He said this last word in a threatening manner. Ogel looked duly intimidated as though he already realised he couldn't help but arrive back late.

"What time is it now Ogel?"

"Minutes past two Mr. Morton" said Ogel without referring to a timepiece.

"No, Ogel, not minutes past two – twenty three minutes past two ... you see the difference?"

"Yes sir" said Ogel but he'd already lost the thread of the conversation and feeling he'd somehow done something wrong tried to smile nicely.

Morton felt satisfied that they were on the correct footing to go for a drive together and, finishing his coffee while giving last minute instructions to a secretary who'd come for his letters, he collected his papers and maps and left for his executive car. *How much can we see in two hours?* Ogel was having trouble keeping ahead of him.

They wound their way through the villages, Morton silent with his maps and plans. In a surprisingly short time he looked out to see they were already ascending Runaway Hill for the top road, the principal villages they'd set out to see were already far below them and Morton couldn't help but feel angry now at one thing and now at another and even at the villages themselves for being so picturesque.

Coming to a rise on the top road with a lay by Morton told Ogel to stop. It was one of his most favourite places on earth -

one of the highest points on the island it had an extraordinary view looking out east over the island and the sea.

Morton stood near the cliff edge with one foot on a boulder in front of him, his hands on his hips. Ogel remained in the car. There was always wind up here even on the stillest of days. He braced himself against the warm buffeting of the trade winds. Cotton-wool clouds sailed close by overhead. Before him the island stood firm against the wind and sea, the kept fields pretty with green and brown lines – the pattern of the farmers' earthen banks. Nearby some swifts seemed to be playing in the turbulent air - flying out into the updraft, scooting to left and right and then wheeling back downwind at high speed, running along under an embankment and then heading out into the updraft again.

Far and away below the extent of the land was outlined by a moving white line where the sea turned to surf and broke upon the rocky shore. The sea was a lazy hazy blue and it merged in the distance with the sky. Morton's gaze was drawn naturally to this far away line but his mind was elsewhere. *That lazy bastard Blackette! Give him an inch he takes a mile! Why is the perimeter wall not complete? Rain? Rain my foot! He'll soon find out who reigns on my property - and it won't be a gentle reign! Oh yes. He'll goddamn well jump when I stick some dynamite up his backside whether it's raining or not!* He smiled inwardly to himself. *Three fifty five. Time for five more minutes here before we have to descend. How beautiful it is!* He turned to see if Ogel was watching him.

He was. He gave him a hard look.

෴

At the hotel swimming pool there was some consternation. Young hotel guests were running up and down between the aluminium and plastic sun-chairs, tables and umbrellas showing each other what red eyes they'd got. The water was indeed very high in chlorine. You could even smell it.

Underneath the pool Peter sat squarely in front of a filter and started stripping it down. Jim stood behind him smoking a cigarette and passing tools. Peter worked easily but carefully, a habit born of a long apprenticeship in a machine shop in Birmingham in England. He had a feel for the equipment and for the materials - bronze, steel, rubber, glass, aluminium, plastic - each had its place, its properties, its use. He unscrewed a bronze butterfly nut to reveal a cracked glass and damaged rubber O ring. He knew better than to correct his workers - they'd get vexed or sulk for days.

"Looks like too much chlorine inside."

Jim stepped forward and squatted down by his side and saw the damage.

"Oh so that what happened to that" he said.

"Go get spares from the store - spare glass, spare O ring. If you see a butterfly nut don't worry to use a spanner - fingers are enough."

"Right" said Alf throwing down his cigarette, "they make these things weak eh?"

Chip was getting tired waiting by Zackie's empty house. He took a last toke on his spliff, held it deep in his lungs and let it out slowly. He felt hungry. Zackie should have been back long-time. His eye kept returning to the fowl that were still inside the fowl house. He had a flour bag with him and he reached down and put some corn in it. Then he covered the entrance to the fowl house door with the bag and opened the door. To his surprise all the fowl walked into his bag. He closed the neck of the bag and tied it. He wasn't sure what to do next. *Me hungry – nobody can steal Jah food.* Noticing that he was picking the bag up and putting it on his back he glanced round the left.

~

The steel reinforcing rods were cut, bent and tied into bundles on a bench adjacent to the bridge by a well muscled immensely strong man of about forty. He cut and bent the steel quickly and angrily like a tough street fighter making weapons - rarely raising his unhappy eyes from his steel. Everyday he did the work of four men. His young helpers buzzed around him in continual agitation. Peter was now back near the bridge watching over the construction work. He counted the bundles piled up ready for assembly. The other steelworkers would carry them to the bridge and set them in place in the formwork. *Well – Malone's ahead as usual, and Henry's behind as usual - so the formwork wont be ready before Thursday and Morton will get vexed as usual.*

"Leroy - give me a shout when the trucks come, I'll be in my office."

Leroy waved. He returned to his office to work on the revision of the construction schedule for the leisure complex. This revision aggravated him as did the continual interruptions that are part and parcel of site management.

"Mr. Finch - there's no tie rods."

"Peter, do you have a minute?"

"Mr. Finch, me haffoo go home now."

"Come outside, a white man is looking for you."

"Listen! Tamarind Tree must buy me a next boot or trouble coming!"

"Peter, the electricity department are cutting off the supply in ten minutes."

"Mr. Finch, some of the cement they sell is hard."

"The aggregate here Mr. Finch. They does drop some in the lagoon."

"What!"

At 4.15 p.m., glad to be rid of the vexations of the day, he headed up the hill, kicked off his sandals and entered his apartment. But one glance at his wife was enough for him to know a heavy mood had entered her.

"Bad day darling?" she said.

"Not too good." He felt constrained, unwilling to go further, wanting to retreat from this atmosphere that threatened to engulf him. He went into the spare room and started sorting out his fishing equipment. After a minute Marjorie came to the threshold of the room. Peter sensed her presence but said nothing.

"Going fishing darling?"

Peter resented this interference knowing she knew he would never set off so late.

"No!" he snapped. Marjorie left at once partly hurt and partly satisfied. He had lost his temper and would have to make it up to her. She returned to her book somewhat relieved as though an unpleasant hovering storm had broken.

Half an hour later Peter entered the living room. The tension between them had subsided. Marjorie considered herself in the right but was ready to show her magnanimity. She waited for Peter to speak first and betray his present state before she exposed herself.

"Like a drink dear?"

"Oh yes that would be very nice." She spoke in a silky voice.

"The usual?"

"Yes thanks."

Two large bright red drinks were duly bought in - vodka and tomato juice. Bloody Marys. There was something wrong in the drink that some part of them found appealing. When she received her drink she smiled into his eyes like a conspirator.

"You know I've been thinking ..." Peter started off in an affable way, his glass already half empty. Marjorie was sitting in her favourite armchair with her legs tucked up under her and was all ears.

"... maybe it would be best for us to return to England. Let's face it we never really settled here did we, and we still have friends and connections back home. The place is beautiful, the weather's fine, the people can be delightful ...." and here Marjorie sat up even more sensing a bit of criticism coming - there was something sweet in a little venom - "but there's quite a bit of hostility here - they don't welcome outsiders like some of the other islands".

"But there's no money on those islands."

"That's true too and that idiot Morton and in fact the whole company shows no gratitude for the work done. Most of our site workers just won't do a thing without supervision ..." Marjorie nodded.

"And I mean take today. Alf and Jim spend the morning in the pool pump room. They clean out the filters, chuck the filth on the floor, load them up with too much chlorine, smash one during reassembly and think it's a kind of joke and I'm the fool when I get a phone call from reception to say there's complaints from the guests again about the pool water. So I have to leave off supervising the construction and go down the pump room sort it out."

"Then on the site - I scarcely see Henry for the day and the formwork is now behind schedule. That idiot Morton wants the leisure complex construction plan revised so we're ready for Christmas knowing full well it can't and won't be done and finally some jokers from the quarry come with the gravel and dump half of it in the lagoon."

"Oh don't go on Peter" said Marjorie who would have been very happy for him to go on. Now she felt in command of herself - the energy inside her surging in a different way.

"Take Mavis today. She finished work half an hour early and told me she was going home. When I questioned her she said everything was finished so I went round checking and there was a lot still to be done - garbage pails empty but not clean, towels on the line and so on and so on. And I'm still wanting an answer from her about the glass horse she broke ..."

"Well they're just a different people Marjorie and we can't change that. And we're in their country. When in Rome ..."

"Yes, but I can't change either" said Marjorie. She felt certain of this. She couldn't.

EVENING

"Me can't find 'em, can't find 'em at all."

Mistress Allen was chasing about her neighbour's yard shouting, disturbing the stock and causing confusion.

"Can't find what?"

"They gone. Missing. Gone."

"What?"

Mistress Allen looked up from surveying the crisscrossing tracks of fowls in the dry soil.

"The fowl them! The fowl them! How can me get a' egg an' bread when the fowl them done gone missing?"

"Well Mistress Allen, me can't help you, me can't help you, me sure. Me nah see them 'round me yard for the day."

"Where they gone to? Who dog eat them? What evil minded can't - read man run wi' them?" And notwithstanding her age and size and the coming of night she set off down the top road at a fast pace.

It was rare to see Doc, the island's senior medical officer, in anything other than white overalls. Rumour had it that he slept in them. Tall and skinny with a quiet slightly pock-marked face he was singularly different from his fellow islanders. There was about him a rather gentle and withdrawn air. Some said he was really a white man – some kind of a spy. He worked long hours, had few friends and fewer enemies.

On his day off he'd visit his parents in Watley Village at the house he'd been born in thirty three years before. They were a well-to-do and respected family - Anglicans and of clear skin.

He'd been educated at the island's high school and gone to university in England - to London. After four years he'd become dully conscious that he was becoming slowly mummified by his education. He'd dated an English girl but found it a conditional kind of love, constrained by opinions and conventions. As soon as his studies were complete he'd returned to Entropica. People told him how English he was. He found this a little disconcerting. He just wanted to be an Entropican, marry a local girl - someone light, easy, shiny eyed, happy ...

He was renting a beautiful wooden 'old time' house near the centre of town. It was far too large for him. Its regal balconies overlooked a well established garden full of fruits and flowers and its many rooms were warmly panelled in local timbers. It seemed to him the house was somehow waiting for a family, for their voices and actions to bring the walls alive. He sat at his desk, a single light burning - his study swelling to music composed two hundred years before, in Germany.

Although it had become his habit to time his arrival at his parents' house to coincide with their return from church, the spiritual yearnings of his youth, buried under years of study and practice, were beginning to reassert themselves again. England's cathedrals and churches had made a deep impression on him - but the massive stone foundations, vaulted roofs and fine stained glass windows seemed to speak of a spiritual certainty of another time – all these 'places of worship' felt like so many empty relics. It seemed to him that they had somehow been abandoned long ago - there was no discernable sacred presence within the buildings and he could find little evidence of it amongst the other worshippers, or in himself. Even the ministers seemed to be playing an agreed part.

He had a portrait in oils of a young woman hanging on his study wall. The portrait was from Haiti and it was extraordinary in that infinite goodwill seemed to radiate from the girl's face. It had become his habit in the evening before retiring to bed to stand and look at it for some minutes. There seemed to be some aspect of the girl's face that contained a secret he was searching for - some laughably obvious reason for her very evident happiness. He looked at the portrait again - what was it?

Night

Three miles offshore a small boat moved silently through the light night wind. Or so it seemed from a distance - a white sail gliding effortlessly forward. On board a young man and a young woman lay on their backs on the trampoline. There was just the night, each other, the sound of water against the hulls of their boat, the great mystery and joyousness of it all. The dis-ease of the day had gone entirely. It was as if they had accidentally found the way they knew they really were. They were, without reservation, entirely glad to be there. When the moon broke from behind a cloud they felt especially favoured.

The helmsman moved the tiller he held in his free hand just a small amount and the back winding of the sail turned to a full belly again. The boat picked up speed a little, heeled slightly and the water gurgled its approval. Behind them was a bending white wake.

"You love me Bill?" said Jacky.

"How could I not?"

"I know you couldn't help but love me."

Silence.

"If I fell in would you save me?"

"Of course."

"If a shark eat you you wouldn't mind?"

"No – I'd be glad."

She sat up and laughed - a clear ringing sound. Delighted. Her laughter fell about him like a waterfall.

THE SECOND WEEK

WEDNESDAY

MORNING

King jumped straight up out of his bed and threw down the sheet on the floor. He felt good. He had a shower, put on his clothes and was out of the house and running down the street five minutes after he'd woken up. There was a faint light from the setting moon and little more from the rising sun.

A pick-up slowed beside him and he jumped in.

"Kong.'"

"Piggy - 's 'appenin'?"

"Going town!"

He stood straight up in the back of the truck taking in the morning. When the pick up slowed as it reached its nearest point to the hotel he jumped out and ran up the road to the hotel, waving to his friend without looking round. He ran into reception, snatched the kitchen keys from the night clerk's hands and ran to the kitchen backyard. *Now for some breakfast ... What to have before the f and b man comes? ... bacon and eggs and bread and cheese and jam.* He gathered his ingredients together while switching on lights, kicking open garbage bins, lighting pilot lights, cleaning off dirty pans, searching for oil, regulating the ceiling fan that had been left on all night, sniffing the coffee, throwing it away and making new.

By the time the food and beverage manager was due he'd had a good breakfast, cleaned up from last night and set up ready to feed an army in an instant. Seeing the girls coming to work through the small kitchen window he opened it and shouted out.

"Eh, Edna, you lookin' sharp today girl! Where Elba? Oh there she is. Elba girl! Come here let me see you a minute ... wha' ... no, here ... the food and beverage man say he want you up here right now for something ... no joke ... come up here now ... eh come back ... come back ... eh, you have a big bum you know!"

"Is the kitchen stock inventory being complete from last night?" enquired the new Austrian food and beverage manager. King hadn't heard him come in.

"Who knows" said King. "I don't see no piece o' paper or some such lying about here and I been here through the kitchen ten times for the morning already. Maybe some fool drop it in the garbage". The new expatriate manager felt put upon. He didn't want to look in the garbage in case he appeared foolish, yet he had to have the inventory and felt the urge to check. He left mumbling something about guests which King couldn't understand but felt was unimportant enough not to have to bother about. King's eyes followed the embarrassed form out of the doorway.

Now he had the kitchen to himself again he wondered what to do. *Oh yeah - make the girls a big club sandwich, wrap it in foil and call them for it. Then when they come me tell Elba me comin' by she to eat tonight.* He set about his new task with relish.

∾

The ceiling fans turned slowly at the Ministry of Labour. The main office, an ancient wooden panelled room with a high ceiling, was a dark jumble of overloaded tables and desks bombed out by cardboard boxes full of forms. The clerks received the flow of forms with a dull stoicism, filled them in, stamped them and boxed them. A small group of Dominicans waited listlessly by the main entrance.

Overhead in his first floor office, the Minister had just completed work on his outgoing mail and was about to leave to see to his own business, a shipping agency, when Prince, his permanent secretary, walked in.

"I been thinking again about our foreign exchange problem. I think I know where we can get some from."

"Oh yeah?" Daley gave him a dark stare out of narrowed eyes. "Close the door."

Prince obeyed, went over to an easy chair by the window and sat down. "Who gets a big wage on the island but scarcely spends a cent here?" Daley didn't answer.

"All the expatriates save money and send money home - right down to the poorest Dominican. We must expect that, they all have family. But at the top end, the big earners, the professionals, engineers and so on, it's the yachties that spend the least."

"Go on."

"The charter business is thriving. There's money there for all the staff and more - but most of the top guys live on boats. You name an Entropican who's got his own big yacht! Not one. And these guys are paying almost nothing in tax."

"True."

"So what do they buy each week? A little fruit and vegetable. A can of paint for their boat. But what are they earning? - five hundred, a thousand bucks a week. So if there's fifty of them doing this that's two million a year in foreign exchange gone! Gone!"

"Sonavabitch Prince." Daley looked a bit stunned. "You damn right. We could sure use that two million right now."

"Sure we could."

"But how to do it, that's the problem. That's not an easy one at all. Not at all damn easy. In fact I don't think ..."

"No listen... you go on ZWX. You say over the radio how people here earning big bucks and contributing nothing to the island, how they taking away our foreign earnings, draining the economy, not renting anything and so on. And you say as of August first anyone who's doing this will have his work permit suspended prior to reconsideration. You'll have the companies here begging you - including those bitches got tough on you over those imports got lost. And the people here will see what we're doing, how we standing up, and they won't forget it at the next election. And you'll get the backing of all those with empty apartments and houses now the season's finished. You could speak to the property owners first so it comes to them like you making a special deal with them - that way you'll have all those big men, Isaac's, Maduro and so on in your pocket when you want them."

"You're a damn politician, Princey, not a civil servant." They both laughed together.

Daley looked pensive.

"We damn stupid you know Prince. We runnin' the government yet we losin' the island. It's our island but we handin' it back to the white man again and again, time after time, day after day. Now he wants it for his winter holiday! What can stand up against the Yankee dollar you tell me? Nothing - not a thing in this world. Who owns the beaches now and the best land, the pretty-pretty land? Who is served at table and who does the serving? We so damn stupid we scarcely even got money enough to pay our clerks a basic wage. We backin' down all the way Prince – is slavery again. They just repackage it that's all. Look at how a man like Morton can still rule things here. He getting' away with murder all over again. We should have stayed village people like we was not modernised like dummies. At least we had our pride then. But we t'row that away for a little flashiness." He trailed off and looked out to sea.

"It's a bitch Prince ..." He stood up and put some papers in his heavy leather briefcase and set it upright ready to close.

"I'm late for meetings. I'll see you later - we'll discuss it some more. Put some figures to it this afternoon. Let me have a summary of those involved."

"Maybe we can get to grips with Morton still you know."

"How is that?" Daley gave him a dark look. They locked eyes for a few moments.

"Let me think about it. Maybe we can arrange another special kind of meeting...."

Daley pushed his two big thumbs down on the two metal clasps of his briefcase locking it. He looked up and they locked eyes again. It seemed that some kind of contract was being entered into, was possible.

"I don't think so" said Daley.

They parted company with averted eyes, like secret agents working in a foreign land.

~

Zackie's grandfather rested on a rock from the heavy work of spiling land. Every now and then his hands and arms gave a jerk he couldn't quite anticipate. He was working some land near his house. It seemed unusually quiet - he sensed there was something wrong. His donkey let out a long bray and it was quiet again. Then he remembered – they didn't have the fowl any more.

In a few years me done this life and none the boys them will care this land which I receive at the hands of me father and am here working fifty years - unless Zackie does take it which have given us sustenance these fifty years gone. Zackie say the young men say working land too low for them make your body stink. Is slavery work. Well me no know about that suh. It hard work but blessed. He looked at his work and the old growth chopped down and passed a hand over the stubble on his chin.

The land adjacent to his had been sold to a white man and he couldn't help but feel surprised again. *What for? Why does these white people want to live here by themself not wi' they own people?* The builder had marked out the building with pegs and string and had shown him where a vast concrete slab was to go at the side of the house. *What so much cancrete there for? What happen to the earth an' the creatures them under the cancrete?*

This last matter continually perplexed him.

"Allen."

He jerked out of his thoughts to see his old friend Tuitt standing nearby.

"Goodday to you Tuitt and me hopin you' alright."

"I am well praise the Lord. But you doesn't fin' the fowl yet?"

"Mistress Allen gone search them since breakfast."

"Well sir, me sorry 'bout that."

Tuitt came down beside him and they sat silently together for some time as though at a wake. Tuitt had emigrated to Puerto Rico in the forties and worked there for twenty years saving money. He'd bought a car the day he'd got back and had driven all over the island since then. Presently he had an old English Morris which he used twice a week.

Allen stirred. "You' car runnin' okay Tuitt?"

"Well" said Tuitt smiling at the opportunity to talk on a favourite theme, "as you know Allen me car like a goat. She never refuse. Any hill she climb. Me brother in England just send me out a new set o' spark plug for her. I put them in Monday after her Sunday outing thinkin' she be glad of them but she doesn't like them and spit them back out."

"O ho" Allen chuckled, "so you put back in the old?"

"I's what I have to do. She refuse them!"

They stood up together and Allen picked up his hoe and started down the hill again. "Until later then."

Tuitt shouted after him.

"Me have two smally goat to sell."

"Me no want you goat to buy suh. Me have me own problems thank you".

~

Morton and Steadman had just completed their daily rounds of the hotel and were returning to their offices. It would soon be lunchtime. Morton's face still retained a trace of the expression it had had when speaking with Henry at the bridge. Steadman cast a side long glance at him and smiled to himself seeing Morton's anger and frustration. He had the hotel to run three hundred and sixty five days a year and knew you couldn't afford to use up too much emotional energy every time you found something wrong. Nevertheless there was a deepening friendship between the two men.

Steadman glanced again at the veins still prominent on Morton's face and neck.

"Ben - you like a cold beer?"

"Tell me Steadman is Henry a complete idiot or is it just me?" Steadman didn't reply at once.

"Maybe after a drink we could discuss that more easily..." Morton smiled at this knowledge of his emotional household.

In a short time they were sitting together on rattan chairs at the poolside bar with two imported beers standing on a glass table in front of them.

"Cheers" said Morton. The cool drink changed them. Everything at once appeared in a more reasonable if diffused light.

"It's my birthday today" said Morton.

"Well let me take you to lunch then! Happy birthday!"

"No not happy birthday" said Morton, "just birthday."

~

"Me nah take him away."

Tyrone gave her a push.

"Me nah take him away!"

He pushed her again and she fell against the wall of the room she'd been cleaning banging her head.

"Remember you place 'oman!" Tyrone stood over her as she slumped down to the floor.

"James nah bright but he stay school! It better for he."

"Me tellin' you - some days 'e come work wi' me!"

"Me nah take him away!" Her face was firm, tears of vexation in her eyes.

"Edna!" Tyrone's voice was hard and authoritative, "you going to get licks! Hard hard licks."

"Jus' you go 'way leave me right. Me got me work a do. Get out the hotel ground before security bang you up."

"You whorin' bitch you!" He gave her a kick in the thigh having revealed what the real argument was about. It was on the street she was going in one of the hotel rooms with the new assistant manager - a white man from England named Jackson. Tyrone's real purpose at the hotel was to see what the man looked like – size him up.

"How can a man hold he head up high when he married a whore bitch" he shouted as he left the unit.

Hearing Tyrone's angry tirade Elba came running up. Seeing Edna on the floor inspecting her thigh, she dropped her cleaning things and let out a scream.

"O don' make noise girl," said Edna, "'e don't start on me yet."

"Le' we go by the kitchen girl. Me get the boys them get you a drink, you look sick."

Edna was in fact extraordinarily strong but this suggestion made her feel a bit sick.

"You right girl me a bit sick."

"You need a whiskey girl."

Edna got up.

"Yes girl you right. An' a chicken leg and bread. I hungry too you know."

⁓

It was the last lesson of the morning. James, about whom this animated dispute had just taken place, was at that moment doing Arithmetic at Point Junior School. That is to say, sitting in a twin desk next to his friend Fish, he was trying to see how far out he could stick his upper lip beyond his lower one. Making a final great effort and distorting his face so that his appearance was most peculiar he placed a finger as a gauge between his lips. When he took down his finger and inspected the wet marks on it his face slowly relaxed into a smile.

"Fish" he said nudging his friend who was preoccupied with other business. Fish turned to him.

"You can't self push out you mout' so far as me one." He followed up this claim with a demonstration of his new skill.

⁓

LUNCH

As had happened during the last few days the lunchtime sandwiches somehow stuck in her throat and the soda she washed them down with bought no refreshment with it. She simply would eat her lunch as a duty to herself and to routine and then return to the office. Now she wasn't so sure she liked the office - often now it appeared as menacing - as though she were doing an exam that she was failing every moment and yet there was no end to it.

"Mistress Skerritt, I 'fraid that Mr. Morton in trut'. I think I getting used to it till 'e come 'ere disturb me. 'e mustn't wait a minute for a t'ing. Not a t'ing. I not used to anyone in such a rush. I never seen a man so busy. Even when 'e sit down to drink 'e coffee 'e look busy. An' when 'e make 'e face go red and cut 'e eye at me - Lord - I just wanna run home to me goat them. Now when I doin' reception and I hear 'e voice on the phone I get the horrors before 'e even get angry. I can feel me head getting hot. Yesterday afternoon I can hear 'e upstairs walkin' up and down in 'e room like 'e trying to keep me knowing 'e up there and can get me any minute an' I know when 'e shout all the brains gone out o' me head. Where he walking to?" She paused in her reflections. "Maybe 'e just like to go for a walk in 'e room. I wish I could 'ave Bill help me. 'e a white man could understand better tell me what to do. An' when 'e call me on the phone it me and Bill go into 'e room together, and when something wrong with the switchboard Bill give it one lash and it come good again. If I give Bill sweet eye 'e can't help but be good to me. If I smile at Morton it' like I not there or something." She bent forward. *Lord help and protect me this afternoon, help me mother at the shop from the manager and help me sister at school from the teachers and protect me from Mr. Morton and any other unreasonableness and keep me to the path of thy Son, Jesus Christ.* Feeling some courage manifest inside her she got up and walked back to the office with her friend.

Henry chewed the last of his sirloin steak involuntarily taking quick regular glances around him. Anger was still in him. He struggled with the bone. I'll *get that lying bitch again tonight and get a next one after the big dance. I sure to hell to get one there. That Morton bastard think he smart but he only know*

how to be smart in the day. That Bates woman – she's sweet meat - roughing up woman helps them get ready.

The waiter came up.

"Ice Cream."

As long as I get even with some of those bastards and bitches it make up for some of the times I get screwed. Maybe I should start carry a weapon. Is Edith tell me 'How you like wake up with a pencil in you' ear?' Anyone can do you anything especially when you is asleep. Apple say a pistol is nice but hard not to use it. He say a knife is best with a woman but with a man you needs practice. That way you keep everything under control. People them think success come easy but you have to struggle for it.

The ice cream came.

"Is chocolate I eat. Take it back." *'e been 'ere long enough to know what I eat. Same on the bridge now. Merchant 'e work hard but 'e stupid. 'e get me in a lotta trouble already. But Morton 'e must be wanting to meet with a' accident. 'e asking for it, begging for it. 'e come round insult all the best men - the biggest men who built this place! Morton couldn't build nothing and Steadman just a black lackey. One of these days they'll get in a car and after a bit the brakes won't work ...*

So his thoughts ran on – a dark turbulent stream carrying him headlong from birth to death.

~

AFTERNOON

Outside was vast, bright and windy. Inside was confined dark and still. Bully and Naman sat inside. It was a country shop, half rum shop, half grocery. Over the front door a hand painted sign read:

'Sunrise Bar & Grocery. M. Davis. Licensed to sell all kind alcoholic liquor and cold beer. No credit and No parking.'

The shop was made of board and had a rough board counter and shelving. The floor had sunk a little and the shelves were no longer horizontal but Mr. Davis knew how to arrange his goods to take account of this. The country groceries all had similar stocks - canned milk, cheese, fish and meat, salt fish, rice, flour, macaroni, margarine, sweet oil, tomato sauce, bread, sweeties, soaps and matches. The rum shop offered rum, beers and sodas.

Bully and Naman sat on wooden stools with their forearms on the counter of the rum shop. The cash drawer held eight dollars and five cents. Naman had five dollars on him. Naman said:

"Me cousin Henry visit we last night down by me sister."

"I see the Toyota park up."

"Well 'e tell me from next week they takin' on men at Tamarind Tree. 'e tell me be on the road Monday at six thirty."

Bully looked at his friend shocked.

"You have a job for true!"

"Seem so" said Naman relaxing into a smile. "How much they pay?" "Three fifty a hour."

"Good money!"

"Now we eat good."

"Right!" *Now I get friendly with Tina.*

He paused, "Things gotta change stop keeping we down."

"True. Me hungry. Mr. Davis let we have a can mackerel and a bag rice."

"I have rice by me."

"Then we celebrate - two rums and a mackerel and a cheese dinner."

~

Rogers clattered down the rough stony road to his house in his pickup. He lived at the west end of the top road high up overlooking the airport and Point Village. Before he had the pickup door open his two year old daughter Janine was toddling out to him, arms raised for balance, her short delicate dress looking quite out of place on her sturdy and ungainly body. She was the character of the family - good natured, energetic and talkative.

"Daddy I have something for you." Her eyes shiny, she raised her left arm a little higher and passed some round stones to her father.

"Janine." Rogers picked her up, kissed her and carried her inside passed their motley collection of dogs, puppies, cats and goats.

"Janet, how are you?"

"You back early Jonathan. I don't have the food ready yet." She came forward to be embraced.

"Claudia not back yet?"

"She said she'd stay late today for games. How's Tamarind Tree today?"

"It's fine. We finished early today because I'm having the men go in early tomorrow to move stores."

"Daddy you like my stones?"

"There's a clean towel in the bathroom - but tell me how the work is going?"

"Well we'll finish within the contract time, no problems there. But you know when the directors are down from overseas they like to change things around a bit. They're a strange people to work with - they seem to have a non-stop impatience that makes for never-ending problems. We're moving the store location tomorrow. No one can make any sense of it excepting Morton of course but no sense arguing. And how was your day?"

"I baked something you like. Janine wouldn't stop talkin'. My sister visit me and the electricity was off so I couldn't sew the dress for Claudia. Nobody phone for you but I not sure the phone working so good. Mother went down the road with the rest the old time women them and I don't see her again since morning."

"Daddy, mummy make a pie for you."

After a shower Rogers sat outside relaxing in the early evening sunlight. He heard a youthful shout from further up the road and soon a boy came into view beating a ring in front of him. *Tin-Can* - a boy with a warm playful nature but small intellect. He belonged to his neighbour Toppy who ran a tiny rum shop and rented three small unfurnished wooden houses he'd built himself as well as working ground and keeping two pigs and some fowl. Toppy described himself as a business man not a family man and he lived rather curiously in the bottom floor of a modest concrete house from which he'd had the electricity disconnected as too expensive. He used oil lamps. His wife lived upstairs with the children and the electricity. Tin-Can was fed by both father and mother but otherwise paid little attention. He had an enormous appetite and played endlessly in the road going home only when he felt hungry. He should have been at school but there was no sense in going. In the village some called him 'Stupid' and the bigger he grew the less forgiving they became. He was beginning to feel hurt, lose his shine and look confused. But generally the Gods still seemed to shine on him. He was famous for his exploits - like the time he'd run down the road after a gigantic cardboard box blown down in the wind. It must have been from a refrigerator. He caught up with it, trod on it and jumped inside and closed the lid. A neighbour had only just witnessed this when a ten ton truck turned the corner heading up towards the box with much noise and speed. The driver steered to pass with one wheel either side of it. Immediately it was passed Tin-Can threw open the lid and jumped out with upstretched arms, shouted, and ran down the road with a special jumping step he'd recently perfected.

Now he was looking up at Rogers with a big smile. "Want oil?"

He delivered kerosene from time to time in the hope of getting something to eat or drink.

"No."

"Egg. Want egg?"

"No." His eyes kept returning to a model car Rogers was making for his daughter.

"Want that car there? Car. Want it?"

"Yes."

"Buy it you buy it?"

"No."

"Make um?"

"Yes."

"You want um?"

"Yes."

"What if someone steal um?"

"They get their hands chopped off."

"Wi' what?"

"A knife."

"You have um?"

"Yes."

"It sharp?"

"Yes." Tin-Can smiled.

"Hmmm" There was a pause. "Egg, you want egg?"

"No Tin-Can, run off and play now."

"You had a shower?" Rogers smiled.

"Look go home boy."

"I gone." He didn't move.

"Run off now."

"Gone!" He shot off up the track whipping his steel ring with his stick.

~

Most of the construction workers had left for home. Morton sat alone at the poolside bar bathed in golden sunlight waiting for a whiskey and soda.

Today I'm fifty – I suppose it's a red letter day. At least it's a time to reflect on the past and look to the future - what's left of it. He looked down at himself. *I suppose I can catalogue some considerable achievements and as well as that some fine moments of personal happiness.* He smiled and reached for his pipe. *In fact I could write a story worthy of a fine autobiography - here I am, once a boy sitting at an elementary school desk being scolded by some stuffy old fashioned school-ma'am, now a man in his prime sitting in a tropical paradise running a successful multi-million dollar enterprise with bright prospects for his future and that of his family.*

Yet despite this analysis there was a disquieting feeling that was always with him to a greater or lesser extent, a feeling that something was wrong, that things were not quite as they should be - something was imperfect, unsatisfactory, cheerless - woebegone. He sat back. If only he knew the cause he could tackle it man to man. *Well of course I regret one or two things - we're not saints - we have to make mistakes to learn. I don't think it's that that's troubling me. Am I sure where I'm going never mind where I'm leading others? I don't think it's that that's troubling me either – I'm used to that. Is it my body? At fifty the body never seems fully operational, there's always some little discomfort somewhere. And we're coming more and more face to face with our own mortality ... Or is it the mind? ... memory fades a bit, but there's an increase in worldly knowledge which compensates ...* On this rather satisfying note the whiskey came. He took a large swig. *Happy birthday* and felt a lot more positive very quickly. *Yes better now but worse in the morning. What is the real problem?* He sat for some time waiting for an answer to manifest. *That stupid fashion woman said at twenty you have the face nature gives you and at fifty you have the face you deserve ... well mine has ... character, seasoned by the world ... distinguished according to some ...* And yet there was something he didn't quite like about it that he sometimes caught sight of in the mirror - guilt, greed, conceit, bitterness - what was it? A mixture? Impossible to say - too fleeting. *Perhaps the problem is my high standards always prodding me to aspire to greater heights and yet never giving me any peace. Yes, it's hard to accept life in a second rate form - I can't stand mediocrity - half assed idiots - they annoy the hell out of me! Lazy creeps! The people here appreciate natural perfection, yes, but they have little idea about its enhancement. Hence few step forward, the rest merely prefer to think they're the best. I am willing to make the effort. I always was, always will be ...* He paused.

I never seem to fully achieve anything ... I'm always heading for the next goal ...surely this is the great twentieth century Western malaise and I'm just one of its many victims ... there's never enough time ... and I want to do a lot more before I retire... He took another swig of his whiskey and sat back again gazing over the low swimming pool wall and out to sea. *If there is an afterlife as those Sunday creeps maintain will I get a place upstairs?* He rather thought he should. He felt his honesty greater than some he knew who were actively involved in the church and yet their lives denied its teachings. *I should get in! I deserve to get in! I've done a lot of good things. And I have plans to do more - the proposed houses for locals are a concrete example!* He smiled. And yet he'd been having a recurrent dream of late - a rather disturbing one. He was marching down a busy city street in his best business suit. It was in England somewhere. He was carrying a lot of paperwork under his arms - files, briefcases, note books and so on. He found himself in an imposing room. A court-room. He was asked to explain himself. He had all his papers in front of him carefully laid out and was just about to start when he realised those in charge were somehow stopping him from speaking and he knew at once that it was pointless to start and that all his lengthy views, opinions, theories and explanations held no water - that there was a clear and universal justice that was different from his own point of view - that he already knew about this timeless universal way, always had, and that despite his skill and eloquence, despite all his careful justifications, his point of view was, after all, just that ... his point of view - nothing more. And it was this dream, this revealed unpleasantness, that somehow seemed to be at the bottom of all this and added to the burdensomeness of his days. And yet, paradoxically, it also gave him a strangely beautiful feeling. *Enough of that. Who's happy at my age? Steadman's not and he's younger. The same for his long suffering wife. Daley's a man in torment. Peter- he's a fish out of water. Bill's a fool. Henry's a spoilt child. Who is happy? No one. Who contains the answer? Not some silly sixteen year old who's divinely happy today and crushed forever tomorrow. And not those religious con-men with their false kindness the bastards!* He felt himself to be snarling and looked around to see if he was observed. A guest of the hotel, a little old lady, sitting across from him, was giving him a rather severe look. He smiled and raised his glass to her. *Why do we have two legs and two arms anyway and why doesn't God, if he exists at all, reveal himself to us in a credible way so we can understand what the hell's going on? Why do we have to be neglected, live absurd lives, struggle and die pointlessly?* And realising he was on familiar ground, following an old train of thought which led only into a dark tunnel, and deeming that an answer was not going to miraculously appear from out of the blue, he left his chair, stood up, and assuming the air of a man who is master of both his own fate and that of others, set off for his room. But on turning a corner beyond the gaze of the old lady, he relaxed this pretence a little and walked along the seafront gardens head down, lost in thought.

Overhead in the last of the evening light, against a luminous blue sky, cumulus clouds, colossal and kind, displayed whites and greys, creams and pinks. But they passed by silently.

∾

NIGHT

"Mr. Prince isn't in?"

"No sir." His son's voice came back from the late night supermarket.

"Well tell him Mr. Daley phoned."

"Yes sir."

"And that he has validated the proposal numerically and is strongly considering implementation pending further discussions concerning that and related matters."

"Yes sir."

"Goodbye."

"Goodbye sir."

∾

The harmony in Jacky's home, the same as in any happy home anywhere, was something both admirable and commonplace. Each was completely glad of the other two. When an emotion held one it commonly passed quickly to the other two. They were like three sisters doing things for each other not from a desire to please but rather because they couldn't help but do them.

Jacky sat close by her sister in the light of a kerosene lamp. A red scarf covered her newly straightened hair. Some blue material in her lap covered her white frock - a silver needle glinted in her hand. Icilma was reading a magasin which lay flat on the table against the lamp. Their mother stood by the open front door looking out into the night. Content only a moment before a passing fear now held her and she kept her face averted from her daughters. She had a dull presentiment of something dark coming before them in the future, something crossing their path, a difficulty, an impasse. Danger...

~

Henry sat sweating in his car on the windless night. He saw Bates' old car passing on the road below him. A kind of smile came to his face. *Now I'll get mines.* He drove down to the village, parked up behind the quarry, sat there a few minutes and then climbed out and went over to Bates' house.

"Open up!"

She was there when the door opened looking a little scared. He went in and closed and bolted the door. He felt thirsty. His face was covered in sweat.

"Gimme a rum."

"No rum is here."

He saw a whiskey bottle on a ledge, took it up and drank a few swigs. Then he let off a great belch and looked at Bates' wife - a wet lipped smile, his eyes fiery. He pushed her toward the bedroom.

When he'd finished his business he turned on his back and fell asleep. The next thing he knew was a loud banging at the door. Bates wife came rushing into the room looking terrified. He felt shock and then terror. She motioned him to go under the bed. *Bates come back!* While she went to unlatch the door he climbed quickly under the bed. His hand came on a steel rod, perhaps kept there for intruders. As soon as he realised what it was he felt an uncontrollable situation had arisen and he might kill Bates. He found himself gripping it hard. He knew some dreadful evil could occur and he feared the night terribly and longed for it to end.

The door was unlatched. He listened earnestly, his heart pounding, his whole being petrified. Some burbled sound came from the next room.

"You's drunk us ... cow ... hand off ... hand off ... gimme back ... no, No! No!"

Heavy footsteps, the last one by Henry's head, then a great crash and he was squeezed to half his size under the weight now on the bed. Bates was flat out drunk, Henry pinned beneath him.

He stayed that way for what seemed like an hour without moving. By then Bates' had quietened down - his breath was rough but regular. Henry could feel fresh air come to him. A door must be open. Bates wife kicked him in the side. He forced his way out and, keeping his face averted, got quickly outside and ran down to the quarry. He half expected to meet a force of men barring his way but to his surprise his car was still there, undiscovered and untouched. He threw away the steel rod, found his keys, jumped in, started up and was gone into the darkness.

THURSDAY

MORNING

A new wind bringing with it a new day - palm trees waving in the new light - grasses stirring in the breeze. Along the shore, small long beaked birds running in and out following the waves, digging quickly for worms. Music from a radio. People washing themselves. Stock standing up, waiting to be taken out to grass. Stoves on, breakfast cooking, children getting up - the sun brightening. Cleaning, washing, making ready. A stronger wind. Clothes taken down off hangers, work done, mirrors consulted. Cars and buses on the road, shouts in the distance, talk up close. A straw hat wheeling down the road and the owner, pleased, running after it.

Elba said "You can't go girl, not looking so bruise up."
"I will too."
"But Mr. Jackson will ..."
"Jackson nothing I going!"
"Well 'e really rough you up in trut' girl."
"'e love boxing."
"'e a rude man."
"An' you never went with Mr. Jackson at all right?"
"With him? Me? You must be jokin'."
"Yet he beat you and beat you."
"You think 'e care?"

Both women stood there indignantly waiting for the bus. It was an injustice. Just gossip. She'd never done a thing in the room with the new assistant manager with his whitey white face. She felt wronged. She was wronged! And Tyrone had his own girlfriend, as she well knew. In fact more than one. She'd never done nothing with Jackson! Nothing. Of course it was true she'd done some little thing with Steadman and King. That had been good fun. No one knew about that. She smiled at the recollection.

~

When Peter checked in at reception that morning there was a telegram for him from England. His mother had died. The telegram was from his younger brother. He went and sat outside in his pickup and looked at it and looked at it. A strange feeling overwhelmed him as though he were lost. After some time he heard someone shout and coming out of his reverie he started his pickup and drove off to the bridge. He was barely conscious of his whereabouts as he moved about continuing a job from yesterday. He couldn't find the two inch spanner. After a while he became dimly aware of two faces in front of him, both full of disdain. *What will Marjorie say? How will she take this? How will she feel?*

"Well where is it?"

"Where's what?" said Peter in an unsympathetic way.

"The spirit level!"

"I don't care where the effing spirit level is!" he shouted back. The figures disappeared from view. *She'll probably get depressed.*

Outside Otley said, "There, see, he a race man orright."

"Yeah, he no good, someone gonna catch that m.f. though, beat his ass."

Inside Peter was fumbling around looking for the hundred foot tape he'd just put down. *I should never have left knowing she was dying.*

൴

But Marjorie was already depressed. Horribly depressed - horrible stultifying depression. Her maid was having a lively discussion with a passing man at the entrance to her house and this was driving her to the end of her tether. The girl evidently expected to be paid for her flirtations when there was work to be done - the garbage was becoming disgusting and it might rain - if the washing wasn't out early it would stay wet all day and they had no spare bed covers. But what vexed her more than this, what made her really upset, was the certain knowledge that this fool of a girl was happy, quite joyous and full of life - that the life force that flowed in these dark bodies and brightened these dark eyes seemed to be scarcely in her at all. She imagined how she must appear to them, an ugly white woman full of the most expensive foods, anger, small-mindedness...joylessness. She felt like an unwanted shadow. Unhappiness embraced her like a second skin. And she was frightened - depression was becoming more and more common to her.

She went to the door. In a mousy voice she said "Come inside Mavis." The girl looked at her and then at her man. As soon as she turned her back there was a peal of laughter. She went busily into her bedroom and stood quite still listening, feeling mortified. The girl still hadn't come in. *What is she saying about me? Why is she so quiet? It's nine o'clock. Peter won't be here for three hours. Until then I have to try and control this ill bred, disrespectful slut.* She went quickly round the room picking up crockery and then sped at high speed passed the front door into the kitchen casting a sideways glance. She was still there! She hadn't moved an inch!

൴

Wealth requires barriers - to be wealthy is to be set a little apart. That which protects and safeguards is also that which separates. Making separate that which is born in unity causes something to become a little cool, a little hardened - a certain indifference sets in. There is a slight turning away.

The hotel buildings erected on coastal land bought, cleared and filled, rose starkly out of the ground with walls that were detached, implacable, inorganic, immobile - white washed clean - the buildings and gardens surrounded by the high boundary wall. These walls provided an indifferent strength, enclosing their agreeable comforts, keeping their pleasures from the endless insatiable poor who passed by ignobly on the outside beyond their charmed enclosure.

~

The general plans for the new leisure complex lay between Morton and Steadman on the desk in the director's office. On the side table lay Doc's report on the medical status of the senior staff. Without exception they all had high blood pressure.

"Well" said Morton, "what do you think?"

He got out his pipe and tobacco tin, feeling satisfied to be working again - his fifty first year. He knew Steadman had reservations about the project.

"I thought you'd already signed the plumbing project Ben."

"Oh come on Steadman you know I can't go ahead without your approval. We need your support."

The structure was defined on the construction plan by thin dark blue lines that were uncompromising - exactly straight or exactly round or exactly oval - precisely vertical or precisely horizontal.

"It doesn't have much life does it?"

"When Emmanuel puts some trees and plants round it and the painters have it coloured up it should look good enough."

"What do you feel it will cost?"

"About half a million. But the potential income from it is enormous!"

"That's true. But potential is one thing - reality is another."

"That's true too. What else?"

"Hmm." Steadman was silent for a while. "It's too far from the units."

"It's a nice walk, a pleasant walk." Morton puffed on his pipe.

"Americans don't like to walk. They like to drive."

"Well we'll teach them to walk."

"But why not locate it adjacent to the swimming pool?"

"No - I want that for my tennis court and games area."

"It's a big lump of a building Ben. It's going to look out of place where you propose."

"We'll landscape it. Anyway that's not the main argument now. Do you generally approve the concept or not?"

"You know what I really think Ben?"

"No - what Steadman?"

"It's a waste. We're not ready for this yet. The whole hotel's in danger of becoming a failure - it could just lose money and lose money and lose money. We seem to be throwing good money after bad. Another half million gone! When do we start getting it back? We've lost two hundred thousand in the first year of operation. Occupancy is stuck at twenty per cent."

"Well the construction's not finished. We're not fully operational." A head came round the door.

"You needed me Mr. Morton?"

"Ah Henry. No we're not quite ready for you yet. We're still discussing the plan itself. Can you come back in an hour?"

"Yes."

"How's the bridge this morning?"

"Coming along well Mr. Morton."

Henry looked a bit anxious and this pleased Morton.

"Good Henry, come back in an hour then."

The door closed again.

Morton sat back quietly. Then he said:

"The reason we selected you Steadman was our confidence in you. We felt you were the one man who could do the job - make this operation a success. We still want you to do that. We've had our teething problems. We expected that. But now we should be looking to real financial success and the people in London feel that with the addition of this leisure centre we'll appeal to a wider market - the casino alone could generate a fortune. I happen to believe they're right and I want to be sure you do before we go ahead with this final phase of the construction ..." He looked at Steadman. Steadman stood up and walked to the windows and looked out.

"Ben – the churches here and the elders don't want a casino on the island. They will make a lot of noise about this and that will make things more difficult with the government. But - apart from that - at the moment we have something that isn't a going concern. It's a white elephant of a sort but not too obvious. It can still hide behind the trees and walls. And we can still have hope for the future, for a change - and I'm willing to work toward that change. But if we put in another half million, or three quarter million or whatever it runs to - well nobody will miss the immense stature of our elephant. Think what that might do to future investment on the island. Outside investors would come here, have lunch, get the jitters and catch the first plane out. And again for the island it would mean the boldest venture yet is a failure - and as you know Ben the history here is not a success story for us - for any of us."

"Yes, yes Steadman I know all that and to some extent I agree with you." He puffed on his pipe.

"I'll leave it with you to think about. Generally speaking I agree with your philosophy - start small and grow organically. But we have to face global realities. And our backers believe it's diversify or die ...

"The fact is in many ways we are in a very strong position here. It's a natural paradise. And our resort enhances those natural qualities and provides much more besides. This leisure complex will make this a very complete resort. Whoever comes here will find everything they want surrounds them. Paradise will be certain for every one. And therefore, for us, it will all be a certain success."

Steadman didn't answer but turned his gaze seaward again - out the window, far away out over the sea.

After some time, as though he wasn't addressing anyone in particular, he said quietly

"Yes, I suppose this is a certain paradise." For a moment a sadness flickered over his face. Morton noted this.

"Good well think about it and get back to me. I want your approval. Then we can make it happen."

~

"Hello, Beatrice?"

"Yes."

"This is Marjorie Finch."

"Oh Marjorie how nice of you to call."

"How are you?"

"Oh fine, fine. How are you and your husband?"

"In very good shape thank you.... Beatrice ... I called to ask if you'll be going to the tennis match at the Sports Club this evening?"

"Oh no Marjorie, I don't think so. The Blenkinsop's cocktail party is starting rather early isn't it?"

"Oh well actually we're not going" gasped Marjorie feeling rather mortified at not having been invited, "we're rather committed this evening." She paused. "Beatrice I really wanted some advice - you've been on the island so much longer than we have, you're older and wiser, you understand things better."

"How can I help you my dear?"

"Well it's my maid ..."

"Oh the usual trouble."

"Yes. Well I'm considering firing her."

"Why's that?"

"Well she just can't or won't work well for me. I've never had such a bad maid in my life. It's as if she thinks she's partly in charge herself. She's clumsy, foolish and idle. She's a perfect menace to Peter's fishing equipment. She's unpunctual and often ill dressed. When she opens the door people must imagine she lives here with her hair in rollers and her 'Who you be?' "

"Ah yes - I know exactly what you mean my dear. It's something we all have to learn to put up with in some way. The fact is if you get someone else you can't be sure if they'll be any better. Often they're really excellent for the first few days and then tail off very quickly. Besides you never know who's related to who or who is a friend of who. She may have friends in the Labour Department and then you could be getting yourself into an unpleasant situation. Marjorie my dear, you'll have to be careful. But do come and talk with me about it any time, any time at all."

"Thank you."

"Oh, incidentally - I heard through the grapevine that your new assistant manager has been having relations with one of the hotel cleaning girls."

"What a local girl!?"

"Yes. I can tell you haven't heard of it."

"No not at all – it's complete news to me. Well really! Mr. Jackson!"

"Perhaps you'll hear something about it. ..."

"I'll let you know if I do."

"Well thank you Marjorie. So nice of you to phone. Please give my regards to Peter."

"Yes thank you for your advice. I will. Goodbye."

~

NOON

A trumpet tree gave shade to some boulders in the grounds of Point Junior School. Three young boys were squatting in the cool gap between the rocks. A cat with an angry countenance regarded them from a distance. They'd just finished their packed lunches and were now about the great business of all people, young and old, everywhere - that is to say, they were informing each other about life. The eldest gave the cat a serious look and then turned to the other two with a solemn air and said:

"Don't let a cat go near you' mout' lick you. You know what happen if 'e do?" James looked up, already a bit fearful.

"You know how cat breathe like motor...well... "

"No 'e can't!" shouted Ash who'd heard the story before.

"Yes 'e can!" countered Shane with the greater force of seniority.

"It can happen to you. An' old lady up east have a big red cat an' she get it. Me Aunt Clarice tell me and I hear her too. It true to God. Her breathing noisy boy just like a big cat. She get licked once an' never stop since."

The bell went. "Quick lie down flat before they see we." James looked worried.

~

Up near Watley Village, overlooking the junior school, Zackie's grandma was preparing food for the day. She had Zackie for company. She felt a bit alone without the fowl and having no children to mind. She'd brought Zackie up. He was her last. His appearance now upset some of their neighbours but not her - she still spoke to him without forethought. She was a Methodist and it was about the Christian teachings that she most liked to talk. They were both consolation and joy to her. She looked at Zackie leaning back against the door frame, eyes half closed, and continued

"... John Wesley say it make no difference in God sight you know. The way I find this out was when Hildred's sister's son was here for the land dispute and I were washing he pant in the yard and I feel something sticking in he pocket and take it out and it a tract. Well I love tract and I stop and read it and it say how John Wesley say 'All people as one before God'." She smiled into the distance. "Lord yes" and chuckled to herself keeping her old smiling face hidden. But when she looked back she saw Zackie was asleep."

"What wrong with you boy you sick or something?" Zackie sat up and shook his locks.

"That ganja have you stupid for true."

Naman's sister was in her mid twenties but looked older. Ten years before she'd been very shapely and could get anything she wanted, but now she'd lost her looks, put on weight and had mouths to feed and bills to pay. Like all poor people she was well acquainted with the sinking feeling of not having enough when all about you have. You are in town, you feel as though you shouldn't be there. You have no money. You may be arrested! Someone might see you looking in a shop window and know it's a joke for you have nothing. And people see your plight and perhaps look sorry and pass on. And you begin to get hungry and the people in the cafés bite their hamburgers at you. And you have nothing and they have dessert. And you are dirty and tired and unacceptable. Nothing. Living trash!

It was past time when she would normally start cooking. The unavoidable housework was finished and she half sat and half lay on her bed with a torn woman's romance paperback on the pillow by her head. She felt a pain round her eyes and in the back of her neck and between her shoulders. Listless, her thoughts wondered in their accustomed grounds - *It terrible here now ... the heat have me and the pain and not a' aspirin nor nothing in the house ... when uncle coming? If me have a shoe this morning me'd a gone town fin' me friend Janet beg something for me pickny them. Town people so wrongful. When they see you they look at you' empty feet them and talk to them. Me tired askin' Hilda for borrow a shoe. She no good ... I tired this bitch house and the sore on me leg them. Me could wear a jeans pant cover them but me still needs a shoe. They so rude it disgusting.*

She dozed off for a few minutes but awoke when she heard a cry from her youngest child. *Where Uncle? 'E promise bring me fish early ... 'e 'ave to be in Daddy Boy's bar drinking and dribblin' out 'e no toot'-mout'. If only me skin come good again. Edna tell me how them white people have a bubble bath and the lady them get out smellin' like roses and dress up nice and they husband care them good ...if me skin good now me'd a go town took a man love me treat me right ... now me even have 'o beg Jacko and the bitch give me nothing for the last I don'' know when.*

Footsteps by the door. Naman and Bully there.

"Where the food?" Naman looked vexed.

Her baby let out a long cry, so she ignored her brother and got up and entered the back room.

∾

King lay on a little frequented but perfect white sand beach - his towels laid out in the shade of a sea grape tree, a position not visible from the point where the path led onto the beach. It was his half day off as it was for Elba who lay close by him. She lay on a huge towel clothed in a purple bikini, a silver crucifix on a silver chain around her neck. They could hear the sounds of the sea breaking, the rustling of the sea grape trees and yellowbirds calling from somewhere way behind in the bush. King looked at her plumpness and felt pleased. He was tall and muscular and he loved short round women. Raising himself on an elbow he leaned over and kissed her on the mouth and then on her neck. She said "No" but then put her hand behind his head.

"Let's go in the bushes."

"No." She pushed him off and rearranged herself.

"I'm going swim cool off. When I come back out I comin' for you".

She watched him swimming through half open eyes. When she saw him coming up the beach at a speed she got up quickly and started running into the bushes behind the beach. Seeing this King started running even faster. There was an old stone ruin in the bushes and she ran around it and beyond it and up over a rise. Here she stopped to listen. She couldn't hear him coming. She paused there, agitated, trying to slow her breath. Then she heard rustling behind and saw King coming at her through the bushes bent half double. As she turned to run she tripped over a root and fell hard on her forearms. He was upon her at once. She didn't look round. The position proved quite convenient. Her elbows dug in. It was a real indignity. Real nice!

~

EVENING

James ran up to Edna as soon as she reached home. "Good afternoon mammy!"

She felt tired, hungry.

"Mammy, can a cat make you breed like motor?"

"Chil'..." she reached in her purse and took out a dollar. "... run sister Ruth get a bread quick quick."

"Yes Mammy."

He started off quick-quick but by the time he reached the shop he was looking for something more interesting to do. He had a foot on the step when a car pulled up. He recognised by the license plates it was a hire car. There were two white men in front and two white women in the back. The driver had on a blue hat with a yellow anchor badge. The women in the back had a lot of make-up on their faces and James wondered if they could be from a circus. They all looked agitated and tired out.

The driver said:

"Can you tell me please, does this shop sell grouper?"

James didn't answer.

"Can you tell me please what does this shop sell?"

"It sell Friko, bubble gum, all kind a thing."

"Can you tell me does it sell grouper? Fish?"

"It sell all kind a thing."

"What did he say?"

"I don't know."

"Please for a dollar."

"Don't give him a dollar. It's too much."

The driver reached in his pocket and found two quarters.

"Here you are boy" he said giving them to James. He drove off hurriedly feeling unaccountably ill at ease. James held a quarter in each hand pressing them into his palms with a finger and watching the hire car turning up dust behind it. Then he stepped up into the shop.

"Sister Ruth, Oh sister Ruth." An old woman started behind the counter. She looked up angrily at the young face looking down over the counter at her.

"Sister Ruth - give me twenty five cent bubble gum and twenty five cent Friko."

~

Marjorie looked up at the wall clock which said two minutes past four and then at her wrist watch which said five minutes past four. Peter had to arrive soon and explain why he hadn't come at lunchtime. The business with the maid still agitated her from time to time and this disturbed her reading. She curled herself up tighter in her armchair, lit a cigarette, reopened her book, took out the marker and put it aside, not noticing it drop to the floor, found her place again, and began reading.

There was a sudden squeal of tyres and a car door slamming. Peter appeared and she at once judged him to be in one of his difficult moods.

"Mother's dead."

"Oh no!" She ran to his side and embraced him. He looked away.

"When did you hear?"

"This morning. I've spent half the day at the travel agent trying to get a flight."

A surge of warm affection for her husband ran through her.

"I'm sorry Peter, so sorry."

He went into the bedroom, moving from her embrace which threatened to come between himself and his mother. She went to make tea. When he came back the phone rang.

"Peter?" Morton's voice.

"Yes."

"Rogers tells me the large cement mixer has broken down."

"Yes."

"I want it running by seven a.m. tomorrow morning."

No answer.

"Can you hear me?"

"Yes Mr. Morton."

"And I think you'd better come to my office in the morning to discuss your return to England. I have more information for you from the Labour Department."

"I won't be able to make it."

"And why is that pray tell me Mr. Finch?"

"I'll be on my way there."

"Where?"

"England."

NIGHT

"I don't know Steadman, I really don't know. You think you're doing the best possible for your staff ..." He took another slice of beef and ate it, "... but somehow they don't see it. They're not even thankful. They get it too easy that's the trouble ... I remember my own youth and apprenticeship. We didn't expect to be driving expensive cars and living in lovely apartments under sunny skies. We were just glad for work, glad to learn a trade. These modern people are spoiled - spoiled - spoiled. And I suppose I'm partly responsible. I've given them too much for too little and now it turns against me. They think they can come and go as they please. They never had a tough father as I did. A good man my father yes." He finished his main course plate of roast beef, roast potatoes, cauliflower, fresh greens peas, Yorkshire pudding and gravy and pushed his plate forward.

"I don't know, I really don't know anymore."

"Well Ben" said Steadman rather pleased with this confession, "you know I think we all have it hard in our own way don't we? It's our common lot isn't it? It's something that binds us together – our common suffering."

Morton sat back wiping his mouth with his serviette and considered this thought.

"Perhaps you're right Steadman. But it seems to me some people aren't suffering enough." They both laughed. But after a while Morton started to feel vexed with Peter again. *If only when you stepped on certain people really hard they wouldn't get up again.*

"How much longer will you be with us Ben?"

"Oh I don't know Steadman. When the bridge is well underway. When we have resolved our doubts about the new Leisure Complex. When I've met with the Labour Minister again, and with the Chief Minister. When I'm sure there's a marked improvement in staff service. When we get that useless painted primadonna in the Tourist Bureau to do something for the island ..." he paused.

"You know what Steadman? I have another project in mind." Steadman looked up curious.

"A personal private one. If you have time over the weekend come for a drive with me. I want to show you something and have your opinion."

Crabs scuttle sideways along the beach in the starlight. Moths appear from out of nowhere and head for distant lights. A cat jumps up the side of a garbage drum, looks inside and carefully eases himself down into it. Men, women and children retire inside their secure enclosures. A wild dog stalks an unpenned goat and bites its throat. A cock far in the distance cries forlornly and one quite close cries back in solidarity. A lizard pounces on an unwary cockroach, gulps once, and looks about him. Everywhere, below and above the sea, millions of diverse creatures breathing slowly in the darkness.

A car takes the same breath into its hot iron lungs, and burning it noisily, careers down the road. A flashlight shines and a sheep turns its head to it in the darkness. A man reaches down his hand and a dog raises up his head to it. In an empty shed a bee buzzes round and round in the darkness banging into the wooden walls - does it not know it will never find its hive again? Dew rises covering all surfaces in small drops of water. A man hears a noise outside his house, looks up, and his cutlass glints back at him. The moon, now waning, rises in the east pulling the earth's waters with it and bringing a light which appears to conceal as much as it reveals. Night-time ...

"Eh, you hear something?"

"No."

"You' sure?"

"What?"

"A noise. Outside."

"No."

"By the door. Sssh. A footstep - listen." Silence. Then a slight noise by the door.

"You hear that?"

"Yes."

"It him. The murderer got free of the jail."

They tense up. King reached out for the cutlass and got off the bed very slowly. He stood in the darkness so even Elba didn't know where he was. A few moments later he had the catch off a window shutter and with one action pushed it open and jumped outside with cutlass raised. A loud bang from the other side of the house. He ran round. A figure running off into the darkness. Elba had the other shutter open.

"I see the bastard!"

"Come inside Kong you got nothing on."

He came in but left the door open. He sat down with the cutlass across his knees.

"Somebody there. Somebody trying to get in."

"Who he be?"

"Don't know. Don't see he good."

"What he look like?"

"A big man. Never see 'e before."

"O Gad 'e come back" she said half to herself.

"Close up the door. Put on all the latch them." The electricity was off. She looked for a match to light the lamp.

In the distance, the sound of a car starting up and moving off.

Very late night but a small group of people outside Sunrise Bar were having an animated argument. They were lit by a single neon light from the shop which, being too bright, had driven them outside. Each held a bottled beer except a Rasta.

"Why you keep wavin' you hand round when you talkin'? You can't keep still?" asked Charlie, a fisherman in his forties, clear skinned, powerful but overweight.

"You can't just talk to me eh?"

"Who?"

"Without jumpin' 'bout an' turnin' you' back an' goin' away an' comin' back?"

"Wha?"

"You can't keep still?"

Chip had been very animated in his defence of Rastafarianism. In fact his animation had proved more interesting than his words. He said, "You was movin' off a little way speakin' down the road just now."

"No I just get drifted off a little with the current you see - I's a fisherman, but you - you can't keep still!"

Chip smiled, but Charlie was feeling heated and vexed.

"I mean what wrong with you - you got on roller skate or something?"

"Rasta don't deal with skate."

"Well stand still now. Tell me your business. How come you can't drink a bottle beer eh? Eh?"

"Rasta don't deal with no alcohol. Rasta deal with 'erb."

"Look don't vex me up orright. I don't stay here late late to talk stupidness. I say tell me your business eh? What you think you is - wanderin' in them hills eh? A goat? You think you is a goat?"

Charlie was playing to the audience now and had everyone laughing with him.

"No. I is up there following the lion - the Lion of Judah."

"Oh ho!" Charlie paused a long time and looked steadily at him - as steady as he could bearing in mind he was having trouble standing up straight.

"Oh so you is a lion. Oh I see. I didn't realise you is a lion." The others laughed again.

"I accidentally mistakin' you for a goat. Well then which zoo you comin' from eh? Which zoo?"

"Ethiopia lion don't study no zoo."

"You is a zoo man in truth. Where your keeper eh? Who he be?"

"Jah. Jah is my keeper." He sang this out after the fashion of Bob Marley.

"Oh so Jah is you' keeper eh?"

Chip nodded.

"Well tell Jah come here. Call 'e right now. An' tell 'e before 'e put you back in you' cage, tell 'e buy we all a next beer or 'e get licks. Tell 'e two Red Stripe an' three Heinekein."

~

One a.m. in the morning, Henry was sitting in his large living room. He sat in an ornate armchair looking forward but not seeing. His wife had been in bed for hours. He'd just returned to the house, hot and sweating, and he wiped his face with a towel.

A sudden thought struck him and he got up and opened the glass fronted bookshelf he kept for works of reference. He took out his Bible and opened it at the first page of the new Testament. A small piece of paper fluttered to the floor. He picked it up and read the handwriting.

"Woman born of God, Woman born of man. Beast woman. I praise you, I glorify you, I take you, I submit to you, I rape you, I destroy you."

A thrill ran through him. He replaced the paper in the Bible and returned the Bible to its shelf, locked the sliding window and went to bed.

FRIDAY

MORNING

It was past eight but Nan was still lying in bed with the shutters closed. Her grandmother had come to tell her to 'get up go school'. But she didn't want to get up. Every now and then she felt frightened, fear coming in hot paralysing waves. Then with an effort she tried to think about something else, but her mind came back to it again and again of its own accord. Her period was late. She wasn't sure how much, maybe weeks. She willed it to come but it wouldn't come. *Come, come please come. O please come. Please come. O please come - I will be good, good, good. O please come out. Please come. Please. Please ...*

~

Morton looked at the Critical Path Analysis prepared for him in England together with the drawings for the leisure complex. It was very attractive in that it was a detailed and accurate analysis of the building sequences beautifully drawn out in coloured inks. But it had its less appealing side - it was a rather impractical planning tool for the Caribbean. *Even if I can make those foremen understand it they'll still ignore it and do things their own way. There's some damn thing in the minds of the people here that makes forethought difficult ...*

By nine thirty Steadman still hadn't arrived to share coffee so Morton thought he'd take a stroll outside and view the construction progress and see how Henry was managing in Peter's absence. He'd spent a lot of time on the phone last night explaining to Henry the importance of taking control for a few days and remaining on schedule.

At the bridge most of the formwork and steel were in place and some pouring had already taken place. But as Morton approached the area he was seized with an overwhelming anger. Not one man was working! The concrete mixer was idle, and the idle men turned idly toward him and turned idly away again. A few of them took the opportunity to stare at him. His face had become quite red.

"Where is Henry?" he shouted at the first man.

"Gone town."

"Gone town for what?"

"Something."

"Merchant, come here!" He could rely on Merchant, a Guyanese man - honest, hard working and indebted to the company. "Merchant, where is Henry?"

"Town Mr. Morton sir."

"Why is he in town Merchant?"

"Gone look timber Mr. Morton." We needs it to finish.

"Oh I see. Well kindly tell Mr. Braithwaite to come to my office immediately on his return. And tell me, I thought the cement mixer was supposed to be working now."

"Yes it supposed to work alright."

"Well is it working or is it not working?"

"Well it not working right now, nobody using it."

"Well why isn't anybody using it?"

"No cement Mr. Morton."

"What do you mean 'no cement'?"

"Cement finished Mr. Morton. None is left on the island."

"What!!"

He hit his forehead with his hand. The more discussion he had, the more he examined the issues, the more they became confused, extended and blurred, covered over by unexpected criss-crossing factors. He was becoming more and more aware of the frequency with which this type of situation arose in the islands.

Why am I paying Henry? Why am I paying Peter? They couldn't even build a dog kennel.

"Just tell Mr. Braithwaite to come to my office immediately on his return! Immediately!!"

He turned away and stormed off.

~

The principal financier for the hotel had his own villa on the island set amidst huge tropical gardens in the hills overlooking the hotel.

When in England he would phone his housekeeper every Friday. The housekeeper had worked for him previously on his country estate in Lincoln.

"Hello Beatrice. Moore here."

"Ah Mr. Moore, how are you and the family?"

"Wife has a bit of flu. England is cold but we have a spell of sunshine. So how are things at the house? We could all be coming out quite soon."

"Coming along very well Mr. Moore. Repairs to the roof Mr. Bailey tells me are good for a hundred years. I'm airing your rooms right now. The garden is looking attractive, the bougainvillea in particular ..."

"Good, good. Well expect us by the end of the month and plan accordingly. I'm phoning Morton later but do you have any news on the hotel side?"

"Well yes I do a little. I understand Mr. Finch went back to England today. His mother died."

"Oh I'm sorry."

"But there's a rumour he won't come back ..."

"Won't go back!Won't go back! Why won't he go back?"

"I don't know Mr. Moore. It was from one of my sources."

"Any other news?"

"Well I understand Mr. Morton is making heavy weather of it - setting up a lot of government people against him ..."

"Hmm ... anything else?"

"Oh yes I almost forgot. I understand the new assistant manager you sent out ..."

"Jackson, yes, I saw him myself before he left England."

"Yes well he's been having relationships with one of the local cleaners at the hotel. In the hotel rooms. I understand she's a married woman." There was a silence.

"Well I'll be out to have a sort out myself soon enough. Very well, continue to keep your ear to the ground for me. Goodbye."

"Goodbye Mr. Moore. So nice to talk to you again."

~

"Henry, what the hell is going on out there?"

"The men are setting the last of the formwork in place Mr. Morton."

"Yes well they may be now Henry - but when I walked there fifteen minutes ago they weren't doing a thing:"

Henry said nothing. All thoughts of interesting Henry in the Critical Path Analysis had quite gone from his head.

"Did Mr. Finch have the cement mixer fixed before he left?"

"Duberry tell me he have it working."

"Well why don't you have any cement in it?"

"No cement is left Mr. Morton."

"But we're meant to keep a stock Henry. A minimum stock of two hundred bags."

"That's not my department ..."

"I don't care whose department it is! How come we don't have any?"

"We have a hundred bags Mr. Morton but they done gone hard."

"So why don't we buy some more?"

"There's none on the island."

"What do you mean none on the island?" Morton's face was red.

"I mean none of the hardware shops has any to sell."

"Good God!!" Morton paused.

"So when are we going to get some back on the island?"

"There's some on the dock but Custom's won't release it right now."

"0 God, why not?"

"I doesn't know Mr. Morton. It's not my business."

"It may not be your business but running out of timber is your business. You'd better not run out of anything else again Mr.Braithwaite or your business will become my business in a very personal way ... you understand Henry?"

Henry sat silent and looked at the floor like a wrongfully chastised schoolboy.

"Well go then, get back to your work. I want to see some real progress. Tell Merchant to have the masons do site clean-up." He turned his back and dialled reception.

"Hello reception."

"Get me the Controller of Customs right now!"

He slammed the phone back and paced the room waiting for the return call.

Underneath in reception Jacky could hear him pacing. She sensed the anger in his walk.

The reply came back from Customs. The Controller had gone town - they didn't know when he'd be back.

~

"Yeah you right girl. The men on the island with cars have it good." Edna and Elba were making up twin beds in unit seventeen.

"You talkin'!"

"Too good."

"Right."

"Any girl know she gotta act sweet to stay in the number one seat."

"Right. An' the man 'e think 'e can do anything to please 'e self an' make she do anything. An' when 'e finish wi' she 'e go look a next girl."

"Right."

"But I ain't like it."

"It not right ... me no like it neither!"

But at the same time they rather did like it and their faces betrayed some pleasure.

The beds made, they set about mopping the tiled floor, cleaning the room and changing the towels. In quick time they had turned a messy living area into an attractive well ordered hotel unit again.

They took their trolleys outside, closed the door, checked for it to be locked and moved to the adjacent unit.

"Tyrone finished beat you?"

The adjacent unit revealed disorder again. They wheeled in their trolleys and set to work.

"I don't see 'e for two night. 'e out limin' some next woman ... Kong by you last night?"

Elba smiled. Then she looked serious.

"We hearin' a knockin' about late late after we was in bed. Kong leap out the window wi' me cutlash - not a stitch o' clothing on!" Edna laughed at this.

"I 'fraid though."

"'fraid what?"

"fraid me boyfriend reach back from St. Thomas."

"O Gad!"

It was 11.35 a.m. Morton was standing at the high counter at the customs office. He had Hilton with him as the young man was the most familiar of all the office staff with the day to day affairs of customs - he ran errands there continually for both the purchasing and accounts departments.

A young custom's officer at the counter was dealing with an island business man clearing goods in. The officer had given Morton such a sharp, penetrating vengeful look on arrival that he'd determined to wait his turn in silence. He'd noticed the time on arrival - 10.55 a.m. Forty minutes later Morton was experiencing extreme difficulty in containing his rage.

But Hilton was feeling pleased. He was standing by the doorway enjoying the idle time. When he saw some girls approaching he pushed his hair in place. They looked sweet.

On the other side of the counter sitting at a desk in the back was a middle aged custom's officer. He had a serene look on his face. His desk was very tidy - a telephone in the far right corner, a blotting pad squarely in front of him, a collection of pens in a holder behind that and four folders to the left. Except for a close trimmed rectangular moustache he was clean shaven.

Opening a drawer under his desk he bought out a small buff coloured cardboard box about eight inches by eight by three. He took off the lid and looked inside. It was full of custom's epaulets. At fifty two, having been in customs for twenty years and in government service before that, he wore the rank of senior custom's officer on his shoulders. The edge of each epaulet was visible and he counted them. Twenty four epaulets. Due to his seniority he was in charge of the distribution of these epaulets which were of great significance, even sacred, to him. He was known as one of the 'Big Men' at customs which he knew was exactly what he was. His car and epaulets were proof. He took them out dividing them into rank and recounted them - four junior officer, twelve officer and eight senior officer. In three years he'd be retired on a reasonable pension. He returned them to the box, now in proper order. Then he closed the box and replaced the rubber band end put it back in the drawer. *Almost lunchtime*. But then he had second thoughts and took them out again and carried them over to the supply cupboard. There he found another rubber band of the same length but much greater width. He returned to his desk and put the new rubber band around the box and then replaced it in his drawer. Looking up he saw it was 11.45 a.m. and that a white man was trying to attract his attention.

Morton was all but climbing over the counter.

"Can you tell me please when the Controller will return?"

"I believe he is unlikely to be back before lunch. We reopen promptly at one and Mr. Bramble will return sometime after that."

Morton tried to suppress his anger.

"I see, very well, please tell him Mr. Morton of Tamarind Tree was here to see him."

"Very well I shall make the appropriate notification." The senior officer was glad be of service, particularly to another man of high rank.

NOON

At midday a fresh boisterous wind drove through the island cutting through its humid indifference and bringing new life. It was the forerunner of a gentler breeze. Flags and sails, trees, bushes and grasses, the skirts of girls and women, the clothing and hearts of all fluttered in glad salute.

A group of Germans, recently checked in, were particularly enchanted. They sat by the poolside bar thawing out. Only hours before, beneath a grey drizzle, after hours in traffic, they had climbed into a cold aluminium bird, been carried far out over the sea and emerged into bright sunlight and a warm timeless place! They now sat, beers in hand, feeling rather pleased with themselves. No not just themselves but with all people and everything and this enchanted moment. They were pleased with the wind – it was warm! - with the extraordinary colours and smells. Pleased with the tiny blue and yellow birds that fluttered in and out of the bar landing on the sugar bowls. Pleased with the easy smiles on the faces of the hotel staff, with the sound of the sea. Yes with life. With life itself! It was incredible! It was marvellous! How had it come to pass that such sweetness could be theirs even for an instant? But here they were - there was no doubt about it. And all thinking was foolishness, vanity and not the thing at all. What was the thing? Eight more beers, Eta's red face, Josey's joke, their comradeship, a humming bird nearby. The deep blue sky.

And two miles away and thirty feet under the surface of the sea a group of north Americans were taking their first sea dive with 'T.T. SCUBA D.' And it was just like the movies. If you wanted to go down you went down. If you wanted to go up one flick of the flippers and up you went. The noon time sun brought light and colour. The water itself seemed to possess luminosity. And the fish - it was like diving into a gigantic tropical fish tank - hundreds of them of all shapes, colours and sizes enjoying the clear waters of the reef just as they were. Their tanks were good for thirty minutes at that depth but it was a lifetime! A visit to another world. And when they surfaced, happy and shouting and laughing and choking they were almost amazed that the world they had left, the world at the surface of the sea and the land, was still there carrying on as it had before - as if nothing had happened!

~

The restaurant bar was beginning to empty out. The vacationers headed back to their rooms and the beach, the locals to their jobs and homes. Beatrice sat at a table for four with three of her friends. Every now and then she eyed Henry who sat in a corner behind a small rubber tree looking vexed. From their guarded expressions, quick sharp glances, and forceful but almost inaudible speech, it might have been imagined the four ladies were planning nothing less than the start of the third world war. When it seemed they had reached a consensus, they simultaneously pushed back their chairs, slung their handbags over their shoulders, picked up their packages and left. Passing by Henry on the way out Beatrice said:

"I'd happily give a thousand dollars to the man who bumps him off." She gave Henry a special meaningful look in the eye. They swept out through the archway, down the stairs and were gone.

AFTERNOON

Doc came back into the room again. She sat on the chair unable to move, looking down in front of her, seeing only the hem of his white overall.

"The test is positive. You are pregnant."

She froze up. He turned away out of deference to her feelings and went and washed his hands, but after some time she still hadn't moved as though, if she kept very still, she could also keep time very still and wouldn't therefore have to proceed forward into the future.

He walked round and put a hand on her shoulder. Tears immediately came into her eyes and coursed quickly down her cheeks.

"How old are you?"
"Fourteen" she stammered out.

"What ya mean he have no big fault? You don't call cleanin' down that old chair with me fresh tea-cloth no big fault? That's definitely a big fault. And you don't call plantin' them slip in front me oven a big fault? It definitely have to be a big fault. That oven is rightfully my business and the way to it is mine by right and he doth always covet my piece o' land and want it for heself and every time I see them stupid slip shootin' up I reminded of he many big fault which is my right to trample down!"

The rough dressed heavy set woman glared in front of her needing no validation from her neighbour, Zackie's grandma. The morning's groundwork finished they sat in the lee of the old woman's house protected from the buffeting of the wind, continuing their habitual talk while waiting for the pan to boil on the coal pot. She was feeling vexed as she took off the cover and gave it a hard stir.

"The man 'e always comin' in me room. Me tell 'im keep out me room but 'e have to keep bein' in it even if it only 'e 'ead 'e put in it. 'e must disturb me sewing. 'e doth covet me peaceable mind and wish to rent it asunder. Thirty years now the Lord giveth me this cross to bear and me have to dead with it. Me only glad 'e hears me and will be in judgment for me and 'ave put me to rule the Woman's Guild. Fahie would be glad to t'row me on the dumpish heap but is work me have to do in His name."

Thus having re-established the exact nature of her grievance she sat back in solemn righteousness to await the day's food.

"Well Henry come in and sit down."

Morton motioned him to a chair.

"How is the bridge going?"

Henry sat down sensing a more relaxed atmosphere. Morton had just returned from a walk on the seafront and the gusty winds had blown away some of his burden - and he'd made some progress.

"All the formwork is in place Mr. Morton. There is only the steelwork to complete and then the pouring."

"So how long is the steelwork going to take?" Henry sat back.

"Half a day."

"Good man, good man. So if the men work a half day tomorrow they can start pouring first thing on Monday."

"But Mr. Morton there is no cement."

"Ah yes Henry you couldn't get any cement. I could."

He picked up his pipe and started to fill it knowledgably.

"You see Henry I've made an arrangement with customs. You don't have to worry what that arrangement is but suffice to say I got the Controller to understand the urgency of the situation. All you have to do is instruct your men to be down at custom's warehouse in the truck tomorrow morning at 8.30 a.m."

"But it's not possible Mr. Morton."

"Not possible! Not possible! Why not posible Henry!?"

"Because I've already sent the men home."

"What!" said Morton taken aback and quickly checking his watch, "but its only 3.15 p.m!"

"Yes but it's Friday Mr. Morton. I just come from paying the men. They already done gone home."

"O God!" said Morton thumping the table, "why is it always the same Goddamn story." He sat back in his chair non-plussed, looking vacantly at the ceiling.

"O go home Henry, please go. Just go home."

Five minutes later when Steadman entered Morton's gaze was still blankly focused at the same point on the ceiling. He sat up reluctantly.

"Ben - you look like someone just knocked you down in that armchair."

"They did Steadman, they did."

Steadman stood half smiling, anticipating a witty tirade.

"I mean really Steadman how do you manage out here? It's impossible, it's unmanageable. We've spawned a brainless monster, a dinosaur. It's amazing. It's incredible. I know of no solution. I see only the tail wagging the dog. Yet I was the one who set it up!"

He picked up the phone and called reception.

"Hello reception - phone customs - tell them not to open the warehouse for us tomorrow."

"Well maybe there is a solution Ben."

"I know of none. Tell me the solution Steadman, tell me."

"Changing the order by a war of attrition."

"War of attrition.... changing the order ... Oh come on Steadman! Its not the enemy ground down, it's me. Good old Henry there will be full of beans tonight. He's had a nice relaxing day watching his men work. But me, I'm exhausted - I just want to go home and cry."

The phone rang.

"Hello reception here sir. Customs is not answering."

"Try them again."

"They go home at 3 p.m. on Friday sir."

"Oh I see." Morton bit his lip. "Thank you."

He put the phone down and gazed upward.

"The only solution for me Steadman is to go back to England where I belong." But at the same time he knew there was a lot more he wanted to achieve on the island.

"Well Ben a good dance tonight will put new life in you."

"You can't be serious Steadman. I don't want to hear any more music. I'm not even sure if there is music any more."

"Well you'll hear it whether you go or not, whether you want to or not. 'Blazin' Brass' is playing tonight by the poolside bar. They have what's called a big sound Ben...big, very big."

~

EVENING

It was beginning to get dark as Hilton walked home from his duty at reception. He was walking home along a narrow road overhung with trees on the outskirts of town. A girl appeared around a bend ahead of him and at once caught his attention - her figure was immediately attractive to him.

When she was about thirty yards away he felt rather then saw her eyes flash at him. She then turned a corner a little more slowly that she could or should have done and passed out of sight. His body jerked alive possessed of a new urgent awareness. He hesitated but then was walking up to the corner she had turned.

She was sitting near the corner as he'd somehow known she would. Young and attractive in a light blue frock. She smiled at him gaily out of the corner of her eyes. There was something inviting about the way she was resting herself on a half broken down wall.

"You lookin' good girl." He was trying to figure out who she was. She looked down to hide her feelings. He came up close to her.

"You lookin' like a ripe ripe mango." He knew just how to rap to these girls. They were easy to get.

"An' I like a taste right now!"

"You full o' rubbish eh?" she said but it was obvious she was pleased. She looked him over, not in a devious way but openly and with interest. She admired his expensive clothes, his handsome face. They talked for a while but she realized it would soon be dark and she didn't want the neighbours to see her in the dark with a boy. She got up. He said:

"We keepin' a dance tonight at Tamarin' Tree. I get you in free."

Up to now she didn't have an invitation to the dance but it had been on her mind for weeks.

She didn't answer him but turned and walked away. But he watched her go and her whole body said "Yes, I will yes, yes, I will, I will go. Yes."

~

Marjorie had taken Peter to the airport in the early morning but hadn't been out since then. Her only real friend Liz, Bill's girlfriend, had been in to see her. But now she was driving to the Grabz's - to a cocktail party. The Grabz's were one of the oldest expatriate families on the island. They were rich. They owned the principal supermarkets. They had a large house, swimming pool and massive grounds protected by steel gates, steel fencing and steel cattle grids. They owned two cars, a jeep, a pickup and a yacht. The children were away in England at boarding school. The family had influence and its parties were quite the thing so Marjorie felt she had to go. The invitation was for 7.30 p.m. She judged it would be best to arrive at 7.45 p.m. which was the time as her car clattered over the cattle grid and entered the grounds of the Grabz's lovely estate.

Even though she claimed to find the company of expatriates the sole consolation of living away from England she felt extremely uneasy prior to entering the house. Perhaps it was the lack of her husband's immediate presence. She parked up and anxiously finished smoking a cigarette. Then she threw it down, trod on it and walked into the house as though she were to be received badly. No one would have thought this was her favoured hour.

Once inside the large reception room she was overwhelmed by the colour, the lights, the opulence and the proximity of the other guests, most of whom were white. A black waiter dressed in a black suit came up and offered a silver tray of glasses. She took one and sipped it while looking over the top to see if she could see her hosts or someone she could join. Happily an old couple who lived in the apartment above her appeared at a doorway and she was soon in animated conversation fuelled in part by the champagne.

"Oh yes I quite agree" she found herself saying "it's quite impossible to buy fresh lemonade anywhere. And yet lemons are so plentiful! You really would think that someone would have the sense to make some locally and sell it."

"But they don't do they" said Mrs. Wilkins pointedly and Marjorie agreed, conspiratorially, that they didn't. The conversation continued in this way for some time - an idle train of thought voiced by several thinkers. Marjorie started to look around again for her hosts or someone else she knew, but her hosts at this moment were in an inner room with a small circle of intimates laughing over the mark ups they put in the supermarkets - 500% on one popular item. The hors d'oevres were brought in, served on expensive platters, tiny and exquisite. She urged her small circle in the direction of the plates and awaiting servants. Trivial though it was the food made her feel better. She decided to stick it out for another hour, then make her excuses and leave.

~

By nine o'clock it had become very still. The sky was clear, entirely free of clouds, and the stars shone down brightly out of the blackness.

At the poolside bar the tables and chairs had been pushed back revealing a large tiled dance floor beautifully lit by small lamps of many colours. Two additional bars had been set up close by and were now open, heavily stocked and ready for business, but only a few small groups of hotel guests sat around tables in shady corners watching the band making its preparations.

"One two one two one two" came endlessly over the speakers. Feedback was introduced occasionally for diversity. The band were delaying, waiting for people to come.

By ten thirty, these same guests were feeling exasperated and tired. If they hadn't already waited so long they'd have given up and gone to bed. It was then that the mass of people started to arrive, mainly islanders, colourfully and carefully dressed, well groomed and sleek. The moon started to rise adding a mysterious new energy and light.

The band started abruptly - an instantaneous barrage of sound that galvanised the floor. The hotel guests immediately forgot their long wait and were swept forward on this brilliant wave of sound, born ahead into the night and into the dance. At first no one danced but the islanders sensed this was going to be a great jam.

In the event the dance was brilliant - it seemed to possess a flawless, entrancing power. The islanders forgot their troubles and danced with no expression on their faces, such was their absorption in the dance, and as the night wore on they entered more and more deeply into it. The band sensed this and played without reservation. There was a heady smell of sweat, perfume, booze and ganja.

Most of the whites found themselves unsuited to these Caribbean rhythms, not quite able to be at one with them. Like old people who find unhappily they cannot quite make the movement they want, their bodies refused to quite reflect the rhythms of the dance and so they remained slightly outside it, dancing energetically but unable to let go of themselves, smiling bashfully into each others faces.

Icilma danced by herself at the edge of the dance floor. Jacky had to work late helping with cashing at the bar so she'd been allowed by her mother to go and accompany her sister. It was her first dance and she was mesmerised by it. Every now and then other girls she knew came and danced with her. Between dances they talked and laughed and held each other, shyly looking around for boys. The band started again and they danced. Henry sat in a dark corner watching her.

By one o'clock the dance was at its peak. Hilton was working at high speed at a cash-till behind a bar but still found time to interest a girl. About six hundred people were dancing with many more on the sidelines. There was no question but that it was a total success. Even some of the elder hotel guests were still going strong.

Henry went up to Icilma and took her hand. She turned round and danced facing him glad of a partner. When the music stopped she didn't know what to say so she looked down and said nothing. When it started she danced again. It went on in this way for some time. She was a bit surprised he didn't find someone else to dance with. Then her sister came up.

"Hey girl how you doin'?"

"Just fine."

"Well we gotta go home. Hello Mr. Braithwaite."

"Hi Jacky. You workin'?"

"We just finish. Management take over. We goin' home now."

"Oh." Henry followed them out talking easily. When they reached the bus there was only room for one. Jacky was already squeezed in the back.

"Go ahead I take you' sister."

The bus drove off.

Icilma followed Henry to his car and got in. They started off. The dance still swirled about her. The stereo player was on and the music was marvellous - she gazed at the instrument panel lit up in green. After a while she realised the car had stopped.

"Let's walk a little."

"No I gotta go home."

"Don't worry the bus gotta go east first."

They were on a beach walking in the moonlight. Henry came close to her and held her hand and led her up behind the palm trees. Suddenly she got the feeling there was something terribly wrong. He sat down and then pulled her down and she knew beyond doubt she was going to be sexed and she was at once as someone a part of whom has died and she realised that this was something she'd always hoped wouldn't happen and was happening right now and she was coming closer and closer to it and he was running his hands over her and grasping at her clothing and pulling at it and she was detached and somehow she'd always known her best hopes would come to nothing, that she was never meant to be anything but be dashed on an empty shore. And as he entered her she started to cry.

On the way back in the car Henry felt disconcerted. She was still crying. He tried putting his arm round her but there was no response.

"I got the money for the honey" he said jokingly, putting on a smiley face. She didn't respond. He stopped the car at some distance from her house.

He took out a twenty dollar note and pushed it in her hand.

"Listen, I'm a big man at Tamarind Tree. Better for you say nothing or trouble for Jacky." She didn't get out but he didn't want to hang around there very long. He reached over and opened her door. She got out and started to walk home. He watched her, then started the car. *Better be no complications.*

Generally there weren't.

SATURDAY

MORNING

The ten minute gun went.

The tactician checked his watch. "Ten minutes."

They had a boat beneath them which could luff them off course and one above. Three were sailing close behind and one was coming toward them.

"Okay."

The helmsman spoke drily. They were under maximum sail for the conditions and the boat was heeled and full, a driving purposeful force reaching at ten knots - near maximum speed.

"Blue hull ahead on starboard," shouted the lookout from the bow. The helmsman had seen him and raised a hand in acknowledgement - there was no other sign of response. The boat to leeward bore off and started to gybe. That gave him more room. He bore off.

"Nine minutes."

He had a moment to look around. The tactician said

"Wind constant, inshore port tack start still favourable."

"Right."

The yacht was sixty feet long, weighed twenty tons and had a crew of sixteen. They were up against fourteen other boats in their class each crew rooting to start in the best position as the start gun fired. The cockpit crew eyed the boats around them, the position of their lines, the wind on the water, the shape of their sails. The foredeck crew sat over the windward edge. Steve got up and took in on the clew outhaul and then on the Cunningham. The mainsail flattened out and looked better for the first beat to windward. They were alert, ready to move fast to take the lead position - wary of collision.

The five minute gun and a blue flag displayed from the committee boat quivering in the fresh wind. They were now under racing rules. The helmsman felt intuitively that today he would race well and win. He called out.

"Today is our day!" hit the wheel and smiled gaily at his crew. The boat surged ahead with happy confidence.

~

Me nah feel so good today. Naman's sister sat at the table with her head in her hands assessing the situation. There were certain things she did at weekends that she didn't do weekdays. *Me nah wash today. Me sick.* Having decided this she felt a little better. She didn't want to feel too much better or she'd have to wash. The wind was unusually cold and brisk outside and she had a sweater on. Her sister had her baby down the road so there was nothing she had to do till afternoon when she should cook. *Me eye heavy. They painin' me. Maybe me get redeye.* She reached out and picked up a knife, wiped it off and looked at her reflection. *No me eye them look orright. It the flu got me.* She looked down realising she'd just scratched the top off one of her sores. She smelt her finger. It smelt bad. A liquid was beginning to ooze out from the sore. She reached for the toilet roll, cleaned it off and threw the used tissue out of the window. It fluttered off in the wind. Then she had a thought and stood up and looked around the shelves around her bed. She opened a small red plastic box. *No fetting phensic. Me nah go pick pumcoolie. Me too sick.* Finding herself kneeling on the bed, which seemed to invite her to lie down, she sat down on it. Then, without thinking, she kicked off her shoes, lay back and pulled the sheet up over her.

~

Years ago Zackie and Tyrone had been regarded as one of the most mischievous forces in Point Village. They'd been great buddies and enjoyed success with the girls. They had six children between them to prove it. Then Tyrone had married and Zackie turned Rasta. But even now in respect of their old friendship Zackie would occasionally pass by Tyrone's house when his day off fell on a weekend.

Today he sat on a rock outside the doorway of the house where Edna was preparing food - mutton, rice and peas, fig, sweet potato and salad. Tyrone had gone to the rum shop for two beers. Children ran around in the yard. There was a shout from a group of boys down the road.

"Eh - come see a man drop top!" They ran off, boy and girl alike to see the top holding itself upright, spinning on the dirt road.

Tyrone came back and sat on the rock with Zackie and gave him a beer. He seemed to be ignoring his wife.

"Them white people stupid eh? You know that Bill work down by the harbour. 'e and me meant to be friend but I finish with that now. Me finish with white man altogether!" Saying this he shot a dark glance at his wife.

"Me car giving me horrors all last week and it break down by Tamarin' Tree this mornin'. So me go by Bill tell 'e give me a spare battery and jump leads. 'e tell me 'e don't 'ave and 'e in a rush for some sailboat race and 'e wish 'e could help me. But 'e lie. 'e lie bad!" he said raising his voice and looking at his friend threateningly.

"'e know 'e 'ave two spare battery for the boat them. White man lie a lot eh?" He took a swig of his beer.

"'e 'ave a white heart - love money. 'e love money more than 'e friend them... Well me finish friendin' 'e and all the white man. They just come here frig up the island, cause confusion try to keep we slave."

But Zackie didn't like this kind of talk. He said nothing in response but after a moment turned to Edna and said:

"You want to sell any the fowl them? Me grandma lookin' some."

"Is none for sale" said Edna without looking up from peeling vegetables. The children ran up and she warned them to be quiet. They gravitated over to Zackie and his bright colourful clothes, red green and gold, and his long brown locks. Junior climbed up behind Zackie on the rock to feel his hair. His face bore the expression of someone entering into an unknown land.

"Zackie you eat wi' we?" said James.

"Rasta man no eat relish - no eat no kinda meat at all."

"Eat chicken?"

"Nah. Rastaman eat I-tal. I-tal good. I-tal give strength" he smiled. All three children surrounded him now looking slightly awed.

"You eat fish?" asked James somewhat concerned for his father's friend.

"Me nah eat fish. Me nah eat no kinda creature 't all."

"Then eat mackerel!"

But his elder sister corrected him.

"Mackerel is fish idiot."

~

The doctor's waiting room was large and bare. It had a stained wooden floor and white washed walls two of which were of hardboard. The patients, for the most part poor and ill kept, sprawled amidst their noisy offspring on the dilapidated wooden benches. The receptionist had a desk, side table and filing cabinet and sat between them bolt upright with disapproval. A few patients sat outside in the fresh air. Jacky and Icilma sat inside in a corner. It was bad enough all these people seeing them there but they certainly weren't going outside to advertise their presence. Mammy, an old village gossip, eyed them from the opposite corner.

A loud buzzer went, something reminiscent of the electrical technology of the nineteen forties, and the receptionist turned to the girls.

"Go in Icilma." The girls got up to go in.

"One at a time" said the receptionist with steely authority.

But Jacky held on to her sister and marched her past the glowering receptionist and her official stockade.

"Is together we be" she said and they walked through the door and into the surgery.

Inside the surgery Jacky did all the talking. Her sister wasn't able and the need of the situation made her brave. Their mother had gone to work early and still didn't know of the affairs of the previous night.

"Good morning" said Doc sensing at once a very personal problem.

"Good morning doctor" said Jacky sitting her sister on the only available chair and remaining standing herself.

"Which one of you is Icilma Malone?"

"She is doctor. We two sisters." The appearance of the girls at once made the doctor feel sympathetic. Icilma's eyes were wet.

"The girl get in some trouble ... Doctor, please for to check her. A man did it. She didn't want nothing."

The doctor took a second to take this in and then got up and in a business like manner told her to undress behind a screen. She did this and he then went inside. Jacky watched over her from the other side of the screen. Then Icilma was dressed and back outside and they returned to their former places. Doc wrote something down on two small sheets of paper and then made an entry on a card.

Then he looked into Icilma's eyes through her wet face and said to her

"Nothing is wrong with you excepting a little bruising and cutting. I'm going to send you to the chemist for an ointment.

It will all heal in a few days and you will be okay again. Then you will be perfectly alright again."

He glanced up at Jacky.

"She will be perfectly alright. If you take action against this man you will have my supporting report. I want to see Icilma anyway in four weeks time."

Jacky acknowledged this with her eyes but said nothing. "Are you going to take any action?"

"We don't know what to do doctor" said Jacky and she stood her sister up, gave her a tissue, said "Come on girl" and took the prescription and note back outside to the receptionist.

She took out her weekly pay envelope which was still unopened.

"Doctor say no charge."

They went quickly outside not looking at the other patients.

Mammy wanted to know why Icilma was crying. It had to be something to do with a man. And a church girl too! She was glad she'd come. This was very lucky, very lucky indeed. The girls were walking down the road. She leaned her head out the window and saw them head for the chemist. The buzzer went and the next patient was announced.

"Goin' to come back" she said and descended the steps at a fast pace. She wanted to get there before the girls were served.

~

Zackie's grandfather returned to the house after the morning's work, put down the polypropylene bag from his back and rested his hoe, his cutlass and himself against the side of the house. His wife came round carrying a large white porcelain mug full of water. He drank it down without saying anything while she opened the bag and looked inside.

"Cabbage look good. Onion and sweet potato. Where the tania? I tell you bring tania."

"Tania nah ready yet."

"Well you did good Allen. The pot is hottin' now."

She was younger and larger than him - it seemed she was twice his size and strength, as though vitality was related to body weight. What the clinic had to say about her heart was largely a matter of indifference to her. Age had made him slim and a little bent whereas she stood straight upright foursquare on the ground looking for all the world as though a hurricane wouldn't carry her off.

"You want more Allen?"

He wanted to rest - this was the time of the week to rest and reflect. No work till Monday. Tomorrow was Sunday and church ... Clean clothes.

"No. Take off me boot them."

She bent down and pulled them off and looked inside.

"Allen, when you last clean these boot?"

He didn't answer but looked away at the hill beyond where she was standing. There wasn't much energy left in him.

He became conscious of generous washing noises behind the house. The government had bought a galvanised pipe right to their yard and this constant easy access to fresh water made their old lives much easier. Before times Mistress Allen had walked with a large pail the half mile to Watley Village and fetched the water back on her head.

Inside the door by which he was sitting Allen could see the pile of cotton he'd reaped to sell at the government warehouse. In the evenings his wife took out the black seeds. It seemed to him correct that God should provide plants for food and plants to make clothes from. This seemed quite in order yet at the same time it filled him with wonder. And trees for shade and to make charcoal for cooking and houses and boats for fishing. And herbs for the healing of the nations! His wife had a dozen kinds growing half wild round their yard. But this wind, in summer, it was unusual. It was drying up the land fast – too fast, faster than the sun could do with all its strength.

He felt his eyelids beginning to close and he lay back a little more, hearing as he did so a slight snoring noise.

AFTERNOON

Nan was standing by the side of the road looking as good as she could and trying to appear confident and light-hearted. After an hour or so she saw what she was waiting for - Garry's taxi coming back over the hill. She stood out in the road and waved him down. He stopped and rather to his surprise she opened the door and got in. There was no-one else in the bus. Nan was glad of this. They started off.

"Where you goin' to?"

"Nowhere special."

"Oh." His voice wasn't very warm. She felt too tense to speak. He drove on to town sensing a problem. Two miles down the road a sheep suddenly ran out. He braked so hard they had to stop themselves hitting the windscreen.

"I makin' a baby for you."

She glanced at him. His expression didn't change. She looked down frightened. He turned and looked at her.

"For me?"

"Yeah I pregnant."

"For me or Hilton or who?"

This was a blow she hadn't expected. She looked away. He looked across and saw his words had scored.

"Better save you'self some trouble girl - get Annabel t'row it down."

She didn't want an abortion.

He took a fifty dollar US note out of his cash box.

"This'll fix you up good."

By now they were near town. He stopped the bus by some bushes. "Get out here. I see you later."

She got out. He put his foot on the gas and drove off.

~

There was a view to the south. The two half doors were held back by stones to stop them banging in the wind. She felt full and sleepy and only stirred occasionally in her chair to scratch herself or wave off a fly. It was afternoon sometime. She could hear her husband snoring in the next room. *Ma bottom a bite me*. She scratched again and half opened one eye. The house was silent except for the sound of wind. She settled herself back but something suddenly alerted her and she opened both eyes wide. It wasn't there anymore but it had been before - a familiar shadow cast by the afternoon sun on the ground outside her house. She half closed both eyes and lay back. A small head appeared from the western side of the door in profile but watching her. *Police Car!* After hesitating a moment and moving his eye all round to take in all aspects of the room he walked down passed the door and disappeared to the east. *No other fowl I know yet ugly like that one.* The fowl passed back from east to west across the door rather faster this time with his tail feathers bent forward by the following wind. Again he went out of sight. *Police Car come back for true!* She smiled happily. He was the only fowl she'd had a name for and been fond of. Born small and ugly without a proper covering of feathers his pink scraggy frame was evident every bit as much as his white and grey plumage. But at feeding time he came into his own darting in and out amongst the other fowl, doing incredible manoeuvres and totally ignoring the pecking order, to carry off the prize of food in his beak, swallow it at a distance and fly back undeterred by the bulk of the others to again do fast turns, interceptions, ninety degree corners and hairpin bends and take the corn, bread or coconut meat from under the very feet of his competitors. His performance at meal times was always quick witted and effective.

Police Car appeared again stopping half way across. Now he saw something more satisfactory. The old lady was standing up near the bread bin. He tilted his head at an angle to better observe a potentially good situation. Pieces of dry bread landed in front of him. He scooted round nabbing them, chasing the last two crumbs being blown down wind. When he came back to the door something crashed about his head. He just sidestepped the worst of it and sped off squawking in a wide arc, his pathetic wings flapping but not raising him off the ground at all. At a safe distance he turned and looked sideways to see the old woman staring at him - broom in hand.

"Where you think you been eh? Huh! Where the other fowl them?"

~

"Less wind inshore."

"Tack out to keep speed."

"What current is there?"

Steve spoke up from the foredeck.

"We passed a fish pot back there. Against us. It's very slight. Quarter of a knot."

"Okay we tack out."

The helmsman turned around to see the boat closest to them a quarter of a mile behind. Rambo following on the same tack. The crew moved to their places for the tack. When the helmsman saw they were ready he said

"Ready about" and then "lee ho" as he put the rudder over. The cockpit crew eased the genoa sheet and let it off as the boat came head to wind. The mainsheet traveller was reset, the foresail clew carried around. The winchmen started to grind the giant silver winch bringing the massive foresail down and in. The main filled and set, the boat picked up speed. The genoa was full but not in tight. The helmsman checked the new course.

Eighty degree change. Boat speed was back up.

"In tight." The genoa was bought in three more inches. The crew moved to their new places on the weather side sitting with their legs outside the lifelines.

"Speed?"

"Five and a quarter."

"What was it before?"

"Five and a quarter."

"Oh, eh, nice, very nice indeed ..." The boat started heading higher and higher toward the finishing line.

"...we have a lift."

The helmsman glanced behind him again. The second boat was sailing deeper and deeper inshore. He could see at once from the angle of the mast that he'd slowed down. The tactician looked with him.

"Looks like Rambo wants to go shore early." They smiled and looked forward again. Rambo's boat was getting smaller and smaller and the finish line clearer and clearer. The crew had given their best and were now quiet and content as the boat slipped through the last water of the course. The wind had lightened and the yellow sun was low in the sky turning the white sails cream. A few yards to go, then a gun fired. First overall. They shouted, slapped each other playfully.

"Well sailed."

"Well sailed yourself."

"Yahoo!"

The crew got up and danced round the deck. Eight hours of concentration was ended.

"Bring down the foresail!"

"Bring up the beer!"

"And the sandwiches! Hey the sandwiches! Bring up the sandwiches!"

"Watch that moored boat ahead."

"Okay somebody get the boat hook."

"You can see the mooring?"

"Over there."

"Beer?"

"In a minute."

"Nick you ready?"

The boat headed into the wind twenty yards short of the mooring. Its way carried it forward till it was scarcely moving, the mooring just out of reach. Then Nick had it and flicked it aboard.

"Drop the main."

The mainsail came sliding down covering Steve's head.

"Eh, it's gone dark."

"Well nice race Bill."

"Yeah nice race."

They felt glad, rolled up the mainsail, secured the rudder, closed the sea cocks, checked the mooring, stowed the genoa, washed the deck.

"Here come's Rambo." They all looked round as the blue hull crossed the line, its white sails luminous in the setting sun.

"Fifteen minutes behind."

Later in the yacht club every one fresh faced, joking, exuberant, discussing the sail. Rambo enjoying being mocked. He won last time, and, he claims, next time ...

EVENING

Seated by himself in a wicker rocking chair on his wooden balcony the doctor rested as quiet as his house in the gentle evening air. He found himself admiring the hand carved woodwork, the trees and flowers in a new more direct way. Through the trees and far off he could see some boats with glowing white sails making harbour. Every now and then a particular thought would come to him and a feeling of pleasure would arise in him. Then he would think of something else, the affairs of the day, or just be aware of the garden. But the thought would come back. He took a sip of guava juice. It had been a very busy day. But one patient had seemed rather, exceptional - different, yes different. There was something about her manner - compassion and resolution, simplicity and directness. He smiled to himself. Yes she was just the right size, not too short, not too skinny. She wasn't a patient even but just an escort to one and he wondered in a tentative yet hopeful way if anything could develop between them. And it appeared to him that it could.

He looked around again. Yes the garden did seem very nice indeed and yes it was pleasant just to sit there. And did it matter if he didn't get up and eat at his accustomed hour? No, it didn't matter at all. Besides tomorrow was his day off. How good it was just to sit back and breathe the evening air!

A bird landed on the handrail in front of him, nodded and flew off.

The doctor stirred in the middle of the night. He had a dim awareness of something ... something he was seeing for the first time, feeling for as if through a mist, and yet something or someone he wouldn't be surprised to find there. It was something he wanted to know, that he felt he might yet know. It was someone there...someone there in the mist... was it a body turned away from him? It was something that had always been there, or been there for a very, very long time.

He wanted to come to know it more closely. And he somehow managed to approach it more closely - afraid to disturb it for there was something terrible and neglected about it – cold, icy and deathly - and as he came closer he saw yes it was someone sitting down naked and cold turned almost away from him and somehow the body turned and looked at him though it didn't appear to move and he was astounded to see that it was he himself.

SUNDAY

MORNING

It was seven o'clock service for the Methodists of Watley Village. At six thirty Zackie's grandma was still at home making her preparations to leave. Her husband had long since left. Checking her reflection in a mirror she felt pleased and started to feel a little religious despite her haste. Her cousin's were off-island for the weekend visiting family in St. Thomas so she would be walking to church today. She set her white hat perfectly straight on her head and left the house hiking down the road with a different step to that which she used the other six days of the week - a straighter, longer step. She scarcely looked to left or right. She had on her white church clothes. The more people she passed who weren't going church the more religious she felt. By the time she reached the church she was feeling very religious indeed. She marched imperiously to her seat on the front pew, sat down, bent forward for a moment and then sat back and looked round sharply. Then, catching a friend's eye - a friend since school-days - she smiled a marvellous smile.

~

When the doctor awoke he was surprised to see it was well past his usual hour of rising. He pushed open the shutters by his bed and the new day burst in upon him with unusual grandeur. He felt exceptionally good - refreshed, almost relieved, as though something that had been shadowing him had left.

After a shower and shave he dressed in his favourite clothes and sat down to a light breakfast with coffee.

He was just about to put the coffee to his lips when the thought occurred to him that he could go church. To even have this thought was astonishing - he'd scarcely been since his early days in England fourteen years before. But he suddenly felt compelled to be there. He knew Pilgrim Holiness Church at Point Village held a service at nine. He quickly finished his breakfast, washed up, donned a jacket, jumped in his car and sped off. Two days before he would have reckoned such behaviour unaccountable and absurd.

Arriving at the simple box like church he entered quickly being unsure what to do. Finding a space towards the back on the right he sat down and then bent forward as he'd been used to doing in his own Anglican church. He sat back and everyone seemed to sit back satisfied with him. He stood and everyone stood to sing with him. They all sat again and something was read. How marvellous that people could come together in this way seeking the highest virtues!

The music started again. A short lady with a red hat and thick glasses was up front encouraging them, moving her arms about as though her life depended on it. She was clearly happy to do it and the others were clearly happy to sing and be waved at.

As he sat down his eyes fell on a young woman to the front left of the church. His belly jolted. It had to be Jacky with her sister Icilma and their mother! He kept looking and looking away. The lesson was being read and though he didn't take in the words he took in the spirit of it and realised with a shock that he had been lost and was now, somehow and in some limited way at least, saved.

And even as he perceived this they called for any visitor to stand up and he stood up and called his name. The music started up and he was moved toward the aisle and each member of the church came and shook his hand and Jacky and he felt like royalty and realised *Yes I am royalty, we are all royalty. Glory in the highest. Praise be for this moment. Yes, thank you, thank you.*

And then all at once the service was finished and he was on the steps of the church and he was glad, very glad, and everyone was happy, there could be no doubt of it, and he jumped in his car and drove off in high spirits singing "Amazing Grace" at the top of his voice.

Steadman was taken aback when Morton stopped in the middle of Point Village. This was where he'd grown up. People were coming out of Pilgrim Holiness Church.

"Uh-oh, look like Doc get lost." He smiled to himself.

"Pardon Steadman?"

"It's here you're bringing me Ben?"

"Yes here Steadman. Surprised eh?"

"Yes. Well what do you want my advice on?"

Passers-by looked into the car curious to know what Steadman was doing there with a white man. But there was no communication - cooled by air conditioning, windows up, they were set apart by glass and steel.

"It's not exactly advice I want Steadman." He looked thoughtful.

"This is the area ..." he paused while he took out his pipe "... that I'm going to propose to the Chief Minister that we clear to make way for clean, decent housing for Entropicans. The work will be done by Entropicans for Entropicans. The house holders themselves will contribute and I earnestly believe I can achieve a unit cost of less than ten thousand dollars."

Morton glanced at Steadman out of the corner of his eye.

"Well that's a kind suggestion Ben, but ..."

There was a long silence.

"But what Steadman?"

Steadman hesitated. "But...you'll have to let me know the details."

At the same moment, in the area Morton proposed developing, Edna was getting herself and her children ready for morning service. She wore a golden dress and bright yellow shoes.

"Come on its eleven. Church start now. James put down that car and fetch you' shoe. Junior come here."

"Mammy we doesn't have any collection."

She looked in her purse and gave them a quarter each.

Five minutes later they were ready and shining, walking down the dirt road to the Methodist church.

"Mornin' Edna!"

"Mornin' sweetheart!" Alice stood in her yard looking on admiringly as the children went passed. Edna felt proud.

∾

Bill was having brunch with his girlfriend. The beneficial affects of the previous day's sailing had quite worn off and he sat at the table not feeling too good. He'd drunk too much at the yacht club.

"You know one of the reasons it's hard to feel good out here is the way people are - you know always grasping for something. In Guadeloupe they say give someone a hand and they take your arm. If you give them something it's not enough, they want something else. But if you gave them everything you had they'd still not be satisfied - they'd still be sure that, as a white man, you had the bulk of your money hidden elsewhere."

His girlfriend carried on eating, neither agreeing nor disagreeing. She disliked moaning.

"I mean take yesterday, I'm in the harbour office in a rush to go sailing. In comes Tyrone looking ready to murder. He says 'gimme a battery and jump leads.' It's not 'can you let me have' or 'please for such and such.' No. 'Gimme.' 'Gimme this gimme that.' Sometimes I think the reason they're friendly is just to get access to what you have - your car, your equipment, your woman."

"Well it's true it's rare to have a completely non-sexual relationship with a black man here. They don't seem to be able to do that. So did you give him what he wanted?"

"Hell no I was about to close up. The batteries are too big for a car anyway. Besides anything you lend you have to go and find yourself - it doesn't come back. And there's a good chance it'll be damaged and yet try and get someone to feel responsible ... words of regret - I never heard any yet."

"Well you chose to come here. You keep telling me how good it is." She wanted to leave, to sail off on the boat they'd sailed in on. Life was getting too complicated. It was simpler on the sea. They'd been happy there before and in England. And she was afraid he was getting to like a local girl too much.

"That's true. Well it is good. Two sides of one coin. But with this pressure from the directors and supposed pressure from the Labour Department and occasional hostility in the streets - I mean we have our friends right but the all too present background resentment of the islanders well ... just be ready to pack your bags quick."

"Wouldn't take me very long." They looked each other in the eye.

~

Elba's house was rented from an Entropican for a very modest fee. He was a man of about sixty, short and strong from years of work. His black head was almost bald but it had a light covering of white hair. He had a strange face or more exactly a strange smile - there was something rubbery and false about it as though he were deliberately stretching his lips upwards and outwards. He was always accompanied by his dog - a small cross bred creature. He'd been married for thirty years during which time he'd built this house, first of board and then later extending it in block with two extra rooms. Then his wife had died and a year later he'd married another woman in the same district. She had her own house and as it was larger he'd gone to live with her and rented out his own. The girls who first rented it had a bad reputation and as they were irregular with their payments he made a fuss and got rid of them. Now Elba occupied the house - or rather all of it except two rooms which he kept padlocked for his own use. This gave him access to the house which he very much wanted as he rather resented having someone bar him entry to his own home. And at the same time the longer she lived in it the more curious he became about her private business and in particular the different men that came and went. In fact by law he had no right of access without her permission but neither party knew this so the situation continued with him appearing round the door with a huge smile on his face saying "Coming in" and unlocking one of his doors and rummaging around inside. Part of his business revolved around the land adjacent to the house which was his and farmed by him. Part of it came from a small fowl house he kept in the yard - so he kept corn in one of his rooms and would go to and fro feeding them. On Sundays he would come down in his working clothes, feed his fowl and then change into his Sunday best which he kept hanging in one of the rooms along with his washing kit - a bowl, soap, mirror and deodorant.

On this particular Sunday he came down to find Edna outside washing her dishes in two large plastic bowls by the stand pipe. She filled one bowl with soapy water and one with rinsing water in the morning and made use of them throughout the day. They said "Good morning" and went about their business. She went back inside. He fed the fowl and then cleaned out the fowl house. When he finished he noticed with disgust he had some chicken shit on his hand. He looked at her twin plastic bowls and quickly cleaned his hands in them listening carefully lest he should be surprised. Then, realising he'd got away with it, and feeling inwardly pleased, he went into his room to change. He put on a white shirt, an old fashioned grey suit, a leather hat and brown and white leather shoes. Then he took out his black umbrella, checked his reflection again in the mirror and, satisfied, turned to go. As he padlocked his door Elba caught his eye and he smiled at her.

"One of these Sundays you must come church Elba." This was an allusion to his previous entreaties to her to give up fornication. She didn't smile but he kept smiling all the way out of the house and down the road.

~

The minister was dressed in black except for a white dog collar. He was in his forties and fatter now than when he'd been ordained twenty years before. The first time he smiled was when he welcomed visitors to the church and to the island. There was a row of white people at the front. Perhaps this was the first unequivocal welcome to the island they had had. Their attendance was spurred by a mild curiosity – 'what did the blacks do in church?' But now they found themselves caught up in the service due to the power of this man's sincerity. The minister's face was not handsome, it wasn't jovial, nor was it melancholy, but rather it had the steady compassionate watchfulness of the man who has looked both himself and life directly in the face.

They stood to sing and their harmonies increased and filled the church and continued after in their silent prayers and in their sitting. The minister looked them over from his new position on the pulpit. He started to speak slowly and firmly.

"We Christians here are glad to be Christians. But I've heard some say 'we're saved' or 'I was saved last year' or ten years ago and still they carry on as they were before."

"But the life of a Christian is not so easy. Only when you turn to God do you begin to realise the continual outta-placeness of your own thoughts and actions - and you are aware of conflict in yourself and of your unworthiness. So even after the high of giving yourself to God and knowing acceptance there are still lows and temptations – constantly! Even Paul experiencing a great painfulness in his eye begged God to help free him of it. But God did not in order to shape Paul, to stop him from being proud."

"Does God turn his back on us? No. But we poor mortals are lazy and full of ignorance and fear. We complain the moment we can't see Him that He doesn't exist. That's true. And our friends agree with our foolishness and we fall away. Stop! This is madness! God has not suddenly vanished or turned cold! The fault lies in us. We cannot see Him due to our defilements. This is a most important point. Only by constant effort to make ourselves pure will we become good enough to see or sense Him a little. Over a long period of time with great effort we see Him more clearly. Yes! And then our lives really do change. We don't have to fake it. Why? Because knowing God you simply cannot keep committing wrong acts. You can't harbour wrong thoughts - malice, envy, greed, anger, vanity. Once real love becomes a part of you everything is seen clearly for what it is. Compassion and understanding arise naturally."

"But don't think the average man will ever reach so high. He may come church but not get much further. To get further requires real effort, real surrender. Only then can we know true peace."

"Most people today spend their life chasing here and there after pleasure. They go movie - four dollars. They go foreign trip - two thousand dollars. They go dance - twenty dollars. They buy present - hundred dollars. But it turns out this pleasure is hard to hold on to ..."

He smiles. Everyone in the congregation smiles - they know this. Edna's smile is a little sad.

"Real joy is under your fingers. But to have what our hearts truly search for, what we long for with all our being - this requires an act of faith. The preachers tell us what is possible - but until we commit ourselves, have courage and perseverance and then take that leap - until then nothing is changed. Nothing! You cannot experience the teaching at arms length! Either you let it become a part of you or you carry on in your usual way with your usual dreary thoughts inside you. Part of your usual habit might be to sit in church on Sunday. But you will still be you - isolated and separate from God, all people and all things. But even if you admit it into you and let it become part of you, a part of you will reject it and will want to keep disregarding it - will want to fight it. Don't worry! That's just the way we are. Even Paul had problems and Paul was especially chosen by God. So much the more so for us. Do not be deterred. Accept these difficulties and in time they will disappear."

"And this is the true nature of the church that we should be together to love one another - to help one another in our weakness. And this is quite different from worldly pleasure where each person is out to please themselves. Be careful in all matters, even the smallest.

"Hymn number three one six."

Ah action, pure action. Sweet words.

"Rise and sing."

~

AFTERNOON

When Naman thought he'd looked at the boots for long enough he turned to Henry and said:

"Le' me have the boots them." They were sitting in Henry's front room.

"Me wear them work everyday."

"Me have a have a boot for work tomorrow." He said this with an accusing air - Henry had got him into this.

"It the onliest boot I have. Wear a shoe."

Naman felt angry. He knew Henry must give him.

"Want a cold drink?"

This seemed a poor alternative to a pair of boots.

"Beer" he said flashing an angry look.

Henry got a canned beer from the fridge.

"You don't have a bottle beer?"

Henry went back to his fridge and Naman followed him. He saw a good sized shoulder of cooked ham in the fridge.

"You have anything to go on bread?"

A few moments later he was taking large bites at the table. A little bread and ham fell on the floor. When he'd finished he belched and said "Got a next beer?"

"Help you' self."

Henry sat with his feet up. After Naman finished the second beer he could see his anger had gone. He knew his cousin would stay now for the afternoon eating and drinking. He put some music on.

"You can have the boots. I buy a next pair."

"Right on brother man Henry!"

He put the boots on, looked at them happily and did up the laces. Family always help you when you need it.

~

"Marjorie."

"Oh Peter:"

"Are you alright?" Her voice was empty.

"Yes, I thought you were never going to call. How are you?"

"Not good, not bad. They buried her today."

"Oh, I'm sorry."

"My brother said she suffered a lot the last two days. I saw her." He stopped abruptly.

"I'm sorry Peter so very sorry."

"I can't talk now. I'll be back as soon as I can get a flight. I'm booked standby for tomorrow."

"I'll meet the flights till you come."

"Don't worry. I'll phone you again. Funny thing Moore phoned. He seemed to have some feeling I wasn't going back."

"I don't know where that came from."

"Nor me."

"Peter."

"What?"

"I miss you. It's hard when you're not here. I'm ready to go back to England."

"I'll be back in a day or two."

~

"You're sure about this Mr. Bailey?"

"Yes Madame Beatrice, definitely sure. As soon as he's drunk it he'll go into a definite coma. For some time he can't do nothing. This is a guaranteed coma mix made by a' expert obeah man from Haiti itself. It's good stuff. It's the best."

Beatrice couldn't help but smile broadly.

"Lovely. How nice of you to take the trouble for me. Mr. Morton deserves the best. The very best."

Mr. Bailey smiled back.

"I'll make sure you're properly reimbursed. After the event of course."

~

Rogers and his wife were making one of their rare visits to the beach. Sundays were normally divided between church and home. They were relaxing on deck chairs under a tree at Kapok Bay. Grandmother was snoring nearby and the children had run off to play with some white boys from a visiting yacht who had a frisby. His wife rested with closed eyes. He looked at her with some affection and felt her tenderness.

He thought of their days courting on the beach, their young brown bodies washed in the shallow waters of the white Entropican beaches - the perfect feeling that comes from guileless action - she, smiling and the clear white of her eyes is joined by white ivory. And then there is only the remnant of a smile on her lips and on his own. The sea swirls about them clear, sparkling, warm, gentle, buoyant. They realise they can trust it, push off and allow themselves to be carried forward into the future together.

A child had come earlier than expected, and seeing her with their fat baby he realised that this was what the woman had wanted - in the same way that his tools, machinery and equipment were what he wanted.

"You like it here?"

"It's nice yes."

"Remember when we used to come here?"

"I was just thinking of it."

~

Since returning from his drive to Point Village with Steadman, Morton had worked alone in his office without stopping for lunch. He looked at his files. Departmental control - finished. Staff attitude - improved. Government wage negotiations - completed, very satisfactorily. New leisure centre - accepted by Steadman. Building schedule - to complete by December fifteenth. Bridge construction - nearing completion. He'd just have to help Henry supervise till Peter returned. Special housing project - underway. Yes there were a few loose ends but basically he'd achieved what he'd come out for. He could think about booking a return flight about midweek. He took out his pipe and spent some time lighting it.

Yet despite this rather favourable account there was a slight uneasy feeling at the back of his mind - a feeling that this analysis of work done was perhaps a bit of a distortion of the real situation, that it wasn't quite like this at all, even that the reality might bear very little relation to this written summary - that the reality was somehow more complex, scattered - less subject to control. But in a few days he had to stand before the financiers in England and give a convincing account of himself. They didn't want to hear theories of anarchy and entropy, of how things out here tended to disorder. *You can feel things start to come apart as soon as you turn your back! But British bulldogs like meat not chit chat.*

The setting sun came through the picture windows of his office. Morton looked out and puffed quietly on his pipe.

~

The young American felt particularly at one with himself and his surroundings. The sky was lit up all colours by the setting sun. He could almost feel how marvellous it was! He carried on walking along the top road which was rough under his running shoes. He really was off the beaten track of the average tourist! As it got darker his feet became less sure and he started to tread on loose stones. He was thirsty and hungry from a day's walking. He determined to stop in the village ahead which he judged must be on the main road to town, get something to eat and drink and then hitch a ride back to the hotel.

As darkness came on the village lit up in little rectangles of coloured light from the open doors and shutters of the houses. But the roads were dark - he could make out only three street lamps. A dog barked at him as he entered the village and he started to feel ill at ease. Heading for the nearest street lamp he rounded a bend in the road. A group of young local fellows were hanging around under the lamp. The nearer he came the more aware he was of eyes fixed silently on him. He sensed that although there were several individuals there was one hostile mind. To his right he noticed an open door out of which a bright light shone. He could make out a counter and a Coke sign over the entrance. He climbed quickly up the steps and went in. There were four people in the shop. He noticed how dark their skins were. They all looked at him coldly except the woman who looked down. Everything was quiet and brooding.

Feeling himself resented and reduced he said

"Can you tell me if I can buy a beer round here?"

"Eh?"

"You t'ink this a rum shop?"

"Excuse me?"

There was no reply forthcoming. He stood his ground for a moment, then turned and all but stumbled down the steps. A small laugh followed after him. He headed down the road away from the street lamp. Try as he might, he was unable to make himself turn and look at the group of men. He could feel their eyes on him. He scratched his back. A stone ran down the street after him. Naman looked with pleasure at his powerful new boots.

"Look like honkey get lost." They put their hands on each others shoulders and howled with laughter.

MONDAY

MORNING

"You gotta go."

"Why?"

"It' late."

"I stayin' here."

"Get up!"

"No."

All the shutters were closed. Elba switched on the light. He looked at her through half open eyes.

"It' passed seven."

"It cant be. I stayin' here."

"No. Go home. You should 'ave left me house long time ago in the dark. You'll be late for work man. You'll get trouble. And me too - me hearin' people see me boyfriend on the island."

"When?"

"Don't know."

King pushed back the bed clothes, got up and pulled on his pants.

"Better no confusion, eh."

Elba unlatched the door for him. He stepped outside. The door closed. He still felt sleepy. They'd been up half the night. He felt he might go home first, maybe take a quick nap, then head for Tamarind Tree.

~

Naman felt confident and ready as he hung onto the back of the pickup as it tore up the road to town. But when it turned into the huge gates at Tamarind Tree he didn't feel quite so good any more. The place was awe inspiring. He'd never been inside it before or inside the gates of any hotel. In fact, he'd never spent much time at all outside his village and this was another world. He looked down at the workers and everyone black and white alike seemed to be full of some strange important purpose and to know exactly what they were about. He decided to try and look as much as possible as if he knew what he was doing as well. He jumped out as soon as he saw one of the men jump out. The men went off to a storeroom. He waited for instruction from Henry but Henry ignored him. The men came back with shovels and barrows. He decided he wouldn't speak too much. He knew some of the men by sight but not to speak to. A concrete mixer he was standing against burst into life and he jumped aside and then, vexed with himself, tried to appear as though he'd expected it to start. Henry came back to him.

"Naman - you mixin' cement. Get a shovel from John. He'll show you the business."

He was soon moving a pile of gravel closer to the mixer and then shovelling it inside. At first the work seemed very hard and he was surprised the men didn't slow up or break for a drink, but by lunch the work was coming easily to him and he was feeling part of it all and to his complete surprise quite enjoying it. *And money on Friday...I buy me girlfriend something.*

~

"Where's the bloody-hell chef?"

"I don't know - haven't seen him for the morning."

"Hotel guests are waiting for breakfasts."

"Can't help you."

"Hell's bells."

Bill replaced the receiver. He had two charter boats due in today one of which had to be ready to go out tomorrow. He could see one of the yachts half a mile off the harbour entrance - it was four hours early. *That gives me a break. Sail number 6 - the Heidelbergers.* He could see the genoa was already furled and the fenders out. The phone rang.

"Harbour office."

"Bill do you know where the chef is?"

"No, the food and beverage manager just asked me the same question."

"Can you come over to my office? I want to speak to you."

"What about Steadman?"

"We'll discuss it then."

"Okay but I've got a twenty four hour turnaround and another check out so it won't be till later."

"Okay. How was the racing?"

"Very good thanks. We won this time. How's the White Wonder?" Steadman laughed.

"See you later."

The boat motored slowly into the harbour. Bill pointed them to a berth.

"Had a nice time?"

"Yes, very good. We have to leave for the airport immediately. Kindly receive this luggage and engage a certified taxi."

~

"... I am very much moved by what the Honourable Member said and vice versa and am very much of the disposition that the people of this country are keeping abreast of what's happening where else in the world and particularly United States territories. Thank you and God help us."

"That was the Honourable Chief Minister Mr. O. B. A. Richardson. And now ZWX brings you a special message from the Honourable Minister of Labour."

"People of Entropica: today, I, Stanley Daley, the Honourable Minister of Labour, have a special message for you. It has recently come to the notice of the Ministry of Labour that there is a large group of persons on this island who are a drain on our economy. These persons earn foreign exchange here but take almost all of it overseas robbing the island of its wealth. These persons are earning very large salaries and contributing nothing to our economy except for a small income tax. The persons I am referring to are employed in our marine service industry. Many of these persons live aboard yachts in order to avoid paying rent. Few of them contribute any of their money or talents to the island in any meaningful way. Some of them have been conducting this selfish practice for many years. But we cannot allow such a group to weaken our struggling economy. We cannot allow them to take our foreign exchange and selfishly increase our foreign debt. The time has come to act and act we must."

He paused.

"The Ministry of Labour is therefore obliged to withdraw the work permits from members of this group. They will therefore no longer be allowed to work in our territory unless they can prove to us that they have been or are willing to contribute properly to our island state.

"People of Entropica: we are no longer in a position where we have to tolerate oppression and theft. We must cut away those parts of us that are ailing so that the flesh may heal and we are fully renewed and ready to enter a new decade as a people with pride. Our country must be based on sound economic principles and justice. Now is the time for us to stand up and be counted - now and in the elections to come. I am grateful for the honour of serving you."

"You can't find some rockers?"

Zackie turned the dial.

"Right."

An easy reggae beat replaced the dry government broadcast. *Sweet music. Sweet, sweet music.*

~

"Where's my typing?"

The girls in the office looked up at him but made no response. "The typing, where is it? I'm in a rush."

"Mr. Osborne said you were to see him."

"I don't want Osborne I want my typing." He paused.

"Well, where's Osborne then?"

"Mr. Osborne is with Mr. Allen."

Bill charged up the stairs, knocked on the office door and entered immediately. The two looked up surprised.

"Morning Bill, glad you could find the time to come over."

"Morning. Osborne where is my typing?"

Osborne glanced at Steadman.

"It's not ready yet."

"Well tell Jacky get it ready it should have gone off last week. It's late already."

"Jacky won't be typing it."

"Oh!" Bill was bought up in his tracks.

"Well who will?"

"We haven't decided yet."

"Well I'd prefer Jacky do it."

"She won't be doing anything anymore."

"What the hell does that mean?"

"It means Bill, she's fired."

"Fired! Fired for what?"

"That's our business."

"What! Your business! Then how come she types for me? I can't remember complaining!"

"Look Bill she was driving Morton crazy on reception. She couldn't handle the job. Besides she was on probation."

"Rubbish! Her probation finished last month. You like to hire and fire too much! Where's that girl going to work next? There's no work on the island. In five years she'll be saying "Yes sir I got good grades at school, worked Tamarind Tree five weeks and got fired."

"Bill."

There was silence. Bill was red in the face.

"How come she wasn't fired Friday?"

"Bill, look, you just stick to your department leave us to run ours." Bill left slamming the door.

"What was that about?" said Steadman.

"I think he love the girl."

Steadman smiled. Then a deep belly laugh rocked the room. Even Osborne, who was unaccustomed to laughing at work, had to laugh.

LUNCH

"Bill."

"I'm busy." His friend Jerry on the next boat phoning him.

"You hear the news?"

"I don't care for any news, I'm busy."

"On the radio."

"No, I'm doing turn-arounds. I'll talk later."

"They're withdrawing our work permits."

"Eh!?"

"Yeah, on the radio this morning! Daley said anyone working here living on a boat is going to have his permit withdrawn."

"You're joking."

"No...serious. Broadcast on ZWX this morning."

"Well they just hit at the right time. The charter season's flattening right out." He paused. "Well they're good eh. What reason did they give?"

"Didn't hear it myself."

"Oh well doesn't make any difference anyway. Damn it. You know what...its payday Friday. I think Saturday Liz and me will take a sail."

"Serious?"

"Yeah serious. I got other problems with the Labour Office myself and here at the hotel and everywhere. I had enough. Time to go."

"We were thinking of staying - maybe unionising."

"Up to you buddy. But right now I really feel I had enough. That sail Saturday was so sweet I'd half forgotten what it's like. Yeah I really had enough. They can keep their bastard little tricks for themselves. Talk to you later." He slammed down the receiver. *Bastards*!

AFTERNOON

It was completely still. Not a breath of wind. The island half closed its eyes - peacefulness.

Morton wasn't feeling placid. The stillness seemed to call for greater action. Hotel reception had been unable to make his travel reservations. He decided he'd go down to the travel agent himself.

Within minutes he was outside the small shop that served as the island's sole travel agency. It also functioned as a grocer's store. There was a half derelict fuel pump in the forecourt, a relic of a previous business. On the face of the building over the single glass window was the sign 'Fahie Travel Agency.

Visit the other islands by plane. Steamship tours our specialty. Ice cream. Closed on Sundays.'

Morton went in. Fahie had already seen the expensive car pull up and the white man get out and he entered from the back room at the same moment with a big smile.

"Good afternoon sir" he said stressing the 'sir'. "Can I be of service to you?"

"Good afternoon. Yes, I want to fly back to England via Zurich later in the week. Wednesday would be ideal."

"To England eh?"

"Yes, via Zurich."

"Zurich, Zurich. That's a good one. Okay, okay. Zurich. Now let me see ... which way do you want to go?"

"Whichever is quickest and cheapest."

Fahie started to thumb his airplane schedule catalogues.

"Yes but the problem is you see Entropica is not a gateway is it not? Therefore I must route you via a gateway to get you there. So which gateway do you wish to proceed through?"

"Well ..."

"There are presently no direct flights from anywhere to Africa."

"Zurich isn't in Africa. It's in Europe. Switzerland"

"I know, I know" he said out loud to Morton and then "Europe, Europe" to his book. He continued to go through the schedules.

"I will soon have you booked up don't worry ... I can send you anywhere you know" he added masterfully.

"Ah Zurich - American gateway is Miami, New York, Houston."

"Miami."

"Good, yes, Miami is convenient, Miami is best. You will fly, let me see: Entropica, Puerto Rico, Miami, Zurich." Fahie smiled.

"And then England."

"Oh yes England of course."

"And how much will that cost?"

"Cost? One minute please."

But after several minutes no cost figure was forthcoming.

"Just give me a ball park figure."

"Well alright, alright I have it. I can't tell you exactly. That depends on the airlines. Until the tickets are ready you can't know. But it won't be less than $1200 US and not more than $1800 or $2000 definitely."

"Thank you. Well get it for me as quickly as possible. B. C. Morton. Tamarind Tree."

"Very well Mr. Morton I'll take action myself straightaway."

"Good."

"Goodbye."

"Goodbye." Fahie's smile, like the airfare, was set at absolute maximum.

During this conversation a powerful dark skinned man with coarse features had come in. He was wearing the rough clothes of a construction worker. Glistening with sweat, he kept making quick agitated movements. As soon as Morton left he said:

"Tell me again how much to Dominica."

"I tell you before."

Morton was getting in his car. Fahie could allow himself the liberty of a scowl.

"Does you do arithmetic?"

"No I does mathematics."

"Well I tell you the price."

"It doesn't add up correct. $228 too high."

"Look get outta me shop don't bother me you no-money man."

"You thiefing black bitch you. Give me the price book before damage done."

~

"She won't go home."

"Well tell her she must go home."

"I tell her. She won't go."

"Jacky go home." No response. Her head bent over her desk, her face hidden by her arms, one hand clutching a pen, the other her bag.

"Jacky." No answer.

"Why won't she go home?"

"She 'fraid tell her mother."

"But she must leave sometime and better now while the buses still running."

"Mr. Osborne she won't go. We tellin' her and tellin' her. She very upset poor girl."

"Well you must tell her again. If she's not gone by six I'll take her home myself."

~

Nan had finished school an hour before. Now she lay uneasily on her back in a small dingy room that smelt stale. A thick material hung over the door and shutter. There was little space for anything in the room except the bed, a chair and table. Her school clothes were folded tidily over the chair as though for an inspection. Steam rose off a pan of boiling water. A metal alarum clock ticked very loudly on a shelf. Flies kept landing on her breasts and stomach. She kept fending them off. She could hear the old woman moving about in the next room. The clock said 4.10 p.m. *By five everything finish.* Although she was afraid for the pain some deeper fear possessed her. The door opened and the old woman came in. She had on a stained brown house coat over a pink nightgown that reached almost to the floor. Under a cloth hat on her head was a $50US note. Nan looked up to see two small silver trays, two needles, a hook and something else besides.

"I don't want." She started to sit up.

The old woman pushed her back down.

"Don't worry soon finish."

EVENING

Bill and Liz were sitting together at a table in the hotel restaurant. The meal finished they were having chocolate gateau and liqueurs. A radio belonging to one of the waiters rested on a nearby table playing calypso.

"So we're definitely going?"

"Yes definitely."

"Saturday?"

"Yes."

"You'll have to give me a couple more weeks."

"Forget them and come."

"It's not possible."

"Why not?"

"I owe it to them to complete the term. They helped me before."

"Okay. Well I'll sail on Saturday. You follow by plane two weeks later. By that time I'll be in Puerto Rico, the boat will be hauled and ready to go."

"Sounds good."

"It will be good." They looked in each others eyes, clinked glasses and took a sip of Cointreau.

The regional news replaced the calypso. Not far away, in Haiti, people were dying of hunger. They finished their drinks, signed the bill and left.

"Oh Peter I'm so glad you're back, I missed you."

She hugged him and the genuineness of her love touched him.

"Well I'm back but we won't be here much longer. I'm going back to my old job. I phoned up my old boss when I was in England. He'll take me back."

"Really!!" she was delighted. "Oh Peter I do love you."

"It rained a lot. I didn't mind that, it seemed right enough... but I don't have a mother any more..." He looked away.

"So what's new out here?"

"Bill phoned. You'll never believe it, he's leaving on Saturday! Don't tell anyone. The chef was late for work..."

"So he's leaving eh the old bastard." He smiled, "Well we'll have a party for him before he goes."

"I heard Morton leaves Wednesday."

"Well that's good news. We'll have it on Friday."

"I'm tired Peter, tired out."

"Let's go to bed. The travelling has finished me too."

~

Naman and Bully sat outside the bar in semi-darkness.

"So how was it at Tamarind Tree?"

"They work us hard boy, real hard." Naman smiled.

"What they have you do?"

"All kinda thing. Me in charge the big cement mixer."

"Yeah?"

"Yeah they have me controllin' it."

"You go tomorrow?"

"Same thing everyday till Friday."

"Then the bucks right?"

"Right."

They shook hands like Vietnam vets. They'd been two years without money – far, far too long.

"How it be there otherwise?"

"As you'd expect, you know how construction is. Nothing special." He thought for a minute. "Oh yeah, there some white man there name Morgan. He keep comin' down harass Henry. He want Henry for slave plain to see."

"Truth?"

"Truth. It' disgusting. If me, Henry me smash 'e face."

"Truth. Too many race man here, try keep we down."

"Truth. Henry stupid eh?"

"You have any bucks?"

"Not a thing - I beg Henry, 'e tell me 'e doesn't have."

"Sammy inside the bar."

"Let we go get a drink from 'e."

TUESDAY

MORNING

"Peter."

"Eh Bill."

"When did you get back?"

"Last night. I hear you're leaving us Saturday."

"Yeah - the bastards in the Labour Office are withdrawing yachties' work permits. I'm seeing Morton later this morning."

"Something came up for me too when I was in England."

"Oh yeah?"

"Yeah. Let's go out for a last meal together. Phone me up after you've talked to that cold fish and we'll fix up a time and place."

"Fine."

Bill put down the phone. *Hmm. That gives me an idea.* He smiled to himself. *They've got several big stuffed fish at the Sports-fishing Club.*

~

"Yes Bill come in I did want to see you."

Morton waved him sternly to a chair. Bill sat down agitated.

"Now we have a quite a lot to get settled before I leave."

"In all fairness," Bill interrupted, "I should tell you I'll be leaving myself on Friday."

"Leaving? For where?"

"Puerto Rico initially. I'm leaving Tamarind Tree. I'm resigning ..."

"Resignations, Mr. Baker, are not handed in in a casual manner in the middle of the season and are anyway subject to three months notice as you well know!"

"I'm not obliged to give notice. Any notice."

"Oh is that right.." said Morton realising the seriousness of Bill's intention "..so what claim do you have to the title of Primadonna?"

"I've just had enough that's all."

"Oh I see. So you drop everything and run." Morton allowed his anger to become more evident. "It's totally irresponsible apart from being in violation of company agreement."

"What agreement?"

"The personal contractual agreements."

"The white staff were omitted."

"What do you mean?" said Morton feigning surprise.

"We didn't get contracts – the locals did."

"It must have been an oversight. I don't believe it. I'll call Osborne."

"I don't think it was an oversight - I don't think Peter does either."

"Oh so he's thinking of copping out too is he?"

"I don't know his plans. I don't think he has any intention of leaving - not now anyway."

"You people have no sense of loyalty. And now you want to run. You've had it too easy, that's the trouble."

"Loyalty is something I don't altogether understand."

"I'll say you don't!"

"I'm not sure you've always stood by your staff." This bought Morton up short.

"I will not allow you to leave. I won't have it. Your salary will be withheld until you've worked out your formal period of notice as is standard company practice. You're a manager not an hourly paid worker. You have no right! And you leave it to the last minute, the very last minute, knowing I'm leaving tomorrow. Such cowardice."

This made Bill squirm.

"I'm sorry I didn't realise you were leaving tomorrow."

"But you knew it was very soon."

"That's true. I made up my mind yesterday."

"Oh yesterday eh?" Morton gave him a shrewd penetrating glance, "And what reasons did you give this peculiar mind of yours?"

"I don't see any advantage in discussing it."

There was a pause in the hostilities. Morton spoke again but more slowly.

"And who will replace you on Saturday? Who?"

"Well as you know there's an excess of experienced yachtsmen on the island right now as the season's finishing..."

Morton looked up at the ceiling, already making plans for a smooth transition and an explanation for the hotel owners.

"...and as you know the Labour Office is withdrawing the work permits of all yachtsmen."

"It wouldn't apply to you."

"Then it won't apply to my successor. I don't believe they have any special feeling for me."

"I can't imagine why anyone should either. Goodbye Mr. Baker." And as Bill didn't leave

"You may go."

~

By eleven o'clock the plumbers had made good progress. The piping for the new lift pump station required for the final phase of the hotel was fixed in place. Having started his men off at 7 a.m. Rogers had worked with them for four hours and then returned to his home to work on the paperwork side of his company - preparing his accounts for the month end. His mother was out working ground and his children at school. After a while he looked up to see his wife going out carrying washing. Looking at her back, her backside, the backs of her legs, he knew she was pleased in what she was doing. She came back in and he caught her eye for a moment. She pretended to be very occupied with her work but he saw her face and front all pleased.

"Coffee please!"

"I'm busy washing."

But in a minute it was there on the table.

"And where's the chocolate biscuits?" he said, "coffee too watery without biscuits." And there they were by the cup. She hesitated by him.

"Thank you," he said, "but I'm very busy with the monthly reconciliation, so run go finish your washing."

"Fresh!" she laughed.

"No, this is hard work. Doing the reconciliation alone is easy but coffee and biscuits make it hard - it too easy to get lost in a problem, stop, raise the cup to your mouth and find nothing there - dregs and the biscuits gone! It takes skill to concentrate first on the figures, then the coffee, then the biscuits, then back to the figures again."

She went off with a smile.

~

NOON

"Hello Liz?"

"Bill, what's the matter?"

"Look I can't speak now but I'm leaving tomorrow."

"Tomorrow! I thought Saturday."

"It was but they're not going to pay me Friday so I may as well go tomorrow."

"You mean they're not going to pay you at all?"

"Don't know. I'll see you later. We'll have a last meal out. We'll take Peter and Marjorie."

~

AFTERNOON

The sun was halfway down from its zenith.

Up on the hill Zackie smiled at a bird passing by. He felt very good. Chip passed the spliff back to him. He took it down in deep drafts bringing it up again through his nose and mouth.

"Zacharious brother man - me a thinkin' you tell me you go Babylon today."

Zackie searched his memory. He looked up for the bird again but it had gone. He looked at Chip to say something but he was sucking in short quick sucks, the end of the spliff going red grey red grey red grey. He found himself saying

"Me was contemplating a bird Rastaman but it vanish from me eye them."

Chip laughed and Zacky couldn't help but laugh too as he took the tiny piece of spliff from his friend's outstretched hand.

"This stuff I-rey." He carried on laughing, unable to stop. "I-Zalta cultivate it."

They looked about them. Was that a footstep? Zackie felt scared. No, a dog turning over a stone. Uncle's dog smelling up the place.

"You go work today Tamarind Tree?"

"Me no feel so inclined."

"Dig it brother-man." They smiled at each other knowingly. Everything seemed just right and perfect. It felt good to take it easy.

~

It was his last working day on the island and Morton was casting a final eye over the detailed job list he'd written for himself in England. All but two of the jobs had been crossed out and he'd given those two all the attention he could. Remembering that one of the reception girls had been fired the previous day he wrote 'Streamline reception' at the bottom of the list then crossed this out in pencil.

Steadman entered the office quickly and angrily as though someone were chasing him. Morton looked up from his list and eyed him over the top of his spectacles.

"Problems Steadman?" His voice was both affable and ironic.

"They're enough to drive you crazy. I've just been with that food and beverage manager that you told me would be such an asset to the company. The kitchen still hasn't been cleaned since yesterday. The garbage containers are overflowing onto the floor. I understand he hasn't yet bollocked King for being late in and we have a Chamber of Commerce meeting at 4 p.m. and nothing is ready yet. And I'm the chairman for the meeting!"

"Well if it's any comfort Steadman I've just received his report on the food and drink costs. Real food cost is averaging 80% and should be 40% selling price. Beverage cost varies so widely it's not possible to talk of an average – it's from 55% to 95% selling cost."

"Good God I didn't realise it was that bad! We're going to have to tighten up - a special campaign - where can it be going?..."

"And listen to this. I had an analysis done of the big dance last Friday. Drinks were 38% selling price which is just about spot on." Morton paused.

"You know where it's going Steadman."

"Theft."

"Yes theft, quite right. I'd say theft 80%, spoilage waste, carelessness, etcetera 20%."

"It has to be theft. With the dance there was no thiefing because office management was there."

"Exactly so. That and the speed of turnover didn't leave time for any funny business."

"Did you ever give thought to a franchised restaurant operation Ben?"

"Wouldn't work Steadman. We have problems now but we can attack them. With a franchise you loose control, standards may come down, then the hotel suffers. You tell me Steadman - who'd operate an effective franchise for us?"

Steadman didn't reply.

"By the way while you are in the mood for problem solving we have another problem in the Marine Department."

"Oh yes?"

Steadman looked up warily.

"Yes Mr. Baker informs me he's leaving on Friday."

"You're joking."

"No, I'm not joking Steadman. I'm going for a walk." He stood up.

"I'm going for a last walk round the site to see if anyone's doing anything - and anyone who's not is going to get a ROCKET!"

~

EVENING

Henry had stayed behind after work. Soon after dark the night security man made his first round. After he'd passed Henry stepped behind the site office, pulled out a large sheet of cardboard and carried it to the staff car park, which, being behind a bank of earth, was in complete darkness. There was no one around. He set the sheet down near the back of Morton's car and lay on it, putting his head behind the back wheel. He could feel the nut in the darkness, the nipple extending from it. He pulled out a three quarter inch spanner from his pants pocket and undid it three turns. Complete silence in all directions. He sensed it was safe to get up. He threw the cardboard by the nearby garbage bins, dusted himself off, walked over to his car and drove away.

~

Henry would have been surprised to find his cousin Naman had also remained behind at Tamarind Tree. He was searching in the half light near the area he'd been working that day looking for a broken pick-axe handle.

Not a man in this world can say that to me, Naman. 'Work harder'. Work harder! Me! Work harder! He's gotta be crazy. He's gotta be damn crazy - and me haffa correct him with a good few lash when me workin' so hard for the whole damn day. Not a damn man in the world can stop me now. Yes, me haff to. An' me do it for me cousin Henry too. And some big cash government man beggin' Otley do it too!

Finding the discarded handle he shook it twice, hit an ornamental shrub with it, and finding it satisfactory, went off to conceal himself in order to be in a position to surprise Morton. He found a good spot.

He doesn't notice how me the one shovelling the damn sand in the mixer? He doesn't know how me work in the sun when a man should rightfully be resting? He think he could do this work? Work harder! Work harder! What the hell! If Henry want to be Morgan's slave that he damn stupid business. But not me boy, not me. Me give 'e some lash tonight. Me have 'o correct 'e. What! The damn man. Work harder!....

~

Henry stopped on his way home at the Sunset Bar and Restaurant. He sat outside on the perimeter wall and downed three rum and cokes. *That's good. No more trouble now from bad man Morton*. It was nearly dark. He set down his glass, climbed into his car and sped off. He'd gone about half the distance to Cornfield lost in thought when a taxi swept passed him very close covering his windscreen with a fine dust. If there was one person he hated completely on the island it was Garry. He'd been bullied by him for five consecutive years at primary school. Every day had been painful. He put his foot on the gas and tore off after him spraying the windscreen clean at the same time. The narrow winding roads made it difficult to pass. Two miles down the road he just managed to squeeze through and was out ahead. He continued at a fantastic pace steering to left and right and travelling deep into the corners of the road gearing up and down, throttle, brake, clutch, gear, throttle. He was conscious of being for moments on that perfect edge between life and death but after the rum his movements were not quite perfect and his mind was in turmoil and he raced it and raced it and the bush whipped him at the corners and the wind blew grit over him and he sped on watching the revs burn deeper and deeper into the danger level - driving the car like a madman.

There was a flash in the darkness ahead and then two headlights over the rise coming for him like lances and he was suddenly conscious of something he'd been uneasily expecting for a long time - the two lights immediately ahead searing through him, his wheel striking a rock, a stunning jolt, the sound of metal crunching and he, Henry Braithwaite, flying through the air in his car out over the cliff edge.

As the car travelled upside down the three hundred feet to the rocks below he found himself pinned by his own weight to the roof. Despite his terror, he sensed the final injustice of a life in which he couldn't even get a decent view, on this, his last ride down.

NIGHT

Darkness. The sounds of night. The sea, disturbed for a moment at dusk, continued now as if nothing had happened, an even breaking sound on the shores of the island.

Bill, Liz, Peter and Marjorie heard it as they sat at dinner in the restaurant. Liz remarked how beautiful it sounded, how even. She used the word 'eternal'.

"Yes that's what we must go after" remarked Bill "to listen to that sound till it becomes part of us and we it."

"That's right," said Liz slowly as if coming across something sacred she'd mislaid long ago in a mist. They were silent for a while.

"Well I guess we'll meet some day in the holy land."

"You mean England?"

"Yes."

"Ain't been too bad working with you."

"Wasn't too bad working with you," Bill smiled, "usually."

"Keep in touch."

"Yeah. Look after the hotel for me. And the director of course."

"Of course."

They smiled. There was more to drink and the talk became more rambling, disjointed and inconsequential. The restaurant became noisy. They parted company quite late.

~

Eleven o'clock. Morton had spent the evening having final discussions with his hotel manager over dinner. He slowly descended the steps from the restaurant and said goodnight. He knew he was unforgivably late for the party Beatrice had invited him to. "A farewell party for you Ben - entrancing dancing" *What a load of old rot.* He collected his car keys from reception and reluctantly headed for his car. Just about to drive away he remembered the proposals from the Minister of Labour that he'd agreed to fax to Moore that night. Moore had recently installed the faxes in his private offices at home and abroad. They were the latest electronic equipment - only recently on the market. Tamarind Tree were as yet unequipped. He switched off the engine and got out and went up to his office. The letter was sitting on his desk in a plain brown envelope marked 'Moore'.

~

It wasn't King's habit to drink while working but by the time he left the kitchen that night he was pretty far gone. It had been a tough day - albeit a short one as he'd arrived about three hours late. First he'd finished a bottle of coarse red wine he'd been cooking with. Then he'd ordered a beer from the bar. The night was warm and still and the kitchen stove was no place to be. He ordered three more and the maitre d' slipped him some left over rum. The diners finished late and by the time he came out front desk told him the night bus had gone. Now he wasn't so sure he'd get to Elba's birthday party like he'd promised to do. He'd have to try and catch a ride.

As he passed by the staff car park he noticed a light in Morton's car. *Maybe me get a ride part the way.* He approached and found the driver's door slightly open. There was no one inside. The keys were in the ignition. *Hmm. Me think me take a chance.. This too good to miss.* He jumped in and switched on, backed up and headed for the gates. He was just feeling he'd made a nice clean getaway when a man jumped out from behind a bush. The headlamps showed him to be armed with a club of some sort. He looked like he meant business. King accelerated and drove at him. Naman was obliged to jump back behind the bush he'd just jumped out from. King made it through the gates feeling pleased. "Me did it, me did it. Clean getaway! Clean getaway! Boy that man Morton don't like nobody borrow his car."

King had no idea of the extreme circumstance he was now in. Every time he braked fluid escaped from the rear bleed screw. The car, like a wounded animal, left a crimson trail in its path.

~

On his return Morton was amazed to see an empty space where his car had been. He hit his pockets. No keys. He'd left them in the car. *I don't believe it. I just don't believe it.* He shook his head in amazement and stood there for some time looking at the empty space with his hands on his hips. Shock eventually gave way to a certain satisfaction. *Well now I can't go to that mad cow's barn dance*. He went back to front desk, picked up the phone and dialled Moore's house.

"Beatrice....oh Beatrice, Ben here. Terribly sorry but I've been prevented from coming to your party. Believe it or not someone's stolen my car....yes stolen! I had to return to my office to collect the Minister's letter and it was taken in my absence. I'm very sorry. The letter must go off tonight though and I'll have it dispatched into your hands by special delivery. In the meantime I have to stand by and sort this mess out. Please make sure it goes off tonight - he's expecting it in his office first thing in the morning.....yes, yes...goodnight. So sorry I couldn't join you. It sounds wonderful!"

He put down the phone with a wry smile and turned to Hilton.

"My car has been stolen. Call night security. Tell him I expect it to be back in the car park by tomorrow morning. Tomorrow morning understand? I have to be at the airport at eight thirty. And tell him to deliver this to Madam Beatrice at Moore's house within the hour. Within the hour! Do you understand?"

"Yes sir"

"Very well. Good. I don't want to be disturbed tonight." Morton headed off for his room.

The night security man used to ride over on his donkey from Point. Hilton picked up the phone.

"Eh tell Midnight Cowboy come here. Tell him bring Champion with him. Morton has some messages for him."

He put down the phone. *Boy, I not sure Champion going to like this. She more used to going back west after she come up east.*

~

A qualified driver would have pulled up at once sensing something was wrong with the brakes, but King was neither qualified nor sober. He half knew something was wrong but he wasn't sure if it was something wrong with the car or something wrong with his foot and he rather hoped he wouldn't have to sort it out before he got there. One thing was certain and that was that he was making unexpected and excellent speed towards his girlfriend's party.

There was a long run down to the bend short of Sapphire Bay. By the time King reached the bottom he was doing seventy, his brake foot was solid on the floor of the car and he was sure it was the car that was wrong, not his foot. There was no chance of negotiating the bend. He switched to the rough unsurfaced road leading to the bay. He must have hit the beach at about sixty and was doing thirty when he went into the sea. Two beautiful arcs of spray flew up into the moonlit sky. For a few seconds they seemed to be suspended in mid air out over the bay – fine gossamer veils threaded with pale colour – ethereal like the aurora borealis. King glimpsed this exquisite sight out of the corner of his eye just before his head hit the windscreen.

~

Morton hesitated at the door to his room. Something told him to be wary. He unlocked it, turned the handle very slowly, and quietly opened the door and looked around before putting on the light. His instincts were right. Someone was in his bed! He was both stunned and excited. *Who is she by Jove?* He slid silently down into an armchair by the door wondering what course of action to take. Several of the female staff had shown a definite shining towards him. Or was it one of the hotel guests? He went through them in his mind. *Is this my last fling?* He listened for some time, trying to hear her breathing to tell if she were awake or asleep. He could only hear his own long heavy breaths. He was tired, the brandy was taking effect. *I always wondered what it would be like with....wondered.... what it would be, wondered what.....wondered.....what...*

~

King sat back and rubbed his forehead. His head ached. *Where am I?* He tried to take in the situation. Water lapped around his stomach. He could see Margarita Island through the windscreen in front of him. *In Morton's car....in the sea....in trouble.* He looked about him. *The damn stereo get wet.* He pushed open the door and stepped down. A small fish swam in.

"You not meant to go in there. You stupid or something? Come out!" He watched it swim round the gear lever.

"Okay stay in there then."

He half shut the door and waded back to the beach. There were two tracks leading down into the sea and he walked up one of them. By the time he'd walked most of the remaining distance to Elba's house his tennis shoes had stopped squelching and his clothes were pretty much dried out. He was beginning to think a lot more clearly. Every time a car approached he moved away from the road and its headlights. He turned up a track to a friend's house, knocked on the door and asked if he could use the phone. He phoned Bill Olliviere, Sergeant in charge of the Fingerprinting Section, Royal Entropican Police Force.

"Bilbo"

"Yeah"

"Kong"

Silence for ten seconds.

"Kong. What the damn hell you phonin' me fuh now!" Then in a whisper, "Doesn't me tell you me have this special chick here Tuesday nights?"

"Listen Bilbo, listen to me man. In case anyone fin' a car in the sea tomorrow don't fin' any prints on it round the driver's side."

"Oh no Kongy. Oh no, I don't believe it! Not again! This the second time now! I can't believe it. Jesus this is great!" He laughed.

"I tell you before Kongy - cars don't work so good in the sea. When you reach the water you have to get out the car and get in a boat. This is great! This is just great! Kongy, you provide some the best action on the island. Whose car it is?"

"Er... me doesn't so much like to talk about that right now. Me see you later. Me have to get to a birthday party."

"Oh I see. Very reasonable of course. I see you later then."

Bilbo rang off.

King continued on down the road. It was 3am.

~

The boat rolled and Bill awoke to find himself on the deck of his yacht, still in his street clothes, but now disquietingly sober. He had the feeling he'd been wasting his time foolishly on the island, and that there was something true in both Morton and Daley's remarks. *What have I given to the island after all, or anyone else come to that?*

THE THIRD WEEK

WEDNESDAY

MORNING

"A fish, a damn fish in 'e bed!" Elba shouted at the top of her voice. She'd just stripped down the top sheet from Morton's bed and been startled by the result. She went racing out of the room not even noticing Morton who was now half awake, sitting up in an armchair by the door.

Morton heard her going off down the pathway.

"It' a fish, a damn fish in 'e bed:"

"What?" Edna stopped her. "What you talkin' 'bout girl?"

"In 'e bed - Morton. A damn fish. A fish . 'e been there lovin' up a fish. A great big fish!"

"Oh boy I don't believe this. You sure 'bout this!?"

"Yes girl" she said striking a pose "'e must 'ave been *so* excited!"

"Oh God this the best joke I get since I work Tamarind Tree. All the island going to hear 'bout this by lunchtime."

"Come see for yourself girl." They headed back to the room.

Morton was standing by his bed. A stuffed hundred and thirty pound Alison tuna stared dully back at him.

~

8.30 a.m. and Morton, dressed again in his English business suit and looking a little the worse for wear, at the airport facing an empty airline counter. His flight for Puerto Rico aboard a small propeller driven plane was scheduled for 9.30 a.m. and he was an hour early as advised. The connection in Miami was very tight. He pressed the buzzer again to no avail.

"No one in the office yet" said Steadman, "they'll be here soon. Let's sit down."

Morton wanted to protect his position at the front of the queue but settled for an easy chair with a view of the arriving cars and his suitcase on the scale.

"Well Steadman - we've made some progress I believe."

Steadman nodded in assent.

"Maybe I painted too gloomy a picture of it last night. It must have been the Napoleon brandy distorted the picture a bit."

"Well it's not easy anyway ..."

"Hmm.." Morton scoffed "..it's like pushing mud uphill."

Our hill, your mud. Steadman immediately regretted this thought.

"Ben in the rush of leaving I forgot to tell you – your car has been found."

"Well that's something. Do they know who took it?"

"That might take a little time – they found it in the sea - in Sapphire Bay."

"Good God! In the sea - in Sapphire Bay – how on earth did it get there?"

"The police will be looking into that now – fingerprinting and so on."

"Well I'm glad they're on the ball at least. In the sea....good heavens!" Morton looked dumbfounded.

"Let me know the outcome."

"I hope you have a safe journey Ben and your affairs in Switzerland are quickly settled."

"Thank you Steadman." Morton looked at his watch. The other passengers were beginning to arrive.

"Keep in touch regarding developments with the Labour Office and let me know who you find to do the harbour.

Remember I can always send you someone from England if you give me a little notice."

"I think we'll find someone quickly enough."

They watched the new arrivals coping with their baggage, children, and taxi-men.

A light flickered on over the airline counter.

"About time" said Morton. *8.48a.m.*

"You should know the airline by now Ben."

"I do Steadman, and that's why they annoy the hell out of me every time." Steadman laughed. They joined the queue behind a Canadian family that looked as though they'd just walked in off the beach.

Morton looked at his briefcase with the Union Jack on it and his single expensive leather suitcase, now standing to the side of the scale. He checked his pockets again for his passport, money, tickets and keys.

"Don't bother to wait Steadman."

They shook hands, their eyes met and they were bonded for a moment in complete and sincere friendship. Morton was deeply stirred by this goodbye.

After Steadman left he found himself looking down at his feet feeling a bitter sweetness. Then he realised someone was trying to edge passed him on his left side. He moved to the left at once and stuck his left hand on his hip in such a way as to prevent any further forward movement. Then he stiffened up his back and stared resolutely at the ticket clerk, while making the fullest use of his peripheral vision.

~

Bill spent the morning unloading stores from his car to his boat which he'd bought to the dock at Tamarind Tree. He then fuelled and watered her – uneasy that Steadman might appear. He was on deck coiling an anchor line when he sensed someone close by. A plane passed overhead. He looked up straight into Jacky's face.

She didn't say anything but her face had a plaintiff look about it and he realised at once he'd scarcely given her a thought, hadn't even planned to say goodbye. Trying to make light of a situation he realised was by no means inconsequential he said:

"Like a soda?"

She said nothing.

"Come down below I just put some on ice."

She followed him down. He struggled with the ice box and then turned and held out a can as though this was in itself what was required. She made no move to take it but looked at him evenly.

"Married me Bill."

He looked into her eyes. Their depth seemed infinite. In them he saw with assurance the future, the present, this whole fine being, this beautiful young woman who could be his.

"You're joking," he said half to his own surprise and entirely to hers.

He picked up a box from the floor and put it on a settee. He knew intuitively that the girl could make him happy, could improve him - that Liz depended on him, and that he was leaving that day.

"Maybe" he said glancing at her and for the first time she stopped looking openly at him, being there for him, and her body trembled almost imperceptibly. He knew the best course was what she had proposed but something froze him and foreclosed this opportunity.

"Tell me you love me ... even if it not true, tell me please." She stood there looking at the floor clasping her hands together.

"Let me hear you say it - just say it please."

There was a pause. He said, "I love you." She cried.

He said "I'm sorry." He felt terrible. He felt monstrous. He knew he was going. She cried still, seeming as if she might dissolve into her own tears and be lost forever.

She said, "I was going to give you my baby. I was going to make you a home. I would do anything for you. Anything! O dear God." And she started to cry again, this time longer and harder, like the endless dreadful rain after a hurricane which stops only to reveal a broken land and a broken people.

~

James stood by his friends in the school playground.

"Me hear Henry Braithwaite dead."

"Who that?"

"Big man Henry. You know ... The stout man have the all black Toyota with the white seat and silvery, silvery wheel. He mash up he car last night. Me hear it from me father this morning. He fly out over the cliff land in the water"

"Not true!"

"True. They take 'e hospital and give 'e blood from a next man but it leak back out again an' 'e dead."

"Not true!"

"True!"

~

The huge sail, now unfurled and raised, waved an idle hello to the wind. The boat pointed head to wind held now only by her anchor. He checked his main sheets were clear and the running backstays not fouling the sail and went up to the foredeck and pulled on the anchor cable. When most of it was aboard he looked down to see the anchor vertically below him. He pulled hard and as it broke from the sandy bay he knew the island's last hold on him was now broken. He walked back to the helm and pulled the tiller to windward. The wind filled the sail, the boat fell off, gathered speed and started to gurgle through the water. He headed south west to the passage between the reefs, through the channel and out into the sea.

Up on a hill sitting down on a rock in an untilled field a young woman watched the boat's progress. After it had passed through the channel and gained the outer edge of the reef it reached the ocean swell and started to pitch. The boat rose as it met the first sea and she breathed in. It fell into the first trough and she breathed out. The deeper it went the more it rose and fell as did her chest. The sea came to her and she heaved more deeply - salt spray blew across her and wet her decks, her eyes and ran down over her face. She was shaking. The waves were parted by her. There would be no turning back. She was parted from him.

"Play with me Daddy."

Rogers looked at his daughter and took his hand off the jeep's door handle.

They walked together on a path through the long grass that moved in the wind coming up the hill's face.

"Sit down." She sat on his lap and started to undo his shirt buttons and pull the hair on his chest.

"Chil'."

He looked over her head down to the airport two thousand feet below. Tiny people were getting into a tiny plane. The plane went away downwind and then came back, lifted off and climbed towards them full of noise and consequence. It turned to starboard and for a moment they caught a glimpse of faces pressed against windows. Then it continued away downwind and became quieter and smaller until it was just a dot in the sky. Very soon the smoke dispersed and the plane could no longer be seen or heard - just the sound of the wind in the grasses.

Two of their dogs had followed them along the path and were now crouching a little way off – facing the wind, panting. A dappled light played on them as the sunlight came through the swaying cedar trees. Rogers found himself to be smiling and looking down at his daughter saw the same smile reflected on her face. *How fortunate we are for this human life*. He did his buttons up.

"Come on chil'" he said "you have to go pre-school. An' I have work to do."

THE END

GLOSSARY

Babylon system set up in accordance with Western values and technology, hence town etc
Bob Marley almost prototype Rastafarian, leader, philosopher, songwriter, musician (1945-81)
clear skin coffee coloured skin of one of mixed race
ducana a sweet food served with the main dish
ganja marijuana
ghaut deep valley
ground work work on land, especially small holdings
head tie / head cook up supposed control of another by use of voodoo (obeah)
honkey derogatory term for white man
I-n-I me (Rastafarian)
I-rey good, beautiful (Rastafarian)
I-tal vital, pure, natural, vegetarian (Rastafarian)
Jah God (Rastafarian)
liming hanging around enjoying a relaxed time, going out with someone
Lion of Judah title taken from Revelations 5 for Ras Tafari
locks dreadlocks, hair grown long and twisted into matted coils
mash up not in working order, beaten up
mistress Mrs
nah not
nut coconut
pear tree avocado pear tree
pickney small child
pumcoolie herb used as remedy for flu

Rasta member of religious movement started in Jamaica in 1930s, believing themselves the lost tribe of Israel, rejecting Western values and technology, eating only vegetarian food, smoking marijuana. Rastafarian. Style copied by some young men without full religious commitment.

Red eye conjunctivitus

red man man of mixed race

s'appenin' ? What's happening, what's going on?

Selassie Haile Selassie I, official title of Ras Tafari, Emperor of Ethiopia

stock cattle, especially sheep and goats

yanking imitating American speech, especially slang

Printed in Great Britain
by Amazon